CARIBBEAN WRITERS SERIES

CARIBBEAN WRITERS SERIES

25

All That Glitters

To Jenny and Sandra

All That Glitters

❋

MICHAEL ANTHONY

HEINEMANN

LONDON · KINGSTON · PORT OF SPAIN

Heinemann Educational Books Ltd
22 Bedford Square, London WC1B 3HH
PO Box 1028, Kingston, Jamaica
27 Belmont Circular Road, Port of Spain, Trinidad

IBADAN NAIROBI
EDINBURGH MELBOURNE AUCKLAND
SINGAPORE HONG KONG KUALA LUMPUR NEW DELHI

ISBN 0 435 98034 3

Set in Garamond by Robcroft Ltd., London
Printed in Great Britain by
Richard Clay (The Chaucer Press) Ltd, Bungay, Suffolk.

✳ One

WHAT AN EXCITING day it was when Auntie Roomeen came! I remember it well, and I remember how she walked into the yard all in a flourish, with her red velvet Panama dress, and the broad-brimmed white hat, and a glittering silver chain round her neck. She had come from Panama and she had arrived in the afternoon, as the sun was blazing down through the coconut trees. Somehow the house looked too old and drab to receive her. To tell the truth, Mayaro looked too poor to receive her. I was the first to see her as she got out of the buggy and walked across to our house under the palms. I cried, 'Look Auntie Roomeen!' Mother rushed out of the house and we both ran to meet Auntie and then she and Mother held each other in an embrace as if they did not want to let each other go again. Then Auntie bent and squeezed me to her, and she said, 'Horace, that's you? God, you look so different; you so big! I didn't even think you'd remember me.'

The man with the buggy had put her trunk down on the sand, near the house. We had stopped in the path and when he was passing back he stretched his hand towards Auntie and I thought it was to shake it but it was for payment, because Auntie gave him a note. She was going to make arrangements for when she was going back, but Mother said, 'It's okay, Roomeen – you forget we have Mr Reid right here?' And she said to the man, 'That's all right, Mister. When she's going back we have a buggy right here.'

Auntie came into the house, and what an afternoon that was! After a little while old Mr Reid came. Then Mr Clunis came. They were old friends and neighbours and they were very happy to see her – especially Mr Clunis, the coconut-picker. They stayed a long while, and I was inside, near to Auntie, and afterwards for sheer joy I dashed outside and made a somersault in the yard. Then I ran out of the yard to the beach.

It was a lucky thing for me that I had come home from school that midday, and I had come only because I had forgotten my composition book. Else I would have never seen Auntie as she was arriving. Now I had already taken off my shoes and my shirt because of course I wasn't going back to school. I stayed on the beach only a short while and then I ran back into the yard and went inside.

I sat on the chair next to Auntie Roomeen, listening to her talk. Her voice was polished, not anything like ours. I looked at her as if I almost didn't believe she had come. Mother, Mr Clunis, and Mr Reid, sat in a sort of semi-circle, and Auntie was telling them about Panama, when suddenly she stopped. She glanced around at me, and she hesitated, then she said, 'Claris, I'm trying hard not to mention it, but it will stifle me. I mean,' and she lowered her voice, 'Poor thing. Gone just like that.'

I could see sadness come over Mother's face. She said, 'Well, I suppose he's gone to a better place.'

Although she looked sad, she did not lower her voice to say this, and Mr Clunis was his normal self, too, when he said, 'Eddie was sick too bad. He get thin as a rake. St Joseph Estate ain't no joke, you know. All this hard work in the cocoa in the wet, mushy place. You think you could play with consumption? Good thing I just picking coconuts.'

There was silence. Then Auntie said, as if to herself, 'That's how he went!'

Mother tapped her on the shoulder: 'We'll talk. I'll tell you everything.'

Auntie was glancing at me from time to time and now she said something to Mother, very softly. Answering in her normal voice, Mother said, 'Oh, he was very upset. He took it bad. Bad, bad. But he's all right now.'

'How you making out?'

'Not bad, thanks to you, girl. Doing a little thing in the factory.'

'I see.'

Mr Clunis said, 'They give her a little thing digging out coconut meat. Instead they should give her plenty money, because – '

'Clunis,' Mother said, 'I always tell you this. *They* didn't kill Eddie, you know.'

2

'Who else?' Mr Clunis said, looking at her as if surprised. And as if it was the first time they had touched on this point. Old Mr Reid looked at them and nodded his head and I did not know who he was agreeing with. Old Mr Reid did not say anything; he never said much.

After Mother and Mr Clunis had argued a little bit, Auntie said to Mr Clunis, 'So you still picking coconuts? Still climbing coconut trees?'

'Eh heh.' He was looking at her very tenderly and he did not hide it that he was very glad to see her. I found he was very jittery in her presence. For instance, although he had been arguing with Mother a while ago, it was Auntie he had kept glancing at. She looked at him for a while now, before taking her eyes off, and then she turned to me. But she did not tell me anything. She only smiled suddenly and then she tried to fix her face to look serious again. She must have found him odd. I smiled. She looked at Mother, then she looked at me again, and she seemed to suddenly come back to the moment. She said, 'Claris, you know I nearly didn't recognise this boy? God! Time could fly! Who would think it's five whole years I'm over there?'

I was a little surprised to hear that it was five years since Auntie had left for Panama. I remembered it so vividly, I didn't think it was possible I was only eight then. But I must have been. 'Cricky!' I thought. Teacher Myra always said something about time and tide. About time and tide waiting on no man. I liked that because the tide was always busy at St Joseph. Either coming in or going out. Right now I could hear the crashing of the waves and so I knew the tide was coming in. Time was always going, though.

Mother and Auntie and Mr Clunis were in conversation but I was hardly listening to them. It was so clear in my memory how nice and bright Auntie had been. Often she carried me to the beach on her shoulders, or bathed with me, and I saw Auntie now, in my mind's eye, going all over St Joseph with me –either with me on her back, or walking holding my hand. She was always taking me to the factory to see my father– when he came back from work in the cocoa plantation – and then we three would walk home under the palms. She was tall and big and powerful, and yet elegant, and I remember feeling so safe and happy with her. And I remember how nice she was to look at– as

3

nice to look at then as she was now – only that perhaps now she was a little nicer. For she stood out with that red, velvety Panama dress, and the broad-brimmed hat, which looked like silk, and the ear-rings, and that silver chain round her neck. Considering the way she looked, the surroundings were very ordinary. Our house, which was old, always looked good to me, but I found it was looking very shabby now. Mother and Mr Clunis and I – all three of us – we must have been looking very shabby too, next to her in our old home clothes. Mother always said: 'Be satisfied with what you have,' and Teacher Myra was always telling us things like, 'Blessed are the poor,' and, 'There is a virtue in simplicity,' but I did not want to listen to those sayings now. It was nice to lead the big life and have rich things, like Auntie. And yet be simple and sweet like her, too. 'Oh cricky!' I thought again. That last saying came right round, like a circle. But we were drab, really drab, sitting next to Auntie. For instance, 'Look at Mr Clunis' – I thought. I turned my head towards him and if I'd been in the mood I would have laughed out. He was wearing a coconut-stained vest and three-quarter length blue-dock trousers, and all he had on his feet were alpargatas. I had heard talk that Auntie had liked him when they were small. I couldn't believe that, but she certainly did not seem revolted by him now. Yet I couldn't imagine her thinking well of him, he was looking so ridiculous. Mr Reid was not too bad. He did not say much as he sat there with his grey hair and his weary-looking eyes. But I knew he was extremely glad to see Auntie and I could see that she appreciated it. Although when he heard Auntie was here he came just as he was – as Mr Clunis did too – his clothes did not look so ruined. It was a good pair of trousers, with only one patch. And although his old-time striped shirt was frayed at the neck, it was clean.

As for Mother, she was always clean and neat, and because of this people always said we had money – which was not true. Even though my father was dead they said that, which made Mother angry. Of course Auntie did send her a little help from Panama regularly. But even I was amazed that she could keep looking so tidy and clean. Because she was always in the smoky kitchen, and also, she was always working at that St Joseph factory – which Mr Clunis said was no joke. But now, even with the neat polka-dot dress she was wearing, she looked drab near to Auntie. I was

4

thinking about all this and hardly listening to their chatter, and it was only when I heard the word 'Braffie,' that I pulled myself to attention.

Mother said, 'So he's in the Canal Zone? What's there like, girl?'

'Oh, it's very interesting,' Auntie said. And somehow she looked a little distant in saying it. As if her mind wasn't really on it, or as if she wasn't sure. It was almost as if she was being false, only that Auntie could never be false. I looked at her charming smile as she turned to Mother. 'It's nice, girl,' she said. 'Beautiful. You know, it's the Americans there, mainly, and you know the Americans have the money and could always fix up a place nice. I hear the pay is great – er – I mean the pay *is* great. Yes, the place is beautiful, and as Braffie always says, the most beautiful thing is the money.'

'And what about you!' Mr Clunis said. Both Auntie and Mother pretended they did not hear him. I found Mr Clunis was out of order, too, and yet I could not help saying to myself, 'Yes– what about Auntie!'

Mother said, 'Glad it's like that over there.'

Mr Clunis was looking at Auntie, 'Claris tell me you holding down a good job.'

She looked at him, serious at first, and then she broke out chuckling, and she shook her head. I felt a pang of resentment towards him. She said, 'So what, Clunis. What's that to you?' I felt the answer was just right, but Auntie could not fix her face to look serious enough. In fact she broke out chuckling again.

He said, 'You working and you can't even help a feller?'

Mother laughed. Auntie looked at Mr Clunis with mock disdain and said, 'What? Help you and leave Clar and Horace? You must be raving mad.'

Then he whispered something and she said, 'I must tell Braffie about you!' All three of them were convulsed in laughter, and even Mr Reid laughed too.

When Auntie recovered she said, 'Mr Reid, you ever hear more nonsense? You are the only gentleman round here. For miles. By the way, so you still have that buggy?'

She cast a quick glance at Mr Clunis as Mr Reid was answering. 'Same old buggy,' said Mr Reid.

Auntie replied, 'You still looking good, Mr Reid.'

5

I was feeling furious within myself because I thought Mr Clunis was out of place and I felt Auntie and Mother were too lenient with him. I didn't hear what he had said to make them laugh, but I knew he was being forward. I hoped Auntie would tell Uncle Braffie about him – but I did not have much confidence in that. Because when she said she would tell she didn't look it. In fact she wasn't angry at all, and I felt it was simply because it was her first day back, and because they had been childhood friends, and – well, because she wanted to be easy-going. But I hoped she wouldn't be so silly as to lend a helping hand to him! She had said: 'You expect me to leave Clar and Horace and help you?' Something like that. I was touched by her speaking that way because she always helped us, and Mother said that since Pa died she did this almost as a duty. Almost every month something came to us from Panama. I liked her very much for this way of hers but now I felt I liked her even more for her own sake. Because she was so nice. It was as if today was the happiest day of my life. Only that Mr Clunis was so pushy and bold. Instead of just coming and saying hello and going, he was sitting down there and talking as if he was Auntie's boss. He was doing as if –

My thoughts jerked to a standstill as I looked up and found everybody's eyes on me. Mother said, 'What's wrong with you, Horace? What happen?'

'Nothing.'

Mr Clunis laughed but Auntie looked concerned. She said, 'I thought you'd be so glad to see me, but I was wrong.'

'No, Auntie,' I hastened to say. 'No, Auntie.'

'No, what? No, you ain't glad? I know that. Because you sit down there looking so woe-begone.'

Mr Clunis said, 'Woe-begone? You mean vexed!'

'No, Auntie,' I cried, feeling tense and almost desperate. 'No, Auntie. I ain't vexed. I'm glad you come.'

'Okay. But I can't believe that. Not with that face so serious.'

Mr Clunis whispered something to Mother. I did not catch what he said. At the same time Auntie got up, crossed in front of Mr Reid, and came and threw her arms around my neck. She said, 'You see this boy? This is my real pal, and we have a long time together. We have a whole month. We have to dig chip-chip and bathe in the sea, go up La Point – we have time for all of that. So attention now ain't nothing.'

Almost together Mr Clunis and Mother said, 'You staying a month?' Not that Mr Clunis was satisfied, though. He wanted more. You could see he wanted her to stay all the time.

Auntie said, 'Well, I took one month's leave. If you want me to go back before, I'll go back.'

Mother cried, 'Don't make joke!' and Mr Clunis breathed hard. Auntie chuckled. She knew she was nice and that everybody wanted her and nobody wanted her to go back.

She looked towards Mr Clunis, who, apart from the hard breathing, did not say anything at all. I for one wished he would get up and say goodbye, but he sat there looking at her, and now he had a silly smile on his face.

She said to him, 'I don't know if I told you, but Braffie's coming over, you know.'

His face changed, and he blurted out, 'Oh no. When?'

Auntie and Mother nearly choked for laughing, and Mr Clunis, seeing it was a joke, twisted his silly face, and looked up to heaven as if to say he was so relieved.

Then Auntie changed the subject. She said, 'But Clar, what about Mona and Ulric? Thought they'd be here already. They knew, didn't they? They knew I was coming.'

Mother said, 'Of course. They knew you was coming today, but they didn't know you'd be here so early. You bet they expecting you to come tonight.'

Mr Clunis said, 'Well let Horace go and tell them.'

Auntie said, 'Oh no, no. They'll come.'

Mother said, 'Perhaps Mona isn't even home, and to walk up all that way for nothing! And as for Ulric, I'm sure he's still in the sea.' She turned to Auntie, 'You know he's in Stanley's seine?'

'Still?'

'Still.'

'How's he doing?'

'I suppose, good. Said he's the second man on the boat. They catch a lot of fish but I hardly see him.'

Auntie simply said, 'You hardly see him.' And she looked at Mother, and she shook her head ever so slightly.

Mr Clunis was at the moment saying something to Mr Reid. I was watching Auntie and Mother, and I knew the understanding look they gave to each other. I suppose I knew the situation so well because I read Auntie's letters to Mother, and Mother always complained because Auntie condemned the others for, as she said, 'passing on the other side'. She was usually furious with them, saying they should keep close to Mother, even if they couldn't stretch a helping hand. She always said Uncle Ulric could at least help now and then, seeing that Eddie died. She always said she expected nothing from Mona, 'the glamour girl,' (as she called her) but she couldn't understand why Ulric kept away. In fact, it was her last letter that touched me so much. I almost learned it by heart. I liked the part where she wrote: 'To tell the truth, girl, they just don't care. Yet when Eddie was alive you know what he was. You know how he was always helping them. But don't you worry. Clar. You know whatever I can do, you could count on me. I want to bring you a nice piece of gold. A chain, like. Over here people keep that for security, and that's what I'm giving it to you for. Because you never know what will happen, and you don't know what might happen to me. (By the way, I have something to tell you, but that will come later.) But just fancy, that brother and sister of ours. And you struggling there with Horace who ain't have no father. No man in the house. Look, Clar, I'll get a nice piece of gold for you to keep and that will bail you out if the worst comes to the worst. Clar – '

I jumped, as I felt a hand on my head. Auntie said, 'You dreaming away again? Come on, man. Tell me something. How is school? Tell me.'

Mother began chiding me and saying she was disappointed, and Mr Clunis said, 'Like he really sorry you come, Roomeen?'

I did not know what to say. I felt so confused I couldn't even talk about school. Mr Reid, who had not said much, now leant over to Mother, and I saw his weary-looking eyes on me. He murmured, 'Claris, the boy day-dreaming because he's so happy. His little heart full – you ain't see how he keep sitting down there and keep on looking at Roomeen? In any case, how could anybody feel sad when Roomeen come?'

'All right, watch it, Reid! Watch it!' Mr Clunis cried, shaking his fist at Mr Reid, and pretending to be jealous. Peals of laughter went up. Then Auntie got up from where she was sitting and said, 'Okay, well Mona and Ulric will come later. Boy, how I want to go and walk about and see the place!'

No sooner had she said so than Mr Clunis got up. He said, 'Well, come on.'

Mother said, 'Let the girl take it easy, eh. She here for a month. A whole month. You, Clunis, you give her a chance. You'll see her some other time. You don't think we have things to talk about too?'

A surge of gladness rushed up in me because it was the first time in my life I had seen Mr Clunis look so sheepish. In fact I wished he would take it as an insult, but I didn't think he was capable of that. Then, too, Mother did not say it as harshly as she should have. She was never forceful. She was always calm and quiet when she spoke, although you could tell from her tone of voice when she meant business. She meant business now, so that was one good thing. And she was so right, too. I thought of Mr Clunis and I said in my mind, 'After all!' I thought, good grief, Auntie just arrived and Mr Clunis wants to take her away for a walk. Even old Mr Reid felt as we did, judging from his face. In fact, out of the four of us, Auntie seemed to be the only one who hardly bothered at all. There was a cool breeze blowing from the sea and all she said was, 'Oh, that's wonderful. This is a wonderful breeze. That's why I love Mayaro.' Mother said no more, and Mr Clunis, after fidgeting a little, got up, walked down the steps, and slinked away. Then Mr Reid said he was going because he knew Auntie had travelled far and that he had seen her yawn and he knew she was tired and must be wanting a little rest. I smiled because he said this as though he was not aware of what had taken place a while ago. Auntie put her arm around his neck, and she said, 'All right, Mr Reid, it's so nice that you came. I really appreciate it. Thanks a lot. We'll see, eh?' And when Mr Reid walked down the steps and went, she came back inside.

Mother said, 'But that Clunis bold-face, eh?'

Auntie said: 'But you didn't have to make him feel so bad, Claris. *Caramba*!' She looked half-joking and half-serious.

❋ Two

IN THE EVENING, after Auntie had looked around the place and was taking a rest, Mother sent me up to Quarters to tell Uncle Ulric that Auntie had come. She said, 'Go up and tell Mona, too. They probably forget – I don't know. I thought they'd be here already.'

'You want me to go *now*?' I said, reluctantly.

'Yes. Just now it will get dark.'

'Well, wake up Auntie, then.'

'Why wake up Auntie? She ain't going. Boy, you better run up the road quick and tell them, eh!'

My mother did not get the point. She was so simple and kind and good that she did not guess why I said to wake up Auntie. I looked upwards and although the sky was still bright, darkness seemed to be already gathering among the fronds of the coconut leaves. I took the main road and hurried down to Quarters, walking and running. When I got to the Manzanilla Road junction, I turned left by Miss Wong's store and went down the Plaisance Road to Uncle's house. I was just in time because he had just come in from the sea. His feet were still white with sand and his clothes were still wet. When I told him about Auntie he was very much taken aback and he seemed to tremble with excitement. He said, 'What you telling me – Roomeen here? In Mayaro? That's what you telling me?'

'Yes, Uncle. Ma didn't tell you she was coming?'

'Yes, Claris said something of the sort, but – my God! I didn't realise it was today.'

'She there now, Uncle Ulric.'

I looked up at him and I could not help smiling to myself, because he was so agitated he did not know what to do. I was standing up in the yard. He went up the steps into the little old house, then after a few moments he came back in front the door, then he went in again, looking very jittery. I had never realised before that he cared about Auntie so much, because he never seemed to show it. I mean, whenever he came home, which was 'once in a blue moon,' as Mother always said, he never asked how Auntie was going, and did Mother hear from her, or things like that. But he really seemed shaken now and as if she meant a lot to him, and I was almost ashamed of what I had been trying to put across to Mother. I was thinking of this when Uncle appeared at the door and said, 'How long she come. I mean, how long she's in Mayaro?'

'She arrived just after lunch.'

He looked very flustered and said, 'Look, I just come from the seine, but I ain't changing. I going just so and call Mona.'

'Oh yes. Nearly forget. Ma said to tell you to call Aunt Mona.'

It was as if he didn't hear me. The little old house was somewhat dark inside, and it never seemed to be inviting. The steps were broken and the door was not straight on its hinges, and when it was open, like now, you could see a rickety old table with tins and seine things on it, some jumbled against the wall. Uncle also had clothes hanging from nails on the walls and I remember how once when Mother was here she kept on talking and looking around with a funny expression her face, and Uncle was upset because he felt she scorned him. Mother did not scorn him but she just did not like coming here. She said the place was too untidy. I stood up in the yard thinking of all this. He had now finished closing up the windows – in fact, tying up the windows, because they had lost their latches and they had strings to be tied on to nails. He came and shut the front door, but even that wouldn't shut properly. Then he stood up before me wearing his vest and short blue-dock trousers. In fact, he was dressed just as Mr Clunis except that his trousers were soaked with sea-water all down the front. I ventured, 'Uncle, your trousers,' and I pointed to the wetness.

'They only a little damp,' he said. Then he said, more to himself, 'This boy always makes me laugh, saying trousers instead of pants.'

I was conscious of it. 'It's a habit,' I said. 'It's through Teacher Myra. She always want us to say "trousers".'

He wasn't even listening to me. He went to the side of the house for his bicycle, pushed it across the little drain and into the road, and said to me, grinning, 'She brought lots of things?'

11

'Ah – well, not sure.' The question took me by surprise.

'Not sure? She give out things already, then. She give Claris?' And when he saw how confused I was looking, he said, 'What I mean is this – she open the trunk yet?'

'Which trunk, Uncle?'

'Any trunk. The big one.' Then he said, nervously, 'This boy so dotish!'

I pretended I was even more dotish than he thought. But what I was hoping was that by now Auntie was up.

We began to walk up the road. I didn't even look back towards Plaisance and the sea, although the fishermen were blowing conch shells down there. Which meant there were lots of fish. Something struck me. Funny how Uncle did not think in terms of fish at all, for his beloved Roomeen. Beloved? I made an ironic smile. We were walking along side by side, but suddenly he must have found we were walking too slowly for the next moment he jumped on his bicycle and said, 'Okay, you can come, eh? I going in front.'

'All right, Uncle.'

I walked up slowly to the junction. All the time I was thinking about him. I was really shocked and taken by surprise. When I had broken the news and had seen him agitated, I had really believed that he had cared for Auntie. But of course I knew better now. In fact, I was right when I had told Mother to wake up Auntie. For I had wanted Auntie to give Mother the best things first, before they came on the scene. As Auntie herself would have wanted to. But Mother did not know what I was talking about! I felt a bit disappointed in Uncle, and every time I heard the conch shell from Plaisance beach, and thought about the amount of fish that must be there, I was even more convinced that he didn't really care about Auntie. Because he was working in the seine. Even if he didn't bring home fish he could have gone back and got some. But no, he was riding away as if he couldn't wait. I walked up slowly and watched the bicycle go out of sight on Station Hill, and all the time I heard the nervous, enquiring voice in my head: 'She open the trunk yet? . . . The big one.' If I was not so angry I would have laughed.

I was walking very slowly for I had intended when I got to the junction to wait for him there instead of going up Post Office Hill, where Aunt Mona lived. But to my surprise long before I got to the junction I saw Uncle Ulric speed down Station Hill on his bicycle and swing into the road I had come along – the Manzanilla Road. On the back of his bicycle, sitting on the carrier, was Aunt Mona. Uncle Ulric spotted me walking up and he made a sign saying I would meet them home at St Joseph.

I felt very irritated because I had come all the way to tell them and now they were in such a hurry they were leaving me behind. Let them go, I thought. Let them rush up there. Getting near to the junction I saw my friend Lennox sitting at the front of his house. He said, 'You down here? You didn't come to school this afternoon. Why?'

I did not answer. I was so upset.

He said, 'How come you didn't come? What's wrong? Something happen?'

"To me? No. Everything's okay.'

'Everything's okay but your face looked vexed.'

'No, I was just – . No, it's nothing.'

I reached him and was standing up.

'You didn't come to school,' he said, 'and Teacher Myra talked about you. She asked for you.'

I didn't say anything.

'Your Uncle just passed down towing Miss Mona.'

'I saw them.'

'Boy, your uncle brave! Towing in front of the Police Station.' Then he giggled and said, 'Anyway, that's okay because Cordner like her.'

I turned on him quickly and clenched my fist but I did not hit him. He thought I was making fun and he laughed but I was not making fun. It was true I was annoyed about Aunt Mona but I wasn't going to let anybody say all sorts of things about her. I did not know who Cordner was but I guessed he was a policeman. Lennox knew that Aunt Mona was a glamour girl and that all the men liked her. But he wasn't going to make fun of her in front of me! I felt like punching him in his mouth. I remained silent and breathed hard as he walked with me towards the junction, slowly, and my temper was dying down fast. The only reason why those two were so silly to *tow* in front of the Police Station was because they could not wait to get up to St Joseph Estate. And it was not that Uncle did not know towing was against the law – in fact he always said a king fish or a carite could smooth out any troubled waters. He meant he could always bribe somebody with a fish. Lennox was talking about how the day went in class, and about the girls, and so on. I listened to him talking and if I wasn't so upset I would have told him that my aunt had come from Panama.

When we got to the junction he looked up the Manzanilla Road and he said, 'Night coming, boy. You'll have to walk fast. You coming to school tomorrow?'

'But of course. How you mean?'

'Well you didn't come today – in the afternoon.'

'Had things to do.'

'Had things to do because it wasn't composition – your favourite.'

'Composition isn't more favourite than – than what happen.'

'What happen?'

I hesitated. Then I said, 'Me Auntie come.'

'Auntie?'

'From Panama.' I felt as if my heart was crying out.

'Oh, that's why Mr Ulric and Miss Mona do that. They excited! Oh, that's why they bolt up St Joseph like a bat out of hell!'

'Getting smart,' I chuckled.

Then he said suddenly, 'But wait. This Aunt in Panama. That was in the composition Miss read out last week. I mean, she is real? Some Roomeen or something so?'

He looked at me as if he couldn't believe and really wanted to know. I just laughed and walked away.

When I arrived at St Joseph, Uncle Ulric and Aunt Mona had been there so long they had already had supper. Their cups and plates were still on the table and they were sitting at the table with Mother and Auntie Roomeen. Aunt Mona and Uncle didn't pay any attention to me when I arrived, although Auntie Roomeen made a great fuss of me and wanted me to have something to eat rightaway; and Mother, who had been looking out for me, said that I had taken ages to walk from Quarters. She said under her breath, 'A pity Ulric didn't bring you down, too.' Uncle heard and he said something about having one bicycle and could tow only one person at a time. I could have smiled to hear him say so because it was a common thing for Uncle to be towing somebody on his carrier, behind, and another on the handle-bar, just in front of him. He went on talking, saying much the same things over and over again, while Aunt Mona was sitting composed, looking on. Then he was silent for a little while, and afterwards he said, 'Claris, girl, I won't lie to tell you, when I heard that Roomeen come, boy, I just fly down here, yes! I was really longing to see this girl.'

'That's why you forgot Horace up there.'

'Well, I couldn't help it. He's me good pal, too.' He turned round to flash a smile at me.

Frankly, I didn't have any time for Uncle and I didn't really care for his smile. Because I didn't think he was speaking the truth. Ever since he had asked me about the trunk Auntie had brought I knew he was more concerned with what she had brought than with Auntie herself. I sat there thinking vaguely of this but watching Auntie Roomeen, and I was full of admiration for her. I was especially pleased to see her still in her red velvet Panama dress and her broad-brimmed hat, for I had wanted so much for Uncle Ulric and Aunt Mona to see how she came. I wanted them to see how gorgeous she had looked when she arrived, and especially I had wanted Aunt Mona to see what glamour was really like. Auntie Roomeen sat there laughing and talking and I was amazed to note how full of life she was and how new and fresh she looked – as though, in fact, she had just come round the corner instead of from Panama. She had such an easy charm and an easy style that she looked like one of those fashion ladies I sometimes saw in magazines. Models, they called them. Only I had never seen a black model. I was so glad she had put her dress and hat and shoes and jewels on again – all the things that she had come in – for when I had left to go up to Quarters she had been taking a rest. And she could not have been resting in them! I sat on the step, nearby, and I listened to the chatter, and I was sickened to hear the flattery Uncle was heaping on Auntie Roomeen.

'Girl, I so glad you come,' I heard him say to her for perhaps the twentieth time. 'And you looking so nice. Panama ain't make you a day older.'

That part was true enough, although it did not ring sincere, because Uncle was hardly looking at Auntie herself. His gaze was flitting from one place to another, all over the room. One moment his eyes were on what she was wearing – especially the jewellery on her hands – and the next moment his eyes were on her trunk, which was left in a corner of the sitting room. Why Mother did not drag it into her bedroom, I did not know.

After paying Auntie a great many more compliments, Uncle said, 'Girl, you loaded like San Juan mule!'

She said, 'Me? I ain't bring so much. Most of what is in there is old clothes.'

He began scoffing, and chuckling self-consciously, as if to say she was taking him for a damn fool. And then he said with a twisted smile, 'Like you have plenty old clothes, girl. Ay, ay,' and he winked at Aunt Mona and she smiled, and with her hands she seemed to wipe the smile from her face.

Mother said, 'How you mean she have plenty old clothes. She have plenty new clothes, too.' Mother, as usual, did not know what Uncle Ulric was trying to say.

He retorted, 'I know she have plenty new clothes. It's she who said the trunk full of old clothes. *She* said so – not me. I only said she loaded like San Juan mule.'

Aunt Mona laughed. You could see it was a sneering sort of laugh and maybe she was trying to rile someone.

'San Juan mule, eh?' Auntie Roomeen said to Uncle. Her voice was gentle and sweet. She said, 'Boy, I could tell you this, and you could take it from me – I worked like San Juan mule too.'

'Roomeen don't give me that,' Uncle retorted. He looked earnest now. 'You? You look as if you worked hard?' And he made stupes. Then he said, 'Look at your face, look at your hands how soft. You know what hard work is? In any case what Braffie doing!'

Auntie Roomeen glanced at Mother quickly and I did not know the messages their eyes exchanged, but Mother looked away, and I knew something was up. Auntie Roomeen stuttered and cleared her throat and then steered the talk off that course by saying something about San Juan mule. Which made my daft uncle 'take the bait,' as he would have said, for he pointed out: 'That's only an expression, *you load like San Juan mule*. You never hear that before?'

Aunt Mona said, 'She in Panama too long.'

I was irritated, because Uncle Ulric should have found out more about Uncle Braithwaite – Auntie's husband. Something was up, but I didn't know what, and although I had got the gist from one or two letters, Mother did not leave certain letters lying around. I really wanted to know, but both Uncle and Aunt Mona let Auntie lead them gently out of that talk.

When Uncle had asked Auntie Roomeen if she had ever heard about the saying, and Aunt Mona had made her silly remark, Auntie had said to Uncle Ulric, 'How you mean? They have one just like that in Spanish.' And she had then said something in Spanish which made all faces light up – including mine.

Uncle cried, 'Girl, you could talk Spanish?'

'So what?' Auntie Roomeen looked amused. 'That's what they speak in Panama – so I just have to speak it.'

'But Roomeen you is a master.'

Auntie laughed, and I had almost forgotten that soft, ringing, flaky, laughter. It was the first time I had heard it since I was very small. I wasn't looking at her now, but I was thinking. Vaguely, I was thinking of her laughter as a sound from the distant past, and at the same time it was as if I was still hearing how the Spanish had rolled off her tongue. And it was as if she had used a different voice to speak it, and I was sure Teacher Myra would have said she used a different soul. I said to myself, 'Auntie, you ain't only nice, but you is a genius.'

I was jerked out of my thoughts by hearing Mother mention my name. Auntie Roomeen said, 'Oh yes, sure.' I looked at Mother enquiringly. She said, 'I was only asking Roomeen to teach you Spanish.'

'Oh yes, Auntie,' I looked at her.

She smiled back and said something in Spanish.

'What's that, Auntie?'

'That's how we say "Of course".'

I was thrilled.

Uncle Ulric said, 'My head is too hard. I can't learn anything. In any case I too old to learn Spanish now.' He was looking at them as if they were pressing him to learn it. As if they were insisting. But nobody had said a word to him about it. Auntie Roomeen smiled softly.

Uncle Ulric continued: 'You see that there?' He was pointing towards the sea. The door was wide open, and ahead, not far from us, was the broad blue sheet, now looking purple-grey in the fading light. The evening was calm and the waves were

17

whispering – not crashing and breaking, as earlier on – but there was still white foam as the water rippled and swept to shore. But the tide was going back. On one side of the water, to the north, was Point Radix, which we called *La Point*. It jutted far out as if hugging up the sea.

'You see that there?' Uncle said again. 'That ocean? That is what I have to tangle with. Every day. That is my life.'

Auntie Roomeen said, 'Well, yes, it must be. Because since long before I left here, you working in seine. I hear you still with Stanley?'

'Still with Stanley. And even if I leave Stanley I can't leave the sea. Maybe – who knows – maybe one day I'll get me own boat. Because I'm almost captain, you know. I'm the second man. So I have the experience.'

'That's good,' Auntie said. I somehow felt he was more impressed with himself that she was with him. The way she was looking at him I knew she really wanted him to make good.

He went on: 'Seine is my life, girl. Fish. You ain't see how I come to see you?' He stretched out his arms to give a full display of his salt-stained and damp vest, but Mother, seeing his arms outstretched, said, 'Yes, that's how you come to see her – with your two long empty hands,' and I could not help bursting out laughing, because that was so apt. I got up quickly and fled down the steps into the yard. Uncle didn't hear me – in fact he didn't seem to hear what Mother had said, for he went on talking as if nothing had happened. From where I was in the yard I heard him repeat, 'You ain't see how I come? You ain't see me clothes? I come straight from the seine. From the time I heard Roomeen arrive I hustled up to get Mona and we come right away.'

'Thanks,' Auntie Roomeen said, and she laughed again and she said, 'Oh Lord!' It was Mother's little joke she was still laughing at, although she was trying to stifle it. She said to Uncle, 'You keeping well?'

He said, 'For that. Oh yes. Thank God.'

'And you, Mona? You are all right?'

'Yes, but don't kill me with big English. I okay.'

Auntie smiled but did not say anything. Mother was just staring at Aunt Mona. Really, this aunt of mine could be so unpleasant. She didn't laugh at the joke Mother had made – although she must have heard it – and I'm sure this was not so much because she liked Uncle, but she was always seeking to make us feel bad. Mother never liked it when I said Aunt Mona didn't care for us, but could I say anything else?

Auntie Roomeen said, 'Ulric boy, I could see that the seine-work agreeing with you – you look so fit and muscular.'

He smiled. Uncle liked to hear that. The muscles on his forearms were big and bulging, and as he had on only a vest, and his arms were bare, they showed up to advantage. Also, big veins were sticking out of them. His shoulders, too, were developed, and I always liked to see when he raised his arms for big muscles rose up under them, giving his trunk the appearance of a 'V'. The muscles which showed then were called 'wings,' and I came to the steps and said now, 'Uncle have wings, Auntie'.

She didn't know what I meant. Neither did Mother. Mother said 'Wings? You mean he is some angel?' Everybody laughed, including Aunt Mona. We laughed because we knew it couldn't be easy for Uncle to be that. I was still laughing when Uncle began explaining to Auntie what 'wings' were, and then he said to me, 'That's the rowing, boy. That's the rowing.' And he said to Auntie again, 'Girl, I really glad to see you.'

Mother said, 'You keep singing a song you so glad to see her. What you bring for her?'

'You didn't hear me? You didn't hear how I come here?'

'You couldn't even bring a fish?'

'I was home when the boy came. And I didn't wait for anything. I just went for Mona and we rushed up here.'

Mother said, sneeringly, 'You didn't bring anything but you know she loaded like San Juan mule,' and as Auntie's flaky laughter made me look up, I was in time to see Aunt Mona give Mother such a sour look, I felt hurt. I didn't think Auntie Roomeen saw it, and Mother certainly did not, for she was just getting up to reach for the lamp on the cabinet. It was quite dusky outside now and she cleaned the lampshade and then went outside for the box of matches. When she came back in and lit the lamp, the place was so bright and silvery I had not realised it had gone so dark. The lampshade had writing around its bulge, and this reflected on the wall in big letters: *Home Sweet Home*.

I saw these words on the wall every night but tonight they had a special meaning for me. They had a special meaning for Auntie

19

Roomeen, too, because before anyone could speak, she said, 'Oh God, Clar, even the lampshade glad to see me!'

Mother said, 'You sure right.'

Uncle Ulric said, 'But now *Home Sweet Home* for you is Panama.'

She laughed, 'Ho, ho, ho, ho.' She wasn't really laughing but pretending to be. Then she looked around at Mother and said, 'Tell him I'm only working in Panama. And that I was born right here, in case he doesn't know. Boy, I was born right here in Mayaro, on this St Joseph Estate, and on this piece of ground. This place is my *Home Sweet Home*.'

Aunt Mona said to Uncle, 'Don't bother with you, Ulric. You forgetting. You forgetting it's not Mayaro so much for Roomeen, it's where Claris is.'

And Aunt Mona tried to laugh this off as though it was a joke but I knew she meant it. And Mother knew it, too, and I was sure that Auntie Roomeen knew it. For Aunt Mona and my uncle were always saying that Mother was Auntie Roomeen's favourite. And come to think of it, she was, too. And I was glad.

Uncle got up now and he had everybody astonished when he said, 'Roomeen, you torturing me, man. Give me what you bring for me from Panama. I can't take the strain. I waiting too long.' He said it just like that and Mother looked shocked, and I could see Aunt Mona was embarrassed.

Auntie just looked at him with her mouth open.

'Come on, man, Roomeen,' Uncle went on. 'I know you bring something for me. Open the trunk, girl. Plain talk, bad manners.'

Auntie Roomeen couldn't help but break out laughing. She said, 'But what is this! But Ulric what you think at all? You think I'm a rich woman? You think I could afford to bring presents for you all?'

✸ *Three*

BY THE LAMPLIGHT Auntie Roomeen took out a few things from one of the trunks, and despite trying to smile, she looked a bit strained and hesitant, and at length she said, 'Ulric, this is a job for the day-time.'

Mother, who had recovered from the shock of his shameless begging, said, 'If she bring anything for you, she'll give it to you. Have some reason.'

Auntie said, 'Let me do things properly, in the day-time, Ulric. I could make a lot of mix-up now. And besides, I'm a little tired. You two could come tomorrow?' She made to close the lid.

'Hold your hand!' Uncle Ulric cried. From the time Auntie Roomeen had unlocked the trunk and lifted the lid Uncle's eyes were like eyes aflame. Maybe it was the lamplight that made them look so yellow and weird, but it seemed to me that it was the wonderful things that were in the trunk. Auntie Roomeen had asked Uncle to help her put the trunk on the table – which he had done willingly – and when she had opened the lid there were such squeaks of surprise from Uncle and Aunt Mona that even I went to the table too, to look.

Auntie Roomeen had said, 'What's all that for? There's a lot of old clothes and old stuff in here.'

Uncle had retorted: 'Well if those is your old clothes I don't want to see your new ones.'

And Aunt Mona had laughed a sort of false, mocking laugh.

The truth was that inside Auntie Roomeen's trunk looked like enchantment. Just like the beautiful clothes Auntie was wearing. There seemed to be only colourful and valuable things packed up inside the trunk. We could not see what they looked like, because, of course, they were folded up, but the colours were rich and beautiful, and there seemed to be velvets and satins in there, and other cloths which I did not know about. And there were other objects, too – wood carvings, trinkets – lots of things,

21

which, to use Teacher Myra's phrase, were 'exquisite and beyond compare.' I did not bother too much with the way Uncle Ulric and Aunt Mona had squeaked because Uncle, for one, was excitable, and Aunt Mona, well, you could never be sure. So it was Mother's face I looked at, knowing she was always calm.

And that was why I felt convinced that Auntie had brought wonderful things, for when Mother looked into the trunk her face lit up, and she said a long, 'Oh-h-h,' as if she was sighing.

When Auntie was going to put down the trunk-lid and Uncle had cried 'Hold your hand,' Auntie Roomeen had stopped the lid half-way and Uncle pushed it up again. At once Mother knocked off his hand from the trunk-lid, and said angrily: 'Is this trunk yours?'

Aunt Mona said, 'But Claris!' Uncle was too excited to take offence. He said, 'It have gold in there. I see something like gold.'

Mother said, 'Everything looking like gold to you. But even if it's gold, it's yours?'

'I didn't say so. I say I see gold.'

Mother said, 'Everything will look like gold in this light, silly. It's night. Roomeen said to come tomorrow, why you don't come tomorrow and leave things like that?'

Then Uncle said something which made me laugh. I laughed because Mother put me in a happy mood. I never thought she could be so firm as to put him in his place. To me, that was the sort of treatment Uncle needed. Aunt Mona was looking at Mother with raised eyebrows, but I did not bother with her. Anyway I had laughed when Uncle said to Mother: 'You said why I don't just come tomorrow. How I could come tomorrow when tomorrow ain't come yet?'

Teacher Myra would have liked that statement. She was in the habit of saying things like, 'Today is the tomorrow of yesterday,' and I knew she would have liked to think of this one.

Mother said, 'You in for making jokes, but not me. Look, Ulric just take things easy. Come tomorrow. If she has anything in the trunk for you, you'll get it.'

Uncle said in turn, 'Is this trunk yours, Claris? You hit off me hand because I talk about gold. Well, for your information, I saw gold, and I just wanted to see what it was.'

Auntie Roomeen was not saying anything but just smiling.

Her head was turned to Mother but she was not looking at her face.

Mother said to Uncle, 'You just wanted to see what it was? Why? It don't have anything to do with you or me. You think Roomeen could afford to bring gold for us?'

'She could afford to bring gold for you!' he said laughing. And Mona nodded her head and said, 'Exactly.'

Auntie Roomeen let the trunk-lid drop, and Uncle said, 'You see, she closing it up?'

Auntie put her arms akimbo and said, 'But it's my trunk. Good Lord, what's wrong with you?'

I could have jumped for joy, and I could see Mother was thrilled, too. Aunt Mona laughed a sort of forced laugh, and she said, 'Yes. Tell them, girl, Roomeen. They don't know you is a big shot now. They don't know you really big.'

Although Auntie Roomeen had spoken firmly to Uncle, she had not spoken harshly, and she did not even look annoyed. She put her arms akimbo, more for style, and she looked so nice in doing it, but mostly I liked what she had said, for Uncle really needed putting in his place – although he never stayed in it too long. He sat there grinning. But the big surprise was that after Aunt Mona had spoken, Auntie Roomeen got as near to being angry as I had ever seen her.

'So you think I'm a big fish, eh,' she said to Aunt Mona. 'Or you think that I feel I'm big. Well you better get that out of your silly head because nobody's trying to play anything. I'm still the same Roomeen and who want to see could jolly well see that. All I did was go to Panama and work hard. That's all. You are my sister just as Claris is, and if I seem to help her more it's because she needs more help. For instance, she has this little boy here and Eddie's gone – '

'Don't come with that,' Aunt Mona said. Aunt Mona was sitting beside her, on one side, but her chair was pulled out and half-turned, so she was almost facing her. Mother was on the other side of Auntie Roomeen. Uncle was alone on the other side of the table, and he was standing just where he could see everything in the trunk when it was open. Auntie Roomeen was standing, too, and now she leaned back on the trunk as Aunt Mona began to speak. She looked at Aunt Mona: 'Don't come with what?' she said.

Aunt Mona did not turn around full to Auntie Roomeen, but she tilted her head on the side and with her large eyes, fixed Auntie Roomeen. I wouldn't say she was disrespectful, but the way she looked it was as if she did not care.

'*That.* What you saying there. Don't come with that. Because we all know you have a soft spot for Claris, ever since we were children. You was the biggest and you used to do what you liked, but you liked Claris more than us. And since you in Panama you never write to me, and yet Claris – '

Auntie Roomeen interrupted, 'You ever wrote to me in Panama?'

Aunt Mona was confused for a moment and she could not answer, and then she kept on with what she was saying: 'Yet there's so many letters from you on Claris chest-of-drawers. Claris is your favourite, why not say that? Don't talk about Eddie because he just kick the bucket last year.'

I was already vexed about Aunt Mona and now I got even more upset to hear her say Pa 'kicked the bucket.' As if he was a ramgoat or something! I wished Pa was alive to hear that. He had never liked Aunt Mona much and it was just because of this sort of way she had. She went on talking and I wasn't even listening to what she was saying – I was so annoyed. I was looking at the sea and saying to myself that I could never like this aunt in my whole life, when the call made me jump: 'Horace.'

I turned around. 'Yes, Uncle.'

He looked towards Aunt Mona and said. 'The boy's face all right. What you talking about. I ain't see any frown.'

I turned towards Aunt Mona but she wasn't looking at me. My face was sweet and smiling. She whispered to Uncle, 'I just thought he looked vexed, that's all.' She had said this in a quiet drone, and she added, 'You know how little boys can be mannish.'

I looked from Auntie Roomeen to Mother and from Mother to Auntie Roomeen, pretending I didn't know what was going on. As expected, they both looked furious, and I could see Mother was going to say something, but she held back. She sat there, rigid, biting her lips and looking at Aunt Mona. I knew she didn't trust herself to speak, and I was glad in a way, because this was not the time to make a big quarrel. Aunt Mona was paying no attention to them, and she sat cross-legged in a casual elegant fashion. I didn't like what she said, but I was trying to keep my face sweet. So I couldn't tell myself now that I hated her because it seemed that all my feelings showed on my face. I looked at Uncle and he too seemed relaxed and casual and he was watching the few lights atop Point Radix. It was during this time, I felt a strange, awkward silence. Then Aunt Mona said, 'Okay, Roomeen. It was nice seeing you. Glad you arrived safe. You look good. Ulric, you ready?'

She got up and walked to the front of the door and everybody got up. And that was another thing with Aunt Mona. When she got up everybody had to get up, as if the world was spinning for her alone. That was how she liked life. If for instance Uncle Ulric had got up first she might have said she wasn't ready yet. She was standing up right in front of the door now, beside me, and the others went down the steps. She said to me, 'You was looking at the sea boy. And I thought you was upset.'

I grunted and smiled. Looking at her I could not deny to myself that she was looking elegant, too, in some way. She was neat of frame, and everything she did looked graceful. For instance, the way she held on now to the edge of the open door, with a leaning posture – even this looked elegant. One knee was bent and the other straight and she was angled against the door and her left hand was across her body and holding on to her right shoulder. I didn't know if she was posing but she did not look as if she was. While the others were talking, she said to me, 'That's what you call pitch-black night. You can't even see *La Point* good. Nothing at all.'

I said, 'But if you look good you could see the light on Paul Urich's house. Right across there.' I stretched my hand out to where the round-off of the point would be. She couldn't see my hand well, although the brightness inside the house cast a faint glow on the step. She said, 'Paul Urich still around?'

'Yes, Aunt Mona.'

'Tide in, boy.'

I knew she was looking at the sea and I turned around. Tide was coming in again. It was only by the roar and the crash of the breakers we could tell tide was coming in, for we could see nothing ahead – only a few faint stars above where the horizon would be. I was not feeling so angry with Aunt Mona now. After looking at the horizon I glanced up to say something to her, but I was taken aback. Instead of her gaze being on the sea it was turned back to Auntie's trunk on the table. I looked back. The trunk was not closed properly, but apart from that I could see nothing to speak of. All this while Uncle, Mother, and Auntie Roomeen, were chattering outside in the yard, not far from us. When Aunt Mona had seen me look at her she had said something funny, about the trunk looking like a crab-trap. This was true in a way – just the angle it had, and the lid not closed right down. I laughed. And this was funny in itself, because it was the very first time Aunt Mona had ever made me laugh.

'Come,' Aunt Mona said, and she took me to where Auntie and Uncle and Mother were. They were talking about Panama, and Auntie seemed to be explaining how the country and the climate and the life there was so much the same as in Trinidad, and yet so different. Then Aunt Mona asked a question which had Auntie Roomeen answering excitedly, but just when Auntie was in the middle of bringing things to light, Aunt Mona said, 'Just a minute.' She was gazing at the sea and then she bent down to ask me something. Auntie Roomeen glanced at her but continued talking.

I was very anxious to hear what Auntie Roomeen was saying but Aunt Mona's question took me aback. I put a finger to my mouth. 'What causes tides?' I asked myself. I was sure that Teacher Myra had told us. If so, it had slipped me completely.

She said, 'You don't have no book – no dictionary or so that have it?'

I began to wonder in which of my books I would find that. It wouldn't be in a dictionary, I thought. Maybe geography?

She said, 'Well come on. Let's see. Where's your books?' As she went tripping up the steps she turned back and said, 'Roomeen, 'scuse us. This boy wants to show me what cause tide.'

When we got into my room she said, 'Where's the dictionary? You have a good dictionary?'

'I think it's the geography book that should have something about tide.'

We stayed a little while in my room, with Aunt Mona tracing with her finger every entry in the dictionary, and with me poring over the geography book. Then Aunt Mona said, 'Let's go and sit down at the table and look for this thing properly.'

At the table she took the geography book from me and gave me the dictionary, and when neither of us found anything, she said, 'Why you don't go and see if it's in your history book.'

'It wouldn't be in history,' I said, and I stopped and thought. Then I got up to go inside and I said, 'But it might be in – '

She said, 'In mystery?' We both laughed. I had been remembering the passages called 'Nature Notes,' that Teacher Myra used to give us. I was thinking it might be in those.

While I was in my room, looking amongst my books I heard her talking to herself. She said, 'I always look at this tide and wonder what cause it. I mean to say if this ain't a mystery, what is?'

I searched for 'Nature Notes' and all the time I was feeling astonished because I had never guessed Aunt Mona cared about the tides or about anything like that. I must have stayed a good few minutes looking for the notes, and another little while trying to find something about tides in them. But there was no such thing. When I came out of my room Aunt Mona was still bent over the dictionary.

She looked up: 'Found it?'

'Nothing at all, Aunt Mona.'

'And nothing here neither,' she said, pushing the dictionary away from her. Then she said, 'What other books you have?' She got up and went into my room.

'They won't have anything like that,' I said. I went and showed her what I had and she looked through them and after a very short while she said, 'Chuts, man. A simple thing like that you ain't have?' She turned around to go and as she pulled open my room door, she stopped short. There was Uncle Ulric standing at the table just in front of the door.

Aunt Mona said, 'What you doing there?'

Uncle Ulric had a frown on his face. 'You going or you ain't going. So long I waiting on you?'

'Where's Claris and Roomeen?'

'Talking out in the yard.'

Aunt Mona looked at me.

Uncle said, 'Look, Claris and Roomeen have all night here, eh. They spending the whole night – not me.'

'Well I only just come up here with Horace,' Aunt Mona said. 'He was trying to show me what causes tide.'

Uncle just made stupes and walked down the steps before us.

Auntie Roomeen and Mother were on the same spot still talking about life in Panama. The story must have been very absorbing because not only didn't they seem to miss us but they didn't even realise that Uncle Ulric had left them. Because when Aunt Mona had joined them again, complaining how Uncle had hurried her up, I heard Mother say, 'Ulric was inside? I didn't know that. I really thought he was so quiet.' Auntie Roomeen laughed and said, 'Cat-foot, boy. You move like the wind.' But Uncle Ulric seemed so peeved with Aunt Mona that he went straight to his bicycle. He brought it before the door in the little light. But Aunt Mona wasn't ready to go just yet. She said, 'Ricky, just give me a few seconds,' and I was so annoyed because she made Auntie Roomeen go over much of the story again. Auntie Roomeen had to talk about exactly where Panama was, and how it was, and I heard her saying how everybody there spoke Spanish, but how workers from the West Indian islands – like herself and Braffie – spoke English together. And I heard her talking about the Panama Canal, and she got worked up describing what it was like, and what people had to do, and at this point Aunt Mona said, impatiently, 'Girl, you like to talk about Panama, eh?'

We were all shocked. There was silence and when Auntie Roomeen caught her breath she said, 'Mona, it's you who asked. I wouldn't go over all this again if it wasn't for you.'

I couldn't see Aunt Mona's face, for the darkness, but I heard little sounds as though she was chuckling. She seemed suddenly light-hearted. She said, 'So all the hats over there are Panama hats, girl,' and she burst out laughing. But she alone laughed at her joke. There was silence with Auntie, Mother, and me, and I heard Uncle make stupes from where he was. He had rolled the bicycle over to a coconut tree and he was lighting the little oil lantern. Auntie Roomeen had made a reply, but although I did not hear it I giggled because I heard Mother giggling in the dark. Aunt Mona just said, 'That's good. That's cute. When you miss me I'm gone, girls.' She walked up to Uncle's bicycle. Uncle said nothing but just leaned the bicycle and in the dull red glow Aunt Mona sat sideways on the cross-bar. Uncle called 'Okay, then,' to Mother and Auntie, and strangely he didn't seem angry now. Aunt Mona said, 'Bye,' as they pushed off. The next moment all we could see was the red glow flickering through the palms.

❃ Four

WHEN UNCLE ULRIC and Aunt Mona returned the next day Auntie Roomeen's face was looking so strained and nervous that the first thing Uncle Ulric said to her was, 'Like you don't want us here, girl – why you looking so irritable?'

'Irritable? Who's irritable? I ain't irritable,' was the reply. But she looked so uneasy, it didn't need Uncle to tell me something was wrong.

I had suspected something was wrong since I got up. Being so moved and not having to go to school I had gone over to Mother's room to see Auntie again – just to make sure that she was real and that she was really here. The reason I went then was because I had wakened up twice in the night, both times on account of Auntie. In one case I sat up on the bed, my heart beating fast, and I was looking out into the black night and thinking about Auntie, and I got filled with doubt because I was not sure whether I had not just dreamed that she had come. But then, thinking about it, I knew that it was real, because of Aunt Mona and Uncle Ulric. But when I lay down again some time afterwards I dreamed that Auntie had not come at all and that everybody was expecting her but she had written and said that she was not going to come. I went out into the sitting room, disturbed, but when I lit the lamp I had to laugh at myself because there was Auntie's trunk still on the table – only that it was wide open now, for Auntie must have been sorting things out after I went to sleep. Still, although I saw her trunk and knew she was here, I got up early and went to Mother's room, because I had wanted to see Auntie with my own two eyes. Teacher Myra had a way of saying: 'Seeing is believing,' and I felt that seeing was never more believing than now. There she was, lying down on the side, with the sheet thrown half over her, and the other half showing the pretty blue night-gown with frills at the neck. She was lying there, her eyes closed, her head sunken in the pillow, but in the light—I had turned the lamp down low—I could see her kind face and her charming big frame. But although her frame was big there was something dainty about it, and she lay there sleeping like a black angel. Only that in all the pictures I had seen, I had never see an angel that was black. I stayed there a little while looking at her, feeling happy within myself that no one else was lying there but my Auntie Roomeen. Mother was sleeping on the far side of her, lying face downward on the pillow. I left, satisfied.

The dawn was hardly grey when I went back again to peep. I always got up early, but this was ridiculous. It was just because I could not sleep again. I did not expect them to be up but I thought I would peep at them and then go out to the beach to have a walk. When I opened the door of Mother's room I was taken aback. Auntie Roomeen was sitting up on the bed. She had her face in her cupped hands.

'Auntie,' I said. She looked up, then her face was bright with smiles. She pulled me to her and hugged and kissed me and she said, 'But look at my nephew! Boy, you've got so big, *carajo!* That's Eddie's face in print. So how you going, Horace?' It was as if she had not seen me at all the night before, so glad she looked. And yet I was sure she had been in tears when I entered the room; and as if to bear me out, her eyes looked red.

'Auntie, you all right?'

'Yes,' she said, 'Why?'

Beside her, Mother was still lying down, asleep. She had turned, and she was sleeping with her mouth wide open. I wanted to say something to wake up Mother for Mother to see Auntie's eyes like that. But she was still sleeping heavily. Beside Auntie on the bed was an empty purse, which she had seemed to ransack—for it was turned inside out—and there were all sorts of things strewn on the bed — pieces of paper, gold bracelets, handkerchiefs—all sorts of things. Auntie saw me looking at that and she said, 'I was just looking for something here. You heard when I was out in the hall?'

'No, Auntie. Oh, perhaps it was that noise that wake me up. The first time.'

'First time?'

I stuttered and said, 'Auntie, I wake up in the night, I didn't know why. Perhaps it was a noise. I was sitting up on the bed and

I was thinking about you. And then I went to sleep again and I dream you didn't come.'

She laughed. 'I am here, Horace. Don't bother about dreams.'

'And then I came and saw you sleeping.'

She seemed touched. 'You came *here?*'

'Yes.' Then my lips trembled. I said, 'You was sleeping like – like an angel.'

She laughed her light, flaky laughter. She said, 'I don't feel like an angel right now. I went out there to the trunk looking for something. I didn't find it. But I didn't panic. I came back and slept and I went back and searched a while ago. It isn't there.'

'Something important, Auntie?'

'Oh, no. Not really.'

'Your eyes red.'

'It's so – early on mornings they are like that.'

'You wasn't – you wasn't crying, Auntie?'

She laughed so loudly that Mother opened her eyes and turned. Auntie looked at me, then put a finger to her mouth and said, 'Sh-h.' I hadn't made a sound. I watched her and she gave me a big smile. I tip-toed out of the room.

I went and stood on the steps looking out towards Point Radix. I was thinking: if it's nothing, Auntie's eyes wouldn't be red. She said that was the way they were on mornings. Perhaps it was true.

Because otherwise her face was bright and cheerful. Especially when she had smiled at me. Although her eyes were watery. In fact, thinking about this now it reminded me of some of these bright days here at St Joseph, when you could see the mist far away on Point Radix, and the sky had a certain bright strangeness you could not describe, and you knew that before you turned around twice it would rain.

I stood there on the steps, looking towards Point Radix and thinking. Then I said to myself, 'Something really wrong. It's something she can't find and she want it.' I thought of the misty, far-away look I saw in her eyes, and I said to myself, 'She's wondering about something – I don't know what.'

All through the day Auntie was like that – the misty, far-away look in her eyes. And as the day wore on one could see she was very worried, although she tried to conceal this by pretending to be bright. And although there were gay cheery moments when Auntie seemed to forget – which almost made me forget too – Auntie was like that until Uncle Ulric and Aunt Mona came, and I could see Uncle noticed it right away, from what he said. Having already told her that it seemed as if she did not want to see them, and that she was irritable, he further upset her by saying again: 'Like we is really a nuisance? What wrong, girl?'

Aunt Mona said, 'Well she only has to talk plain, and we'll go back.'

Auntie Roomeen repeated that it was all right, that it was nothing. She was looking down at the floor, seeming harrassed, and Mother said sharply, 'The girl said she ain't vexed, you can't take that? You have to insult people?'

Mother did not usually talk like that – she did not usually snap at people – but she was always very nervous when it came to Auntie Roomeen. She was looking from Uncle to Aunt Mona, but she was looking at Aunt Mona more so. Aunt Mona opened her eyes wide to reply to her. 'Who you mean – me?'

Mother did not follow it up, for fear of causing a row. She began talking to Uncle Ulric about something quite different.

All the while they were sitting there I could see Auntie Roomeen was under a strain and she did not want to talk. And after a little while she said she wasn't feeling well and that she was going inside to rest.

Uncle said, 'Oh! Well. Oho!' And he shook his head knowingly. 'I know when something wrong. That was not Roomeen – Roomeen is a bright, lively sort of person – I mean to say, I was wondering what happen. As a rule the girl is like a new shilling. I knew something had to be wrong.' He turned to Aunt Mona, 'You didn't see how she was nervous and fidgety, and looking at us underneath? I know something was wrong. It must be this change of climate.'

Aunt Mona said, 'I didn't know change of climate used to make you watch people underneath. But if people feel you come for what they have – well.'

Uncle Ulric looked at her reproachfully.

Mother did not hear what Aunt Mona said, for she had just taken Auntie Roomeen to lie down. And it was a good thing too that she did not hear because Mother would have surely given

Aunt Mona the right answer. Not that Mother was quick to give any answer, but it was a fact that when it came to Auntie Roomeen she was as touchy as a setting hen. She would have wanted to know what the hell Aunt Mona meant by saying that. Only that Mother would not have said 'hell.' But still she would have wanted to know what Aunt Mona meant. I wanted to know, too, but I had to keep my mouth shut. Mother came back from the bedroom and Uncle asked, 'She all right?'

'Yes. She ain't too bad, you know. Just nerves a little frayed.'

He said, 'Nerves? Why?'

'Maybe it's the long travelling.'

Aunt Mona said, 'Well, she was all right last night. Anyway, my nerves getting frayed too, so I'd better go.' She perhaps meant this as a joke, because she laughed, but Mother didn't take to it kindly.

She said, 'Mona, you mean even for Roomeen you wouldn't have a little compassion. The girl travelled from Panama.'

'If it's anybody it's you who should have compassion for Roomeen. You are her favourite.'

Mother said, 'The girl down and out with tiredness. She ain't herself at all.'

I looked at the floor and smiled to myself. I said to myself, 'Boy, you have a mother and a half.' Mother had pretended she didn't hear what Aunt Mona said, and had begun to speak even before Aunt Mona had finished. And yet she came very near to giving Aunt Mona just the treatment that she was needing. I saw when the anger flashed to her face, and I saw the blaze in her eyes, her mouth was already open – but she swallowed, and began to talk about Auntie Roomeen not being herself. Not that Mother was a hypocrite. She just didn't want to clash with Aunt Mona. Especially as Auntie was here. In any case she didn't believe in what people called 'bacchanal.' She hated rows. She was always trying to make peace. I didn't find it was paying now, though. I found Aunt Mona was getting more and more out of hand.

Uncle was leaning over to Aunt Mona, mumbling something, and I heard Aunt Mona say: 'It really don't make no sense.' She was shrugging her shoulders. 'Stay here for what? If we want to see Claris we could always see Claris – Claris ain't no novelty. She's here morning, noon, and night. We came to see Roomeen.

If she's resting, my dear, it makes no sense staying.'

'But she has something for us.'

'Who told you so? She said so?'

'Well she said come today.'

Aunt Mona looked towards Mother and at the same time I saw Mother give a sleepy-headed nod. She was tired too! I looked away and smiled. Playing with Claris! I thought. Mother wasn't a trickster but I was sure she did that so that she would not have to say anything. And I was sure she didn't mind Aunt Mona leaving. Mind you, whether her nod was genuine or not I really did not know.

Aunt Mona looked towards Uncle: 'Ulric, it really ain't make no sense waiting. You can't hear she ain't feeling well? If I had my own bicycle I'd just go.'

Uncle said, smiling, 'You ain't have a bike but you have your own two feet.'

She couldn't help chuckling. She said, 'I ain't walking that distance.'

I smiled too. Briefly. I was sitting on the steps, and I had turned to look, but I turned back now, looking at Point Radix. 'That aunt of mine!' I thought. Aunt Mona was pretty. To be honest, she was the prettiest, most glamorous, of the sisters. But the way she talked – good grief, she wasn't nice at all. Just imagine saying that. I shifted around slightly and after a few moments I glanced sideways at her sitting there, stylish, her head slanting, her big black eyes so attractive on her smooth black face. The fact was, she looked prettier tonight than usual, the way her hair was. She often pressed it straight, but somehow she had not done it these last few days and it looked beautiful and thick and black. Like Auntie Roomeen's. And she resembled Auntie today, too, and she resembled Mother a little bit. At least you could see right away they were all sisters. Pity this one was so silly. Because she had poise and charm. From here, sitting on the steps, I could not see her hands resting on the table, but you bet her long, thin fingers were looking special with the nails cutexed and well-manicured as always. She was dressed very elegantly in her sailor bodice and blue skirt, and I really did not know if it was meant as a tribute to Uncle that she was dressed in the colours of the sea. Aunt Mona was the sort who would pay tribute to no one but herself. Yet, if you did not know you would say she was such a sweet person. Everything on her was charming and nice – except her tongue.

It was only early afternoon and Mother started talking about other things with Uncle. Aunt Mona was staring Uncle with her big eyes, and Uncle said now, 'Well, look, I'll come back Claris. I'll have to go now. But I'll come back because I'm positive that girl won't come all the way from Panama without bringing anything for me. She must bring me some kind of thing. And when I say something I mean *something*, you know. Panama have gold. So don't bother about any shirt or any – '

'Or any Panama hat,' Aunt Mona cried, and they burst out laughing. Then Uncle getting serious again, said, 'And you Claris, I ain't harping on it but don't tell me "no" about gold you know, because I saw gold.'

Aunt Mona said, 'Your eyes good boy. You saw more than me.'

I didn't know if it was because Uncle said he was going but Aunt Mona was now in a bright, cheerful mood. Uncle said, 'But I said so last night. I said I saw gold. Claris, ah lie?'

Mother said, 'Ulric, whatever we get we have to take.'

Aunt Mona said, 'Because you know you getting the best – eh Clar?'

'You always say that kind of thing.'

'And they always true.'

I was glad that Uncle got up just at this time, because Aunt Mona was ready to pick a quarrel. When he got up she remained seated – I suppose because he got up first. And because she was hot to have words with Mother. Her mood had suddenly changed. It was bright just a while ago, but now it was the sort of mood Teacher Myra would have called 'churlish.' As for me, I would call it 'vicious.' She seemed ready to snap at anything. As Uncle turned round talking to Mother, Aunt Mona got up. Uncle said to Mother, 'Let Roomeen rest, because I'm coming back here for what is mine.' He seemed to be making fun and yet he seemed deeply serious and counting on what he imagined Auntie Roomeen brought for him. He said to Mother, 'You know what I want? Gold, girl, gold.'

'Because Roomeen is a gold-mine!'

Aunt Mona was already down the steps, else we would have been sure to have a biting remark from her. She was already standing by the bicycle, and she was looking impatient.

Uncle said to Mother in a low voice, 'That's yours? The thing that I saw inside there. I didn't look at it good. She bring it for you? What I – ' He stopped short when he realised Mother was looking sharply at him. Before Mother could speak he said, 'You too damn stupid, Claris. You know anything about Panama? Roomeen bring gold.'

'Yes, because Panama is El Dorado!'

I heard soft laughter, and when I looked round it was Aunt Mona passing up the steps. I was surprised that she was laughing now. She said, 'Ulric, you going or you spending the night here.' She went into my room, perhaps to fix up herself nicely, because when she came out again she was preening herself. She had a hair-pin in her mouth and she loosened some hair on the side, and she fixed it in place and then she took the hair-pin from her mouth and pinned it. As she came down the steps Uncle was walking towards the bicycle. She said to Mother, 'Roomeen still sleeping? Tell her we gone.'

'When you coming back?'

'Coming *what?* Back? I don't know.'

Uncle heard, because from where he was beside the bicycle, he called: 'Clar, oh Clar, we coming back tomorrow. At least *I* coming back. Come on, Mona.'

He rolled the bicycle off the coconut tree and leaned it, and Aunt Mona sat on the cross-bar. The wind was blowing her hair and she had one hand near to Uncle's on the handle-bar and the other holding her hair, and just in that pose she kept her balance as Uncle was pushing the bicycle out of the heavy sand. I was out in the yard and looking at this and I couldn't help saying to myself, 'Style you style!' I felt a gush of admiration for Aunt Mona, despite the sort of things she said. And despite the fact that I knew she did not like the closeness between Auntie Roomeen and Mother. It was just that everything she did was so stylish. And she was really so glamorous-looking. And on top of all that she really knew how to balance on the cross-bar. 'Jeese and Ages!' I said, as I watched Uncle push the bicycle out to the hard track, with Aunt Mona still balancing, holding her hair. Then Uncle jumped on the saddle. I watched until they disappeared amongst the coconut trees.

✳ *Five*

WHEN I WAS coming up the steps again, into the house, I was surprised to see Auntie Roomeen was up, and then I was even more surprised to see Mother with her hands to her head and looking at Auntie Roomeen as if awestruck. Neither of them seemed to notice me. Mother was looking as if she could not believe what she was hearing, and then she said, 'You mean that, Roomeen? Oh God!'

'What happen, Ma? Auntie, what happen?'

My Mother now had her hands over her face as though she was crying. But now, hearing my voice, she quickly removed them, and said, 'Horace, all right. It's all right. You could leave that alone.'

I knew what Mother meant then, and I knew she wanted me to go. Before I could move off to go back down the steps, Auntie Roomeen said, 'Just a minute.' She went to the dish-cabinet and from the middle shelf she took a glass and from the top she took out the goblet with water and filled the glass and drank. She looked at me and it was as though she had passed through a storm. Mother looked well shaken up, too, and her eyes were red, but she was not crying now. Auntie Roomeen said, 'Sit down, Horace.' And she looked towards Mother and said, 'You ain't wanting to sit down?'

'No, it's okay.'

I looked at Auntie and all the time I was wondering what sort of news it was. After Auntie and I had sat down she said to me: 'Your mother is saying it's all right, but you have to know. You should know. You remember when you got up this morning you said you thought you heard a noise?'

'Yes, Auntie.'

'And later on you came in the room and you saw me sitting up?'

'Yes, Auntie.'

'Well I was worried and really feeling terrible. All night I was worried. I couldn't sleep.'

I looked at her, waiting anxiously to hear what had happened.

'It's something I was looking for in the trunk. I couldn't find it. I looked in everything. I looked all night and this morning. And I'm sure now. That's why I didn't come out to Mona and Ulric.'

'What, Auntie?' I was still puzzled. 'What it was you was looking for?'

'You have to know exactly what happen. You remember your Uncle saying he saw gold in the trunk?'

'Yes.'

'And he kept on harping on gold?'

'Yes, Auntie.'

'Well, he *did* see gold – but it ain't have no gold in the trunk now.'

She looked at me, at the same time trying to force a smile, but her face looked very pained.

'Auntie, how you mean?'

'How I mean?' And in a mock American accent she drawled, 'It just ain't have no gold, kid.'

Mother shook her head and pursed her lips. I said, 'Ma, what Auntie talking about?'

'They thief the gold.'

It was as if something exploded inside me and left me weak. I wasn't expecting gold, but I wasn't expecting this sort of news either.

'Who?' I asked Mother. She did not say anything and I looked at Auntie.

Auntie said, 'Who? You asking me? It's one of them, that's all I know.'

There was silence. Then Mother sat down, rather heavily. Her face looked as if she was trying to figure out something. Then she was nodding her head slowly. Her eyes were still red.

Auntie looked at me and said, 'But with all that, I have my own suspicion.'

'Auntie, you sure it gone?' As I said this, Mother raised her head. The question seemed to put a little extra hope inside her. She said, 'Yes, Roomeen, you sure? Positive?'

'I looked everywhere, in every, *every* thing. The chain is a big heavy gold chain. Big links. It just can't hide. I looked through every single thing I brought. It's just not there. Come, you could see for yourself.'

We went in to Mother's bedroom, and Auntie went and sat before the half-opened trunk. It seemed to be packed neatly. She said, 'You know the number of times I open these things and search them and fold them and put them back?' As she said that she proceeded to take every article from the trunk and searched each fold, each pocket, and put it on the bed.

She said, 'But the thing is – this is only a waste of time. If it was here you bound to see it.'

I said, 'Yes. If you said it's big.'

'It's a big heavy gold chain. Thick. Claris couldn't wear it – it isn't made to wear. Just to keep the gold.'

'And Auntie, you sure it reached here with you from Panama?'

Mother said, 'She showed me last night.'

Auntie took out clothes and all sorts of things from the trunk until it was empty. Everything now lay on the bed. There wasn't a single thing more in the trunk, and the red velvet bottom was just glinting in the evening light. Auntie got up now and sat on the bed beside the pile of things. I remained there, kneeling beside the trunk, and my heart was hurting. I looked up at the faces of both Mother and Auntie. It was amazing how at this moment they so resembled each other. The way their faces were both twisted with anguish and shock, the eyes a little swollen – you didn't have to look twice to know they were sisters. Only that one was a bigger version of the other.

I began wondering what we could do. But before I asked that, I said, 'The gold chain worth plenty money?'

'You asking that so quiet!' Auntie cried. 'That was almost me life's savings – which I put in gold. Because you know what Panama gold is!'

'Your life's savings, Auntie, and you brought it for us?'

'Well,' she shrugged. 'That's nothing. You see, I might be going back, and – '

'*Might*?' I cried. For the moment I forgot all about the gold. Could Auntie be thinking of staying? My heart raced.

I looked at her eagerly, and she looked at Mother, and I did not know what language their eyes spoke, but she switched the conversation back to the gold.

'That chain's worth thousands,' she said. 'Thousands, you hear me? Money to change your whole life.'

Mother said, 'Good Lord.'

Auntie said, 'Anybody could take that anywhere in Port-of-Spain. To any bank, or pawn-shop, or even a money-lender, and he's a rich man right away because that is good good Panama gold.'

Nobody said anything for a while. Mother had her head turned towards the window, staring blankly towards the sea. She turned round now and looked at Auntie: 'That's exactly where he'll take it.'

I said, 'Who you mean – Uncle?'

She said, 'I ain't calling no names.'

Auntie said, 'But who else? Who was the one talking about gold, gold, all the time. I know he was trying to push his hand inside the trunk, but I didn't see when he took it.'

'No, Roomeen, it couldn't be that time you know. He couldn't take it then. The chain too big for that, we'd have seen him.'

Auntie agreed. We were all puzzled. We were all very uneasy and we went and sat down at the table in the hall. Mother was leaning against the table, her elbow resting on it and her hand propping up her chin, and Auntie was sitting up, her arms folded. They were both looking woe-begone, and I guessed I was looking even more woe-begone. I got up and went and sat down on the steps and my eyes were on Point Radix, but my heart was feeling depressed about the missing gold. It was getting dusky over there at Point Radix. The sea was unusually calm out there and there was only a spot of white where the sea washed the tip of the point. Usually there would be a crash of breakers and there would be so much spray that the tip of the point would be covered with white. Nearby, the murmuring of the sea told that tide was going down. It was growing dusky amongst the coconut trunks, too, and as I looked, there was the flickering light of a candle-fly.

I turned back. 'So what you'll do, Auntie?'

'Trying to figure out.'

Mother said, 'I think the first thing we have to do tomorrow morning is to go to the Police Station and report it. That is the first thing.'

Auntie said, 'But if it's Ulric – '

'We have to report it,' Mother said. 'We must do that first thing in the morning.'

Mother was resolute. In fact, she had seldom looked more resolute. Of the three sisters she was the mild, gentle one, and normally she would be the last to mention the Police Station. I was sure she had never gone inside the Mayaro Police Station in her whole life. She was talking to Auntie now and they were agreeing that they must go and report the theft first thing in the morning.

Mother said, 'We ain't telling the police it's Ulric. We just making a report, and if it turns up anywhere, if anybody try anything, well they'll know.'

'That's right.'

I sat there, my heart thumping. It was much duskier over Point Radix now, and I saw this without looking too closely. But I was aware of the fire-flies, their flickering light passing before me every now and again. I sat still and my thoughts were wandering far.

I was thinking about Uncle. Why oh why did he do such a thing! When Mother and Auntie made the report the police would know right away that he was the thief, because they were bound to ask who was there and when Auntie said Uncle had been talking about gold and that he had put his hand in the trunk, they wouldn't want to hear any more. The first thing they would do would be to go down to his place to find the gold, and then they would arrest him and put him in the cell. But at least Auntie would get back her gold chain – her riches, her life's savings. *Her* gold chain? *Our* gold chain. Riches that could change –

Auntie's voice roused me. 'Eh?' she was saying. 'Eh, Claris?'

'You mean go to him?'

'I feel so,' Auntie said. 'I feel we should go now and confront him and ask him back for the chain. After all, he must give it up, because he knows we know it must be he who took it. Sure he wouldn't want us to go to the police.'

Mother said, 'He might say he didn't take it. A whole day passed. He might say somebody came in the house while we were sleeping and took it. Let's go straight to the police, but if you prefer to face him – '

'Yes, I think that's best. Just let's go up right away.'

'How we'll go?' Mother said. 'It's getting dark. Old Mr Reid will take us, but I didn't want – '

'Put on your crepe-sole shoes and let's walk it.'

I got up and was going to put on my crepe-sole shoes, too, when Mother said, 'No, Horace, you stay here. Funny things happening. He could make a tack and come right back here.'

Then Auntie said, 'You think it's best to go up alone? What about Clu – ' And then she herself said, 'No, no, we can't let Clunis know about this. Although the police – well, hurry up, Claris.'

Mother was busying herself getting ready. She had gone into her bedroom and emerged with an old felt hat on her head and her crepe-sole shoes, and she had changed the frock she had been wearing for a brown hard-wearing Panama one which Auntie had given her. When she and Auntie were ready to leave she went into the kitchen and took up a cutlass. She said, 'This is in case we meet any snakes in the road. Come on, Roomeen, you ready? Let's leave Clunis out of this for now. Let's go up the road.'

It was the first time I had seen Mother so determined and forceful and strong. Mother dashed up the steps and went to her room and came back with the torchlight and then they both went down the steps. I was standing in front of the door. As they were walking out of the yard, Mother turned back and said to me: 'You ain't scared?'

'Scared about what, Ma?' I asked, surprised.

'That's my boy,' she said. 'We won't stay long.' In going, she stopped, then she came right back in front of the steps. She said, 'Look, don't let nobody come inside. I don't care who it is.'

'Right, Ma.'

I shut the front door and the windows and I sat at the table. I turned the lamp down low. If anybody came and called, once it was not Mother and Auntie Roomeen, then nobody was home. I was sitting facing the door and I had already gone into Mother's bedroom and brought out the knotted stick that my father used to walk with in the night, and I held it in my right hand as I sat. 'This is for snakes,' I said to myself and chuckled. Since Mother had said don't let anybody come inside I didn't intend to let anyone whatsoever come in, and if anyone came and called and heard no answer and still wanted to tamper with the door, then he would have to tamper with me! I didn't really want to think about it because I really didn't know what I would do if *he* turned up. But I knew I wasn't letting anybody come inside. My mind was on Uncle Ulric and although I didn't feel he'd make a tack back I didn't put it beyond him. Because there might be other valuable things he had set his eyes on. I didn't want to take any chances with those lovely and wonderful things from Auntie's trunk – those rich things which were piled up there on the bed. Satins, velvets, things of splendour. All sorts of beautiful Panama clothes. Carpets, rugs – to go where, I did not know. I even saw things intended for me, but my mind was not on them now. There were cups and plates and pots and pans – all from that massive trunk. And beautiful ornaments, too, which seemed to be worth much more than the gold chain we were trying to find. I couldn't risk anybody crossing the doorstep while my Mother and Auntie were out. I sat there for what seemed hours and waited while all sort of chirps and croaks and whistles punctured the night. It seemed an eternity that I sat there, and at last I heard footsteps. I waited and listened and when they came right up, Mother's voice said, 'Horace.'

I unbolted the door. 'Success?' I asked anxiously, even before they got inside.

✳ Six

WITHOUT ANSWERING, they came in and sat down looking despondent. Mother said, 'Anybody came here?'

'No. Why? What Uncle said? You didn't get it back?'

Of course, I could see on their faces they didn't get it back. Mother said, 'We didn't even see him.'

'You didn't see him? How come? He wasn't home?'

Mother did not answer. She was very upset. The way she had sat down heavily in the chair I knew she was extremely troubled. Auntie's face was very strained, too. I said, 'Auntie, but how come you all didn't meet him?'

'Because he wasn't there, that's how come.'

She said no more for the moment. I could see that the journey to and from Quarters, along with the disappointment, had taken heavy toll of them. But what was uppermost in my mind was the clear sign of Uncle's guilt. Uncle wasn't at home at this time of night. True, one could go out – go to see a friend, for instance – but it seemed very suspicious in this case.

I looked at Mother and Auntie sitting there. I thought to myself, that journey isn't so much really. I walk it to school and back every day. But of course I went in the morning and came back in the evening – not right away, as these two just did. It was two and a half miles to Quarters. They had walked it each way in vain. And as for the gold –

I said to Mother, 'The bicycle wasn't there?' She shook her head. Shaking her head must have made her remember the felt hat, for she took it off now. She had already taken off her crepe-sole shoes. The cutlass was lying on the floor beside her and the torchlight was on the table, standing on its face.

Something flashed to my mind. 'And you didn't go up Post Office Hill? Oh gosh! He's by Aunt Mona. Ma, you didn't even think about that?'

Mother said, 'He isn't by Mona.'

Auntie said, 'Even Mona ain't by Mona, far less Ulric.'

I fell into silence. Uncle wasn't at home, nor was Aunt Mona. Yet they both left here some hours back, to go home. I looked at Auntie Roomeen yawning in the chair, but I wasn't thinking of her very much – only about Uncle and Aunt Mona. I was wondering whether Aunt Mona was in it too. I did not feel so. I didn't think Aunt Mona would be in anything with anybody – just that she was that way. I looked at Mother to see if I could guess what she was thinking. I could see she was dog tired, the way she slumped back there on the chair. Every few minutes she gave a big yawn.

'Ma, why not go to your bed?' Then I asked, 'You think Aunt Mona is in this business too?'

'Mona don't want riches,' she answered, ending the sentence with another yawn.

'What make you say that, Clar?' asked Auntie Roomeen.

'Just the way she is. Mona takes life easy – she doesn't care about a single thing. All she wants to do is to look nice.'

'Well that's true. But you noticed she was very keen on what I brought from Panama? The things in the trunk. So I won't say she doesn't care about anything. I agree she wants to look nice. And she likes luxury. She likes nice things. But to have nice things you have to have money.'

Auntie said that so casually, it was as if she wasn't thinking much about it. But I liked the way she took those two points and made them one. It was true that Aunt Mona wanted to look nice and liked nice things. And Auntie was saying if you liked nice things then you'd want riches. That was it in a nutshell. I liked how Auntie tied up those two points.

Mother and Auntie Roomeen continued talking about Aunt Mona, and now I heard Mother mention the word 'jealousy,' with emphasis. I looked quickly at her. Teacher Myra was always saying: *Jealousy is a crime.*

Auntie Roomeen said, 'I agree. Mona is like that. That's the main thing about her. Otherwise she's no great harm.'

'She doesn't care about people – let's face it. People's feelings. But the jealousy is the part I can't stand. That girl believe everything you bring is for me.' And Mother looked across to Auntie's chair and said in a different tone: 'But she wouldn't steal the gold.'

45

'Of course not.'

'It could only be one person,' Mother said.

There was silence, and after a few moments Auntie sat up. There was no sleep in her eyes. She said, 'I'm not vindictive, Claris – God knows. If Ulric was to bring back that gold chain, I'd be so glad, I'd have nothing more to say. Everything would be over right there. No going to police or anything. Just for him to bring back the gold, that's all. It's for you and Horace, but Ulric could share in it too.' I was looking at her. She was talking so clearly and loudly it was as if she felt sure Uncle Ulric was standing outside in the yard listening. At one time she even got me feeling he was outside, listening, and my heart was racing. But the only sound I heard was a 'clix,' and that was a sand cricket. I was still looking at her. She said, 'Horace, what I'm saying is true. If he'd only bring it back he'd get something.'

After a few moments' silence Mother whispered to Auntie, 'You heard something outside?'

'No.'

'But you just thought he was there?'

'Well, you said he might sneak back.'

'Not now. When we went up Quarters. I was frightened for your things on the bed; with this boy alone in the house.'

'Oh, I see. But who said he can't be outside now.'

Auntie was saying, 'Oh, I see,' but her eyes were closing. I knew they both would soon be asleep. As for Uncle, I didn't think he was anywhere near this village. I said, 'Ma, Auntie, so what we doing? Uncle is going in the sea first thing in the morning and then you won't see him till evening again. You can't leave him to go in the sea without seeing him. You have to catch him before he leave the house.'

Auntie Roomeen opened her eyes. She said, 'We know. We going up there early.'

I hesitated, and then I said, 'And suppose he say – '

Auntie put up her hand. 'Boy, don't say that. Because in that case we going straight to the Police Station.'

I didn't notice that Mother was wide awake, too, but she said, 'Make up your mind that we going to the Station. Just make up that mind. I don't know him as a thief but the way he was getting on, gold could make that man go mad. Perhaps he even gone and hide it – perhaps that's why we didn't see him.'

46

'But where is Mona?' Auntie said.

'But where is Mona? I don't know. So she have to be with Ulric? I told you Mona has her po – ' Mother suddenly remembered I was there. She glanced at me and then continued: 'Mona has her own little life to live, she ain't have to be with Ulric. Maybe she went walking.'

'Yes, but it's a funny time to go walking.'

'You find?' Mother said, and I turned towards her just in time to see her mouth shape 'policeman.' I marvelled to myself that Lennox was right. I had nearly boxed his mouth, but he knew more about my own aunt than I did.

Mother was talking and my heart gave a sudden heave when I heard her say, 'Once he doesn't let it slip and fall down to the bottom of the sea.'

Auntie Roomeen said, 'Oh God, don't say that.' She had been getting sleepy again but what Mother said seemed to chase all the sleep from her eyes. She sat up. My heart was thumping and I was having all sorts of fears.

'I was only making fun,' Mother said. 'At least I hope that won't happen.'

'Just don't make that kind of fun,' Auntie said. Then she yawned again, and at the end of the yawn she said, 'Look, Claris, we better go in and take a rest. Because we have to get up real early – don't forget.'

'It's early already. Girl, it's morning.'

Auntie Roomeen got up right away, murmuring something which I did not catch. Then as she was fixing the chairs in place to go inside I heard her say, more to herself: 'You see that gold chain? If it's the last thing I do I'll get it back for you all.'

For you all! I thought. So Auntie had really brought the gold chain for us! When they had both gone in I put out the light and went in too. My heart was throbbing. I said to myself, 'What an Auntie!' In her letters she had often said that since my father was dead, if anything happened Mother would know where to turn. And earlier on didn't she say she had brought if for our 'security' – or something like that? It hadn't sunken in then, but it did now. I sat on the bed and I could hear my own heartbeats. I was thinking all sorts of things but there was the big question in my head: *Where is the gold chain?* Auntie had kept saying if anything happened we wouldn't know where to turn, but of course if anything happened we'd turn to Auntie. Unless she meant in case she happened to be dead. God forbid! My heart thumped wildly and I had to lean over on the pillow. If the worst came to the worst we could never turn to Aunt Mona and we could never turn to Uncle Ulric. Thinking of Uncle Ulric I sat up, suddenly tense and fearful. I hoped that when we saw him in the morning he would just hand over the gold chain and say he was just making a joke and that he had just wanted to scare the daylight out of Roomeen. I hoped to God it would be something like that. Even if he didn't say anything I hoped he would hand over the gold chain.

I suddenly stopped talking to myself and listened. I could have sworn I heard a cock crow. It must be very late, or as Mother said, early – early in the morning. I smiled. I'd better lie down and try to sleep now and wake up in time, I thought. Because Mother and Auntie would be leaving before day broke, and I was going too. My little bedroom lamp was burning low. I stood up, changed my clothes quickly, then blew out the light. I said to myself, nervously: 'Oh God, that gold. Good Lord, boy. I wonder what happen? You think we'll get it?' When I lay down I could hear my heart thumping against the mattress.

❋ Seven

I WAS AWAKENED the next morning by the sound of Mr Clunis'
voice in the yard. At first I heard his voice and I did not open my
eyes and I was not thinking about him at all. But suddenly I
remembered and I opened my eyes and when I saw the broad
daylight I jumped out of bed frantically.

I hurried out into the hall and there was nobody, and I went
into Mother's room but there was nobody in the house. 'Good
God!' I said to myself, 'They gone!' I was feeling wild and
depressed. Mr Clunis' voice still sounded from the yard, calling
'Roomeen, Roomeen.' I went and opened the front door.

'Ay, Horace, it's you? Where Roomeen and Claris?'

'They ain't here.'

'That's what I was thinking. They ain't come back yet? What
happen?'

'Don't know, Mr Clunis.'

'Where they went – Quarters?'

'I think so.'

Although I was feeling wild and frantic I still kept my head on.
I would never tell him they went up to Uncle to ask about a
missing gold chain. But I was wondering how he knew they
weren't here.

He stood up just there in the yard, wearing a torn-up stained
merino and blue-dock shorts. The shorts were frayed at the
ends. In one hand he had a cutlass and in the other, his big oval
hoop, which we called 'bicycle'. I didn't know how it got that
name. Coconut-pickers climbed coconut trees with that. I was
looking at him but I wasn't really bothering about him at all. I
was furious with myself for having over-slept and for having let
Auntie and Mother go off without me. Also, it seemed so late it
was as if it had passed my school-time. Mr Clunis said something
which I didn't hear, and then he spoke again: 'Like you ain't want
to answer me? I talking to you and you wouldn't answer?'

'Oh, I didn't hear you.'

'You didn't hear me and you standing up right there? I ask you when she coming back.'

When *she* coming back, mind you; not *they*. Mr Clunis only wanted to know about Auntie Roomeen. I said, 'But Mr Clunis, I only just wake up. I don't know. I just just wake up, and I have to rush to school.'

'School, now?'

'It late?' I felt frantic. All the time I was standing there I was thinking of how it was looking late for school, and of how Auntie and Mother had gone, and I was wondering what time they left and how late it was now. Mr Clunis looked towards the sun, which was big and round and glinting, and was not too high from the sea. He said, 'It's about a quarter-to-eight.' I looked at him as if I didn't believe, and he said, 'About a quarter-to-eight, I telling you.' And he laughed and said, 'That sun, that's me time-piece, boy.'

I felt a little relieved. If it was a quarter-to-eight then I'd better hurry up and foot it fast down the road because I could still get to school in time. Perhaps I'd get there just a little after half-past eight. Mr Clunis was still standing in the yard. He said, 'Who went out last night, with a torch-light?'

'Mother – and Auntie.'

'Something wrong?'

'No. They had to go out.'

'And they had to go out this morning too? Early, early I seeing the light going up to the main road. I was just getting up to have me strong coffee to go to do me work. Early, early. I could make out Roomeen hustling up the track. When I say early I mean early, you know. Day didn't break yet.'

I said nothing.

'And you want to tell me nothing ain't happen?'

I turned my head to the floor and to the wall as if I was looking for something. I couldn't think of a proper answer. As I began to stutter, he said, 'Okay, I know you want to go. You have to get to school in time. But Horace don't look at a big man like me and say nothing ain't happen. Look, for the morning I climb nine coconut trees already, and I woulda climbed more if I wasn't looking out for those people. Not a sign.' He looked disappointed. He went on, 'And as a rule smoke pouring out from you kitchen because your Mamie making tea. This morning nothing. So I know something wrong. At least I know she ain't come back yet.'

I said to myself, 'Oh, you know, and you still come calling.' I stood there looking at him and feeling jittery to go and dress and hurry to school. But I couldn't walk away from him. He said, 'The only reason I ask is because I only want to help.'

I nodded but I did not say a single thing. It was nice of him to say he wanted to help, but I knew the only person he was worried about was Auntie Roomeen. Because we were there all the time and he was never usually so nervous about us. I knew how silly he was over Auntie Roomeen but I had to pretend I didn't know anything. And to tell the truth I was almost frantic for him to go because the minutes were passing and I had to hurry up and get ready for school. He saw how uneasy I was and he began to move off. As I was turning to go inside he said, 'Don't forget, tell them that if it's anything at all, I right here.'

'Okay, Mr Clunis.'

After he left I was busy like a windmill. From the time he said it was a quarter-to-eight it must be a quarter-past-eight now. I turned round and dashed down the steps into the kitchen, then I dashed back inside. I took up my tooth-brush then I dashed down again to brush my teeth and to wash my face, then running back up the steps and making for my room, I collided with a chair, and myself and the chair came crashing to the floor. It was a good thing, too, for when I tried to get up, holding on to the table and grimacing with pain, my eyes caught sight of a slip of paper on the table under a spoon. I had seen the spoon but had not noticed the slip of paper. I took it up and looked at it. It read:

Horace, you still sleeping so we gone. I have biscuits in the kitchen in the green tin, and you'll find cheese in the safe on the third shelf. Make some chocolate tea and eat something before you go to school. Try and don't oversleep. Claris.

I wasn't what they called 'mannish,' but I made stupes. Just fancy reading 'don't oversleep', when you already woke up late. Of course, Mother wasn't to know that I was going to over-sleep, but if somebody is sleeping, could he read? And fancy signing 'Claris.'

51

I put back the slip on the table and I put the spoon on it. I dashed to my room and quickly changed from my night clothes. I took out a pencil from the pocket of my school-pants and held it in my hand, then I put on my school-pants and shirt, then I combed my hair, put on my crepe-sole shoes, and I took up my book-bag. When I came out into the hall I rested my book-bag on the table and with the pencil I scribbled on the piece of paper, 'Gone to school'. How could I be gone when I was writing a note at home? I didn't have time to worry about that. I put the pencil in my pocket, rushed into Mother's room, reached for the key which she kept hanging from a nail, checked my book-bag, went outside and locked the door.

As I ran and walked through the track towards the main road I heard coconuts falling 'boop! boop!' I didn't even look up among the tree-tops to see if I saw Mr Clunis and I hoped he didn't call me. Because I knew he was seeing me. I wasn't thinking of him much. I said to myself, 'I wonder what happen up Quarters this morning?' I was thinking of Uncle and the gold chain. I wondered if he handed it over. I was thinking of this wildly, and I was thinking of school, too.

When I got up to Quarters I had to forget school right away. I was already at the school gate, in fact, when, just glancing up the hill towards the Police Station, I saw Aunt Mona's face at a window, and I knew that the worst had happened. I knew that Mother and my two aunts had come to report the matter to the police.

School had only just called, but instead of going in, I walked up Station Hill and turned up the gravel road to the Police Station.

When I got near enough, Aunt Mona called, 'What happen, boy – you ain't going to school today?'

'No, Aunt Mona. I want to see Mother. Mother here?'

'Yes, she's in the Charge Room. She and your favourite Auntie.' And she laughed. She was talking to one of the policemen, and they were both standing very closely together, looking out of the window, and Aunt Mona looked relaxed, even happy. I was taken aback by this. And then, too, I found it very odd that Mother and Auntie Roomeen should be in the Charge

Room and Aunt Mona out here. I looked at them stealthily –
Aunt Mona and the policeman. She was leaning against the
window, and the policeman was bending slightly, looking down
at her face, whispering, and I was sure he wasn't talking police
business. He was neat in his black boots and what they called
puttees, and his black shorts and grey shirt, and he had his cap
fixed at a cheeky angle on his head. There was a bench in the
open, platform-like gallery, beside the window, and I sat down
there and I thought, oh, that was who Mother meant last night
when she had whispered, 'policeman'. From the bench I peeped
towards where the Charge Room was, but I couldn't see anybody
inside. I got up from the bench and I went round and looked
through the Charge Room window and my heart raced suddenly.
For I saw that not only Mother and Auntie Roomeen were
inside, but Uncle Ulric was there as well. A strange-looking,
dressed-up Uncle. Auntie Roomeen was talking to the Police
Sergeant. None of them saw me. On the other side of the Charge
Room was another open window and through it I saw the little
concrete house, strong-looking, with the big round hole in the
centre. That was the cell! You could see that place from the
road, too, and I had often passed looking in to see if I could see
who was inside. To tell the truth it was inside there that I had
expected Uncle to be now. I went back and sat on the bench.

When I sat on the bench I turned to glance at Aunt Mona and
the policeman, but that window was closed now. Aunt Mona has
no shame, I said silently. I told myself I could never like her.
Although I couldn't see inside the Charge Room from here I
wasn't too far from it, and I could hear the gruff voice of the
sergeant and I could hear Auntie answering, and sometimes
Mother, but as much as I listened, I couldn't hear Uncle saying
anything. At intervals, against the voices of the Charge Room, I
could hear whispers coming from Aunt Mona and her policeman
friend. I was conscious of them but the big question knocking
against my head was: 'What happened this morning?' I didn't
expect to see Uncle there in the Charge Room. I did not really
know what to expect. What happened? I asked myself. Did they,
rightly, charge him and were just taking down a few details
before they dumped him in the cells? Or was he challenging
what they accused him of? Did he come to tell the sergeant that
the gold chain was his? But nothing of the sort seemed to be

going on. I could not hear what they were saying but there didn't seem to me to be any heated dispute. I couldn't understand it. I knew Mother was withdrawn, but Auntie Roomeen could explain things, and forcefully, and I was sure she could put the matter beyond any doubt. And in any case, why didn't Aunt Mona go and join them and tell the sergeant exactly what happened? She was there. She was there when Auntie opened the trunk and was going to close it back when Uncle cried out, 'I see gold!' He had even held back Auntie's hand. Why didn't Aunt Mona go and join them instead of shamelessly whispering there with that policeman? I got even more infuriated than I had been. The window which faced on to the road from where they were, was wide open, and anybody passing in the road could see them. Anybody –

I jumped. Uncle said, 'What happen, boy? You look so tense and rigid. I didn't even know you was here. Nobody see you yet?'

'Aunt Mona saw me.'

'She saw you. That – ' He didn't say it. He continued in a low voice, 'You mean she saw you and she wouldn't even tell us you here. Too taken up with that so-and-so.' He was breathing fast. Then he put his hand on my shoulder and said, 'Boy, they tell me the gold gone. Good Christ. I wonder who slip in there and thief that? We just making a report about it. God, I wonder who thief that!'

It was a good thing I did not open my mouth because I might have said, 'You, Uncle.' And heaven knows he did not slip in but had come in the broad light of day. Or was it in the night? Was it in fact that time when Aunt Mona was in my room and opened the door to find him standing at the table? She had been trying to find what caused tides, and when she opened the door she said, 'What you doing here?' Auntie Roomeen's trunk was on the table then. Was it that time? I was confused and I was feeling pain and desperation. Despite the kind way in which he had greeted me, and despite the harsh things he had said about Aunt Mona – which I liked – inside me I felt very resentful towards him. For apart from doing such an awful thing as stealing the gold chain, he was bold enough to go to the Police Station and report its theft.

I sat there motionless, looking at the concrete floor, and I wouldn't say a word. Uncle was standing there beside me, his hand on my head now. After a few moments of silence he said, 'Not you alone so depressed, boy. I in agony. Oh God, I wonder who could do that wickedness.'

I looked up at him. My lips remained silent but my heart cried out, 'Nobody but you.' He looked at my face and said, 'Boy something wrong with you? You look so terrible. You eat this morning?'

'No.'

'Oh, that's why. That's it. Why you don't go down to Assam and buy two buns.' He put something in my shirt pocket. I put my hand and felt it was a shilling. He said, 'I have to go back in with Claris and Roomeen. I only came out for a little air and I bless me eyes on you. Look, you better go down by Assam now and put something inside you. Your health is more important than all the gold they could thief.'

'Okay, Uncle,' I said, hardly wanting to look at him. I found it very hard to speak, let alone to say 'Uncle'. In fact, it was harder for me to call him 'Uncle', now, than to call Aunt Mona, 'Aunt'. As he left I looked, and there, in front of me, just putting his head round the door, was the sergeant. Uncle said, 'Sarge, it's me you looking for?' The sergeant mumbled something and they were both inside.

A flash of hopefulness surged over me when I realised the sergeant had wanted him, but what followed was the same dull questioning, instead of the sergeant putting him in the cells. At least it sounded like questioning, for Auntie Roomeen's voice was responding all the time, with now and then Mother's. I reflected on Uncle and on the falseness of his conversation with me, and the falseness of his dress. Because that was what his dress looked like to me – false. I had been accustomed to seeing Uncle in that stained, three-quarter length, frayed pair of trousers, with a vest – in fact very like Mr Clunis – and to me that was the true Uncle Ulric. But today he had on a brownish serge pair of trousers, a striped shirt, and a white drill jacket, with tie. When I had looked at him in the Charge Room I was astounded. I had never known he had those clothes because I had never seen him wearing them. Teacher Myra had always said something about the leopard changing its coat. She called it 'metaphor'. This metaphor suited Uncle so well, I was amazed. I was still thinking about this when Mother appeared.

'I didn't know you was here. Ulric just tell me. You didn't go to school?'

'I was going but when I saw Aunt Mona up here, I came.'

She said softly, but with disgust: 'As for your Aunt Mona! She just wouldn't come and talk, she said she didn't see any gold. She just prefer to stand up there chattering. I think it's Ulric she's trying to protect, but – '

'What Uncle saying?'

She looked around and she whispered: 'Saying he don't know anything about it. Talking as if he's more shocked than we. You could beat that?'

'And you didn't tell the sergeant?'

'Tell him what? We didn't see Ulric take the gold.'

'But who else, Ma?'

'I know, and you know, and Roomeen know. But we didn't see him take it. If the police asking questions you have to answer to suit. And you have to grind your teeth and take it easy.'

'You always taking it easy.'

She turned to me sharply. 'Look, you watch yourself, eh! And you better go on to school.' Then she said, less harshly, 'You never liked missing school. I know you upset about this – this gold; but you didn't have to come here.'

'I wanted to know what happen when you went to Uncle's place.'

'Well, I told you. If he was acting he could act good. He nearly dropped down when we said the gold chain gone. He said he didn't even know we had that.'

'Yet he nearly dropped down?' I gave a derisive laugh. Mother knew what I meant by that, and she looked at me and said nothing. Then I said, 'Ma, who is that policeman feller – Aunt Mona know him?'

Mother cleared her throat and looked around her, then she took up my book-bag from the bench beside me, dusted it and gave it to me, and did a lot of other little things, except answer. She began saying something about not having got much sleep, and hurrying up to Quarters in the dark with Auntie, and about how Ulric rushed up Post Office Hill to get Mona and brought them here to make the report. Then she said, 'Look, Horace, you better go to school.'

'Now, Ma? Nearly time for lunch-time. I'll go half-day.'

As I was talking she kept looking towards the Charge Room. She said, 'Let me go back with Roomeen. We'll come right now. Wait here.'

Mother certainly did not come 'right now', and although I had said it was nearly lunch-time, it wasn't at all, for it was a long while afterwards that I heard the bell ring for twelve o'clock. Mother and Auntie Roomeen emerged just before this time, and then Uncle followed, and then Aunt Mona and the policeman came out and stood up in the gallery not too far from us. I hardly noticed them because Auntie came straight and put her arms around me, and said, 'How? You all right? You cool? How long you here?'

'Oh, a long time, Auntie.' I was so glad to see her. Mother said, 'He turned up late but he'll go to school half-day.'

I guessed she didn't want to say that I saw Aunt Mona and came up here. I suppose she didn't want to call Aunt Mona's name. Aunt Mona was close by, and although she was looking towards us as if she wanted to say something, I could see that Mother and Auntie were trying to avoid looking at her. The policeman was standing beside her. Uncle was by himself, at the far end of the open gallery, and he was looking over the coconut palms to the sea.

Auntie Roomeen said, 'Look at these school-children in that road. Goodness. Boy, I'm fagged out.'

She did look worn out. I said, 'Auntie you had a hard time?' I couldn't hide it that I was pleased to see her. She was wearing an elegant blue dress with a brooch, and I had seen that velvety dress in the trunk when she was taking out the things. But even the dress looked a little faded now after the trying time she must have had in the Charge Room. When I asked her if she had had a hard time I saw her lift her head, and when I raised mine, Aunt Mona was looking our way. Auntie did not say anything. Mother said to us, 'Okay. Well get up. Let's go now.'

We got up, and Uncle Ulric came, and we began to walk down the slope. I glanced back and was surprised to see Aunt Mona walking down too. When we reached the main road from the yard of the Police Station, Aunt Mona said, 'You all going home now?'

Mother pretended she didn't hear and Auntie Roomeen said dryly, 'Yes, we'll see you.' Uncle was walking in front of us and I didn't know whether he had heard Aunt Mona. We had turned left, and as we walked down Station Hill, with the Government School on our right, I began to think of class and of my friends. The road was filled with children, and whatever cart or bicycle passed, it passed very carefully. As we walked down, the Plaisance Road lay straight and flat in front of us, and there was a glimpse of blue sea. To the left, just in front of the school gate, the Manzanilla Road swept away. The sun was hot on the road surface. We crossed, and Uncle said he was going straight down home, and Mother and Auntie went towards Miss Wong's store, at the corner of Plaisance Road and Manzanilla Road. Mother said to me, 'Well you better go on to school. By the way, you ain't have money to buy something to eat?'

'Uncle gave me a shilling.'

'Oh. And you had what I left for you this morning? Go on, then. We'll see you later. There must be some cart or something going up St Joseph.'

She went under the eaves of Miss Wong's store. Auntie went inside, talking to Miss Wong. I was feeling very hungry now. I thought I'd go and put my book-bag in school then go over to Assam's to buy something to eat.

When I came back running over the hill from Assam's parlour I was just in time for a big surprise. I was really taken aback. Mother was too. Mother was still under the eaves of Miss Wong's store, sheltering from the sun and looking for some sort of ride up to St Joseph, and Auntie Roomeen was still inside the store, when I heard, 'Woa!' and a horse and buggy pulled up. Mother was almost stunned. She was so surprised that she had to burst out laughing. Miss Wong, who saw this from the counter through the open door, cried to Mother, 'That's old Reid.'

Of course it was old Mr Reid. He was right there, holding the reins of his horse, and looking towards us, half-smiling with his weary-looking eyes – and inside the buggy itself, who could be grinning out at us but Mr Clunis! I suppose that was why I didn't laugh. Although, in a way, I was glad to see him.

Miss Wong called again: 'Take that buggy, Claris.' And she

said, 'Reid. Wait, they going up.'

Mr Clunis laughed, 'Heh, heh,' and he said 'It's them we looking for. Don't get excited, Miss Wong.' And the next thing he said was what I was expecting. He looked at Mother and said, 'Where's Roomeen?'

In all the commotion Auntie Roomeen had just looked on. Mr Clunis did not realise it was she who was chatting with Miss Wong inside the store. She came to the front now and walked down the steps. When Mr Clunis saw her his face changed. You could see he didn't care about anything else. Auntie Roomeen just smiled. Mr Clunis looked at Mother and said, 'You know how long we looking for you people! We pass up and down the Plaisance Road, because we thought you was by Ulric, then we went up the hill by Mona, and now we come here.'

Mother said, 'Oh, is that so?'

'Where you all was?' he said, but he did not get any answer. He came out of the buggy and he said, 'Get in, ladies,' but as soon as Mother got in he went in too, so he was bound to be sitting beside Auntie Roomeen. When he got in he stretched his hand to help Auntie Roomeen inside, and Miss Wong, who was now at the front of her store, laughed and said, 'Clunis is gentleman!' I laughed too, not because of Mr Clunis, because I was getting used to the silly way he behaved when my Auntie was around, but I laughed to see how Miss Wong laughed so much that her eyes crinkled up into two tiny slits. Also, it was funny about Miss Wong. Auntie was her good friend and they had both gone to my school – that same school across the road. Yet often when Miss Wong talked it was in the Chinese style. She ran the store alone because her parents were dead.

The buggy was not long in moving off and both Mother and Auntie waved to me. And I suppose it was only then that Mr Clunis saw me because he looked back and gave me a smile. I watched them turn the corner, then I said, 'Okay, Miss Wong. Going over to school.'

'Kay, Horace. Mind how you closs the road.'

'Kay, Miss Wong.'

❋ Eight

WHEN SCHOOL CALLED and I got into class everybody seemed glad to see me and wanted to know where I had been. Teacher Myra wasn't there yet. It was going to be English Grammar this afternoon and I took my book from my book-bag. There was constant chatter and I was a little shy because most of my classmates wanted to talk to me. Cedric, who sat beside me, showed me his copy-book to see what they had done in the morning. In the morning it had been Arithmetic but this afternoon it was going to be English Grammar. I felt excited about that. I glanced up at the blackboard and right away my heart gave me *voom-voom*. Written under the heading, 'English Grammar', and the date, were the words: Analyse and Parse: *Gold is where you find it*.

The whole class was chattering together because Teacher Myra had not turned up in front of the class yet. Nobody was attempting the exercise, which Teacher Myra must have written at lunch-time. Just behind me one of the girls was prodding my back.

'Yes, Lenore?'

'Why you didn't come this morning?'

'I was sick.'

There was a wave of sympathy around but Frank Fridal spoiled it. He cried, 'Sick? The boy went fishening with his uncle,' and hilarious laughter rang out in the class.

I laughed too, but I couldn't help thinking of the sentence on the board, and I was not only thinking how strange that it should be about gold, but I was already thinking of the analysis. In this subject I always wanted to be the best in the class. Cedric beside me had turned back, talking to Claudia, and as Lennox on the far side tried to attract my attention, I heard the voice say, 'Eyes front'. Teacher Myra came in front of the class. She said, 'Attention, class. Silence. There is work on the board.' She was looking around and then her eyes fell on me. She stopped short with surprise. 'Well, if that isn't Horace Lumpres!' she said. 'Well, well. Where were you this morning?'

About half the class cried in chorus: 'He was sick.'

'Good gracious,' she said. 'How are you feeling now?'

'Much better.'

'What was wrong?'

'Just fever.'

She came up to me and put the back of her hand on my cheek. Then she said, 'You don't have it now, though. Not so much. Good of you to come half-day.'

Then pointing to the blackboard and looking round the class, she said, 'Has everybody done this yet?' She looked at it and said: 'Analyse and parse: *Gold is where you find it.* Anybody finished?'

Nobody answered. She put her arms akimbo and said, 'Well, well. Do you know I put this on the board during my lunchtime? I went to lunch with my father and I came back early to put this on the blackboard. Come on, class, get at it. Has everyone a copy-book for Grammar?' She was looking around the class. 'Not your Composition book, please. Come on, get there now and work.'

As she was talking I started and finished it. It was easy. The boy just behind me, Clevin, nudged me, and then he looked over my shoulder to see how I was doing it. I covered it up with my hand. Then he whispered, 'Sums,' and I removed my hand. To me Clevin was a genius in arithmetic, and as we were both sitting towards the end of the desks, he could always pass me his book along the side of the desk without anybody seeing. That was the reason I got so many of the sums right. After I let him look, stealthily, by lowering my shoulder, I put up my hand. Teacher Myra came and took my book, then she went over to her table. Then after a few moments she looked up and smiled at me. That meant that what I'd done was right. She kept the book so that I wouldn't show anybody.

I looked down at my desk, contented.

After a few moments I heard her footsteps, and she was coming towards me. Everybody was quiet, working out the exercise. She came and put her hands on my cheeks again. While doing it, she said, more to herself: 'He's so good at English.' Then she told me, 'You haven't got fever now but you aren't looking so well, you know. Your face is warm, isn't it? Maybe you are feeling some strain. Do you want to go home and rest?'

'No, Teacher Myra. No it's all right,' I said anxiously.

'Well when you get home this evening take a rest.'

'Yes.'

'By the way, I saw the man – your uncle, isn't he? The one that fishes.'

'That's Uncle Ulric. I have just one uncle.'

'Yes, I saw him. I met Lennox on Station Hill and he told me that it was your uncle.'

'Yes, he was up here today,' I said, my heart beginning to race. I guessed that it was now I was looking tense. Teacher Myra was silent for a moment, then she said, 'He was with Mona.'

'That's my aunt,' I said, looking at her. I didn't even know Teacher Myra knew my aunt's name. She smiled when my eyes met hers but somehow in a way it looked as if it was she herself who was under strain, although she was smiling. It was strange because for a moment it seemed as if she was smiling and crying at the same time. Maybe I was really feeling sick, but I thought I noticed that. I looked away a little but now as I turned back, Teacher Myra was walking off and looking towards the class as though she meant business. I knew I had been wrong about her. Because there was no strain at all now on her face.

'Class,' she said, 'Come on now. Who's finished?' Several hands went up, and Clevin was punching into the air, trying to draw her attention. She ignored him. She said, 'Okay Claudia collect the books and bring them up.' She went back to her table.

When she had finished correcting the books she came and stood up in front of the class, smiling. She said, 'Most of you were right, but let's be honest – this was an easy one. Look how quickly Horace did it. He was the first boy, and he did it a long time ago. And he only came to school half-day,' she said, looking around the class. 'And he had fever,' she added. She looked at me and smiled. She said to the class, 'He still looks a little drawn.'

I was feeling so strange, it was hard to explain. Because of what Teacher Myra had said I was feeling quietly proud, but running through my mind all the time was the sentence: *Gold is where you find it*, and bigger against my mind was the gloom that had settled over me because of the loss of the gold chain. I

62

thought of it as 'the loss' although I knew that it was Uncle who had stolen it. After thinking about it about twenty times I knew it was Uncle and I was sure about it. When Teacher Myra had mentioned Uncle he came to the front of my mind, but of course I would never tell her what had happened. And she had mentioned my Aunt Mona. She had seen Aunt Mona and Uncle together on Station Hill. I began to get anxious about that. When? Was it midday? Was it – were they coming down from the station yard? My heart was going wild. Good thing she didn't spot me then, I thought. Good thing she –

I jumped as Lennox nudged me, and when I turned he made a sign with his head that someone was calling me from the back of the class. Teacher Myra was writing something on the blackboard. I looked back and it was Effy Thorpe who had wanted to offer me tamarind she had brought. I could see that many of those behind were sucking tamarind, the seed showing on the sides of their mouths. Teacher Myra must have either found them too quiet or she must have smelt the tamarind, for she left off writing on the blackboard and turned round. She saw nothing but angelic faces and she turned to the blackboard again. I smiled. I looked at her as she tip-toed to write on the top part of the blackboard.

I thought of her a little because I felt in some way she was strange. She was very prim, always dressing tidily, always dressing in fancy clothes. I suppose that it was because of this she made me think of my Auntie Roomeen. And oddly enough, Aunt Mona too. Auntie Roomeen had the fancy clothes and looked nice in them, but Aunt Mona was so stylish she made almost any clothes look fancy. I looked at Teacher Myra dropping the duster on her table and dusting her hands. Although she was our teacher, at some moments she was just like the girls in our class, and I could see that she herself was not much more than a girl. She was not from Mayaro – in fact she came from Rio Claro, but I was sure that the people from Rio Claro did not speak like her. I thought she spoke beautifully and I always liked listening to her. I sat down there looking towards her and the glint of the belt round her waist made me think of the gold chain we lost. I started suddenly thinking of how Uncle stole the gold chain and how today we had all been to the Police Station, and of how today of all days Teacher Myra had seen Mona and himself on Station Hill, and how Lennox had pointed him out, and how lucky it was for me that she did not see me coming down from the station yard. And then I thought of how much I wanted that gold chain back, and of what a big difference it would make to our lives, and then I could not help thinking how odd it was that with all that was happening, and having to search all over the place for the gold chain, the sentence on the board should be: *Gold is where you find it*.

I jumped when I realised that Teacher Myra was standing in front of me. She was saying, 'Yes? Yes?' and I had been hearing the voice like one distant and far away, but it was only this moment I realised she was speaking to me. The class was laughing. I said, 'Oh. Sorry, Teacher Myra.'

She laughed. 'What was my last word, Horace Lumpres?' She silently moved her lips to tell me what it was but I didn't understand. The class did not see that but there was a wave of laughter again. She turned round to the class, 'He's still not well, so his poor mind's not with us. Horace, you should have stayed at home and have more of a rest.'

'Yes, Miss.'

She had the pile of copy-books in her hand and she walked round the class handing them out. She said, 'Now what I have on the blackboard are really tricky ones. Not hard, but tricky, and mind you don't trip yourself. Don't forget your Extension of Object – that's the key.' Then she said, 'The comprehension passage below – you can do that for homework.'

'But why, Miss?' said Claudia. She meant why for homework.

'Because now it's composition time.' What Teacher Myra had written on top was 'Homework'. Claudia had not noticed it.

Teacher Myra looked at me and smiled. 'That should get you better,' she said.

I gave her a faint smile. Teacher Myra knew composition was my favourite subject. She said, 'Class, take down the homework. Come on.'

On the board were several sentences – some to analyse and parse, some to correct grammatically, and some to punctuate. The very first sentence on the board set my heart racing again. It was *All that glitters is not gold*.

Before I started to write someone from the back said, 'Gold again, Miss? That first sentence. It's like the other one we had, Miss.'

'Oh, yes? Let's see.' Teacher Myra stood off from the blackboard and watched the sentence, then watched the class and chuckled. She said, 'Come to think of it, is this a coincidence? We spoke of the word *coincidence* before. Isn't it a coincidence? Still, this is a golden afternoon, isn't it? Look at the sun through the palms. Look through the window on your left and you'll see the sun playing with the patches of blue between the green leaves. I don't want to be poetic, but it's beautiful. Horace, what did Kingsley say again?'

She did not catch me unawares this time because I had been listening to her. I said now, 'Kingsley? Charles Kingsley, Miss?'

'Yes, in that lesson about the Kaiteur Falls. That nice phrase you used.'

The class remembered it and said it, for she had read out my composition to the class. I pretended I didn't remember, but she was looking at me, waiting for me. Then she said, 'Oh, he is still ill. Let's leave him alone now. But they were beautiful words. Okay Horace Lumpres.' Then she told the class, 'He's not hot, but he still has the fever within. But his choice of words is good, because a thing of beauty is a joy forever. That's Keats.'

I was wondering to myself how come she liked things like that. Nobody else seemed to care. In fact, sometimes my class-mates laughed about her and most of them felt she was a little crazy. Only during this period, though. But I liked her for the things she liked because I liked them too. And most of all I liked listening to her. Especially when she said things like, 'Isn't it?' I didn't know where she got that from. I was looking up at the ceiling and thinking, when her voice came suddenly louder and broke through to me. She said, 'All right, class. Come on, now. Settle down. No playing about and no dreaming.' This last phrase pulled me to attention and I sat up and looked at her but she didn't seem to be thinking of me. Her head was turned away. She said, 'Get out your composition books and I want each of you to write a composition. The subject? Let me see. A big event in your life. Any big event. Something that happened and stunned you. Something unforgettable.'

The class fell silent. Everybody was wondering and looking worried. Teacher Myra turned towards me. She said, 'Feeling better?'

'Yes, Miss.'

'Okay, see if you can write,' she said, and there seemed to be something feverish that came to her eyes, but I knew that there was really nothing at all. I was sure that it all came from inside me because I wasn't feeling well. Strange how I wasn't feeling well because Teacher Myra said so. The class was beginning to rumble again, and Miss cried, 'Silence now, class. Work!'

It was a little while before I got started but once my pen started it would not stop. I was writing – and I did not know why I was writing like I did – but I was putting into my composition what I would not tell anyone. It was the truth – I knew it was the truth as the Gospel is the truth, but it was the sort of truth, I suppose, that Mother would not have liked me to tell anyone. Nor Auntie Roomeen. Nor even I myself – I would not have talked about it, but now that I began to write it all came pouring out. It was as if I could not help it. It was as if my heart was ruling my hand, and my head could do nothing about it. I wrote effortlessly, my thoughts flowing like a river. I just kept turning the leaves of my composition book every few minutes. Once I raised my head to look at the big clock and my eyes caught Teacher Myra's and for a moment – I didn't know where I got this from – for a moment she seemed to be looking at my book with wild eagerness. But I knew that this feeling came from me, and that I was seeing all sorts of things because I wasn't feeling well. So I knew I was wrong – especially when she smiled and looked away. I suppose she must have been looking at everyone in the class, and it just happened that her gaze had lingered – and looked like that.

I went on writing all the time, frantically, as if my thoughts were like the tide, and as if the tide was not just rising, but rushing up. I could not even remember what time I had seen on the clock. My hand was just moving and I was stopping only to turn pages. What I was writing was the living truth. Because I did not *have* to write it. Only that as long as I did not stop to think or to reason it out, it came flowing out. Good thing a composition did not have to be taken for what was really happening! I thought. And good thing Teacher Myra did not know anything of what was happening at home and would say it's imagination. I rejoiced in this, because when something was on my mind and I took up my pen to write, whatever it was just came spilling out.

It just came out with the ink just as though I had no control over it.

Until now I did not know how deeply I felt about those close relations of mine, nor did I know what I really thought about what had happened. And I had not put into words my feelings for Auntie Roomeen. Now as I wrote I knew exactly what I felt about her. I truly admired Auntie Roomeen and Auntie Roomeen loved us. Oh how I loved Auntie Roomeen who had come from Panama. And how Auntie Roomeen worried about us and cared for us! She had not even bothered about losing Braffie, who had gone off. I was not going to call him Uncle Braithwaite any more, and I did not want to. Just imagine he had gone off. Where? In the wilds of Panama, maybe. She did not care and she did not want to see him again, and the same could be said for Mother and for me. Forget Braffie. Auntie Roomeen brought such lovely gowns and dresses and other lovely Panama clothes. She brought many shirts and trousers for me, too, but I had not even seen them properly yet. Because of the gold chain! We lost the gold chain and my Uncle had taken it. He said he didn't know a single thing about it. We spoke to the sergeant this morning and the sergeant said the police would find it. He said that was his job. Give him a chance on the evidence and he would find it. He would have to search, though. That's what Mother had told me he'd said. She was not sure how and what and when and where he would search but he'd better search now. The sergeant had a long curling moustache and he did not smile and they called him 'Sarge'. Aunt Mona was at the Station this morning but she did not bother to go up and answer any questions and she was not called. She had been talking to a policeman all the time. When they left to go home Uncle went down towards the beach to the seine where he was working, and Aunt Mona went home without bothering to walk down to Miss Wong's store with us. But Aunt Mona would not rob us of the gold. And Uncle said he did not take it but I am not sure that I believed him. Where is the gold chain? Gold might be where you find it but where can we find the gold chain? The gold chain is for us two – Mother and me. The gold chain is worth thousands of dollars and Auntie Roomeen bought, no, brought it for us. I love Auntie Roomeen perhaps better than all the people I know. Perhaps except Mother. Because Mother is my mother and because –

'Stop, class.' Teacher Myra's voice made me jump. 'Just round off your compositions now. Don't forget to write the date. Has anyone forgotten the date?'

A chorus of voices cried out, 'No, Miss.' I did not say anything. I was nervous and perspiring. I was not finished and I wondered how I could round it off. I heard Teacher Myra's voice as in a dream. I did not look up. My hand was moving again.

I heard her say, 'And don't forget your names.' I looked up. She was laughing. She said, 'I mean don't forget to put your names – that is important. So you will have *Mayaro Government School*, and your name and the date. Round off, now. Round off now, Lumpres. Horace Lumpres, have you heard? Thanks. Claudia, take up the exercise books, kindly, please.' I already had my name and the date and I quickly wrote on top, *Mayaro Government School*. I had always been inclined to leave out *Mayaro Government School*, for I had always felt that at least that much the teacher knew. Until the day she told me: 'Well, I'm from Rio Claro. Suppose these papers through some mystery were to turn up there, how would I know where they came from?' I saw the point she was making, and in any case it did not hurt to write *Mayaro Government School* on top.

Claudia was very swift. She had already taken up all the other books and now she reached me. I did not have the time to read over even a single line. In fact, the school-bell had already rung for recess, and Teacher Myra was already saying we could go downstairs to the yard. And when we came back, what's the subject to be? Benches and desks were being pushed around and children were filing – almost tumbling – out of the class. I put the rest of my books in my desk and I turned round to find I was the last person in class. I looked towards Teacher Myra but she was not looking at me. She was sitting at the table, and I was surprised because she was reading one of the compositions as if her life depended on it. Her head was going from side to side. My heart gave a heave because I saw that she had *my* exercise book.

❋ *Nine*

THAT EVENING when I got home Mother was in the kitchen, cooking, and I went in to talk to her but the kitchen was filled with smoke so I ran out again. I went up the steps to my room and put my book-bag on my bed, and when I came out again she was out in the yard. She said, 'You come back? You wanted to tell me something?' She said this with a sort of vacant look, as if her mind was not really on me. I found it strange because this was not so much like Mother. Her eyes were red from the smoke.

'How you mean, Ma? You all right?'

She looked around her first, then she said, 'How could anybody be all right with those thieves around.'

I said, 'Who?' I thought she had a new idea.

'How you mean "Who"?'

'You still believe it's Uncle?'

'Sh-h!' she said. She went and cast her eyes to the back of the kitchen and when she came back she said, 'Don't talk so loud. And don't call no names. This is a very slippery man. Any thief have to be well slippery to make that raid from Roomeen's trunk.'

'But the way he talked this morning. You still believe it's Uncle?'

She looked at me surprised: 'Who else?'

'Ma, after all the questioning this morning – from the Sarge?'

'He could fool Sarge but he can't fool me.'

'And why you didn't talk?'

'Because I didn't *see* nothing,' she said. 'You can't talk by guess.'

I thought about it but I didn't say anything. Mother was not sure and yet she was so sure. I didn't say anything for a few moments. Then I said, 'Where's Auntie?'

She pointed to the beach. Almost at the same time she spun

round, and saying, 'Me pot burning!' she dashed into the kitchen into a cloud of smoke. At other times I would have laughed.

I stood there for a few moments wondering if the culprit was really Uncle, although I could not think of who else it could be. And I remembered him as he was this morning – his whole manner – and I thought he must be one of the finest actors in the world. For it *had* to be him. Who else? There was nobody else it could possibly be. I remembered how when he first learned what happened he had hurried up Post Office Hill to Aunt Mona, and I could not help wondering now if Aunt Mona was holding any secret for him. I remained there, my head wrapt in thought, and then I tried to shake the thoughts off and I walked towards the beach. But the thoughts were still with me, and a certain depressed feeling had taken over my whole mind. As I got into the heavy sand my footsteps were very slow because the sand kept sliding away under my feet. The evening was still bright and Point Radix was bathed in light, and the rock just a little way off it, the rock we called 'Rock of Ages', looked like – I could not bring myself to say it, and then my heart whispered – *like gold*. And now like a flood sweeping my mind was the feeling of the bright gold of the chain that was lost, and mingled with this feeling were the thoughts of the Police Station this morning with Mother and Auntie Roomeen and the other one and Uncle Ulric. And then there was the class in my mind and Teacher Myra and then in my mind I was seeing myself frantically writing the composition. I could not bear to think of what I might have put into that composition. I knew when I was writing it my heart had felt brimming like a river, and overflowing, but I could not bear to think of what I might have said. But I knew that in a certain part I said something about *Gold is where you find it*. I felt thrilled because I knew Teacher Myra would like that. I knew that I said –

I stopped short, my heart thumping and my mind excited. I stopped because I was sure I heard my name. I looked towards our yard but there was nothing but smoke pouring out of the kitchen. Mother was nowhere in sight so it could not be her. I was about to dismiss it when I heard again, 'Horace!' this time distinctly, and now I turned the other way up the beach. And then my heart went *'voom!'* I saw Auntie leaning against a coconut tree talking to Mr Clunis. Mr Clunis was wearing a new, multi-coloured shirt, which I realised had come from Panama. I had a sudden resentment seeing him there and also seeing his shirt. Auntie made a sign for me to come.

As I approached she said, 'You just come from school?'

'Yes, Auntie.' My thoughts were in confusion. I just did not like her there. I just did not like her letting Mr Clunis play the fool sitting there talking to her.

She said, 'Boy, you know you could really walk! That distance nearly killed me. And you do this every day, from Government school to here?'

'Yes, Auntie.'

'You don't even wait for donkey-cart – like we used to do in the old days?'

Mr Clunis laughed derisively. 'And what about donkey-cart! That is distance to walk too? And for a young boy like that?' He made a long stupes, then he said, 'You think Government School to here further than here to Government School?'

Auntie said, 'You always talking nonsense.'

She said this lightly, almost playfully, and I was amazed and put off. Because I had wanted Auntie to tell him firmly that not only was he talking nonsense, but the matter was none of his business. I looked at Auntie and I noticed that although she was bright, she was a little subdued. I noticed this particularly when she put her arm around my neck and she did not say anything to start with. It was afterwards that she said, 'What Claris doing?'

'Cooking.'

'Still?'

'Yes, Auntie.'

I knew she only asked this to say something, because once Mother was in the kitchen, and the kitchen had smoke, Mother was cooking. Mr Clunis looked at me without saying anything, and inside of me I wondered if he wanted me to go. Then Auntie said, 'I think I'd better go and see if I can give Claris a hand.' I was thrilled. She looked at me and asked, 'Think she need me?'

'Yes, Auntie.'

Mr Clunis jumped back in a funny sort of way, and gesticulating with his hands he said, 'Yes, Auntie – yes Auntie! How you know Claris want her. Eh? You is a fortune-teller?' He said this in a boisterous sort of way and the way Auntie laughed I could see she felt he was making fun. He laughed too. But I knew he was more than half serious. I could see he did not want her to go. As he talked my head was turned towards the St Joseph factory.

'Eh?' he went on. 'How you know Claris want her? Horace I am speaking to you.'

'I didn't say Mother want her, Mr Clunis.'

Auntie said, 'The boy said "need".'

'You could keep your big English,' Mr Clunis said, looking at me. 'Like you swallow a dictionary? Go on, you'll bite your tongue!'

I couldn't help smiling. I smiled not only because of what he said, but he himself had said: 'I am speaking to you,' and that was not at all like Mr Clunis. He was only trying to impress Auntie and now he was talking about my biting my tongue. He would certainly bite off his tongue if he tried to keep up any more of that 'I am'. He was standing there looking at me with quiet amusement.

Auntie had leaned off from the coconut tree and now she said: 'Look, I'll go and see if I could help Claris a little.'

As she moved off I was on one side and Mr Clunis stepped on the other side of her and said in a low voice, 'You'll think about that thing, eh? You know what. What we was talking about.'

Auntie looked at him as if she didn't remember what they had been talking about and just when I thought she was going to tell him off, she quietly said, 'I'll consider.'

He stood up and she stood up too. He said, 'You ain't have nothing to consider. Look, it's like this – ' He stopped and glanced round at me, and at the same time I turned away and spun round, digging my heels into the sand and then eased off as though I was walking to the water's edge. Then when I glanced at them they were walking on again and I eased back. I was feeling heated inside because I really did not like the way Mr Clunis was getting on.

I didn't see when he nudged Auntie but she suddenly said, 'Eh?' and Mr Clunis said, 'You notice what I notice?'

'What's that?'

There was a little silence. I did not look at him, and I did not know what he was doing, but Auntie began looking at me, amused. I heard Mr Clunis whisper, 'Don't like to see me talking to you at all.'

Auntie Roomeen chuckled, and I suddenly got all confused and embarrassed. I looked at Mr Clunis but he pretended he was not talking about me and he looked up into a coconut tree. Auntie chuckled again and she said, 'You could talk nonsense, boy.'

We had reached the yard and now stood up near the kitchen, with smoke billowing up, blueish among the coconut trees. I would have gone on but Auntie had her arm around my neck, and I was glad. Mr Clunis looked very self-conscious about his multi-coloured shirt, and he was pulling down the sleeves and trying to button them at the wrist. He said to her, 'It fit me good, girl.'

She said, 'At least you looking decent, for a change.'

He gave a funny little skip back, pretending he was appalled that she should say this, and she chuckled. He said, 'What the hell you mean by that? So you more decent than me?' Then he said, suddenly looking more serious: 'Look, Roomeen, I know something's wrong, but you just ain't telling me the story. But today just ain't your day. I could see that. I could read you like a book. But, anyway, about that thing. I want to hear what you say tomorrow. Right? Matter fixed?'

I did not know if she answered or not but if she answered it must have been very, very softly. Then he turned off and went towards his house by the factory, Auntie stood up there and watched him go, and I looked up at the blue smoke amongst the leaves of the coconut trees. I wasn't really paying attention to the smoke. I was gazing in space, and if my eyes were red – well, could I say it was the smoke? I was feeling more pained than I could describe. I stood up there, with Auntie's arm around my neck and I did not say anything to her. Neither did Auntie say anything to me. We started to walk on a little, and as she removed her arm from my neck to go into the kitchen, she said, 'I notice you don't like Clunis. Why?' She said it as abruptly as that. It took me so unawares that I was shocked and did not know what to say. She was looking down at me, questioningly.

'But Auntie – ' And I stopped. She remained there, looking into my face, waiting for an answer.

'But Auntie, I don't like Mr Clunis?'

'No, you don't,' she said. 'And he's noticing it.' There was silence for a little while, and she began speaking again. 'Clunis is really a nice person. With all his antics, he's simple and genuine. He likes to talk a lot of nonsense but he's nice.'

'I didn't say anything, Auntie.'

She said, 'I know you want to protect me. Think I don't know? I know very well.' She looked at me and smiled. It was a soft sweet smile that made me feel to cry. But I was still upset about Mr Clunis.

She said, 'I hope you'll get to see the pleasant person that he is.'

That made me feel that she was getting to like Mr Clunis even more than I had thought. In a way I was feeling very much alarmed. I wasn't very clear in my mind as to what had happened about Uncle Braithwaite, but it came to me that he could turn up at any time and he mightn't like what was happening. I blurted out: 'Uncle Braithwaite mightn't like him.'

She looked at me with astonishment, and then she burst out laughing. Then she said, 'Oh, you don't know. Okay, we'll talk. I'll tell you something soon about your Uncle Braithwaite and me. Let me go in to Claris now. Okay? Let me go in and help her.'

I went round behind the kitchen, where there was a clump of zecack. I went and stood up against a branch, still upset, but embarrassed, too, about what I had just said to Auntie. I was standing up where I could hear her talking to Mother in the kitchen, and I was listening to hear if she would tell Mother what I said.

But after asking Mother what there was to do, I heard her say with great eagerness: 'He asked me, you know. Clar, you know he asked me? He asked me to consider.'

Mother said, 'That's no news. I knew he'd ask you.'

'What you think?' Auntie said, and there was a nervous giggle.

'Girl, it's not what I think, it's what *you* think. When he asked you to consider, what you said?'

'That I'll consider.' Auntie started giggling, but I did not hear anything from Mother. Afterwards there were the sounds of spoons on plates and I knew Mother was almost finished in the kitchen and that the food would soon be on the table, indoors, and I'd be called. I started to move away from the zecack clump. Mother said something which I did not hear very well, and Auntie said, 'Girl, I know that. Nobody can't decide for me because it's I who would have to make it.' I wasn't sure exactly what they were talking about but I guessed. A storm of despair lashed against me.

As I was going to cross the side of the kitchen I heard Mother ask her, 'Where is Horace?'

I stood up, because I did not know whether she could see movement between the creases in the kitchen boards. I didn't hear anything else, though. I did not even hear Auntie's reply, but my head felt hot when Auntie said, 'Claris, that boy of yours – '

'What about him?'

'Smart too bad.'

'How you mean?'

'Braffie. Why you didn't tell him everything?'

Mother did not answer.

'Why you didn't tell him Braffie's gone?'

'He's only a child, you know.'

'He's only a child but he's watching me and Clunis.'

'Oh yes?' Mother said.

'But I like him. All he's thinking about is protecting me. And then too he wants all the attention, so he's a little hurt. But what a nice boy. If we could only get back that gold – '

'If I know anything that gold is already at the bottom of the sea.'

'Claris!' Auntie said. There was anguish in her voice. There was sudden anguish in me, too. Mother's saying that almost made me faint. I felt so weak I went back towards the zecack clump and leaned on a branch. I stayed there for quite a few minutes while I heard the kitchen door being opened and shut – which meant things were being taken out to the table indoors. I was glad no one came round here. I remained here until I heard Mother call 'Hor-race:' thinking I was out on the beach. I ran behind the house and out to the beach, and began coming in where she could see me.

✳ Ten

WE HADN'T QUITE finished supper when Uncle Ulric walked in. When he came in everybody was silent and stiff and you didn't have to ask if something was wrong. He said, 'Aye, man, how everybody? No sign at all of that thing?'

'What thing?' Auntie said.

'The gold chain.'

There was a pained smile on her face. She said, 'No. No sign of it, boy.' Mother did not even look up. When he asked her about the gold chain Mother flashed a look at me.

I was feeling hurt and subdued. I could not look at Uncle for the moment, but when I did he was sitting in the old basket chair on the other side of the dish-cabinet. Auntie got up and collected the plates and began taking them outside to the kitchen. Mother remained at the table. When Auntie came back in she came in with a cloth and wiped the table, then went back into the kitchen, and when she came in again, she went and sat down in the corner opposite Uncle, in the old rocking chair. Mother had not lifted her eyes yet. Normally, when Uncle came, the first thing she would say is, 'You eat?' Now neither she nor Auntie had said anything of the sort. In fact, neither had spoken for a little time. Things looked so odd and embarrassing that I was relieved when Uncle spoke. He said, 'I just finish in the sea, yes.'

Auntie said, 'You had a nice day? You strike it rich?'

I looked at Auntie and stiffened up for I was sure a quarrel would break out. Uncle said, 'No, girl, not today. Today wasn't bad but we went just half day. But these days it have plenty anchore and sometimes we could strike it rich. I just came in from the seine – see I'm still wet? This thing was on my mind all day. All day, all day. Stanley even had to say, "Boy, what wrong with you?".'

When I heard his line of talk I was very relieved, for I was sure

Auntie meant something else by 'You strike it rich?' and I was glad he did not catch on. He was wearing his three-quarter length blue-dock shorts and a merino, and they were both wet in parts and his legs were sandy. The fishermen may have just hung up the nets at Plaisance and he must have walked right down the beach to us. I was looking at him when his eyes caught me. 'Horace, how?'

'Okay, Uncle.'

He looked towards Auntie again. 'That's how it is, girl. Lord, where the hell that thing gone?' Then he said, 'We'll find it, you know. We'll have to find it.'

'Aha,' was all Auntie said. Her face had looked strained from the time Uncle had come in. It had looked strained before, but not that much, and she had almost seemed back to normal when she had been talking to Mother in the kitchen about Mr Clunis. Uncle looked businesslike, in a way, and serious, and at times he made his face look worried. Just for one moment, when he appeared, I thought he had brought back the gold chain, and my heart thumped. But that was only for one moment.

He said now, 'But Claris you ain't saying anything yet.' He looked at Mother sitting at the table, staring at it as though examining the mahogany from which it was made. He looked towards Auntie. 'I know how it is. Everybody depressed and disappointed. You know how much money gone if that thing is really lost. But I don't think it's lost, you know. It can't lose. You'll find it but you'll have to give a good look in this house.'

Mother turned sharply towards him. 'Not in this house. Perhaps in some other house. We already turn this house upside down and it ain't here.'

'Oh well,' Uncle said, a look of despair on his face. He either did not know what Mother had meant by saying 'Perhaps in some other house', or he did not want to know. I looked at his face. His words, 'It can't lose', kept clinging to my mind. He seemed so serious in saying this that it made me wonder if he meant to bring it back one day. And then my mind shifted to Teacher Myra and it was as if I was hearing her voice: 'Analyse and parse – *Gold is where you find it*'. I was seeing myself in the class-room again, looking at the words on the blackboard, when Uncle's voice brought me back to the moment.

'It's the funniest thing,' he said, 'The way this gold just went.

In all my born days – ' He stopped. Then he said, 'I don't know what to say. You sure you brought it, Roomeen?'

Auntie retorted: 'But you saw it.'

He looked as though he didn't know what Auntie was talking about. Mother looked him full in the face and said: 'You didn't see it? You didn't say, "I see gold"? Roomeen didn't hit off your hand from the grip cover?'

'Well, yes. Who's saying no. I mean I saw something shining – sparkling, you know. I thought it was gold.'

'So it wasn't gold?' Auntie asked. Mother was still staring him full in the face.

'But I don't know,' Uncle said. He seemed to be getting irritated. His voice was a bit raised and he opened his eyes wide. Then he nodded his head to himself and bit his lips. Then he looked at Mother and Auntie and he said, 'Wait, nah, you all think I thief the gold chain?'

Auntie said, 'It's not for me to accuse anybody, it's for the police to find it. I don't care where they find it, I don't care who they arrest. I give the sergeant a full statement.'

'I gave the sarge a full statement, too. And I talked to the sarge as man, in front of you and Claris. But it's a good thing I come here this evening, because I didn't know you watching me as the thief.'

Mother said, 'Roomeen never said that. She said it's the police to find out.'

'Well let them find out. In any case the sarge said he sending here to make a search.'

'Here?' Mother and Auntie cried almost together. Auntie said again, 'Here? What for?'

'I heard Sarge say so when we was walking out. And let me tell you this – and I talking frankoment: if the gold chain left Panama at all, it in this house. So if the police come, I satisfy.'

Mother said, 'So the police must come here and search to satisfy you?'

'Claris, I want them to come to find the gold chain – not to satisfy me. To tell the God truth this is a mystery. I can't tell what happen. I really don't know.'

Mother and Auntie sat down there and I could see they were tense. I knew they wouldn't get very far with Uncle because he seemed to have taken a stand. So I myself didn't know what to think or do. I wondered if we would have to give up all hope of finding the gold chain. As they went on talking there behind me, my thoughts were far away and I was looking across towards the sea. While the discussion had been going on the evening had been turning to night, and now I could see a light twinkling on Point Radix, and I could not see the 'Rock of Ages', in front of the tip of the Point, nor, in fact, where the sea met the sky. For the darkness was deep there already. Mother had long got up and lit the lamp, and the *Home Sweet Home* of the shade was there in big unsteady letters on the wall. As I turned to look at the darkness under the coconut trees, my heart jumped. I saw the beam of a torchlight under the coconut trees. I quickly ran down the steps and I looked out towards the estate road, and I ran up the steps again.

Before I could speak, Mother said, 'What happen?'

'Somebody coming with a torchlight.'

Both Mother and Auntie hurried down the front steps and Uncle followed. They watched the light coming through the coconut road. It was much nearer now but it was mainly on the road itself, although now and then it lifted and rested directly on our house. At first Uncle said, 'It must be Clunis,' but when he saw the light rest on our house he said, 'No, it's somebody coming here.' Mother and Auntie stood up there without saying anything and I could not see their faces in the gloom, but after a few uneasy moments of silence, Mother heard voices and she said, 'That's Mona's voice.' A few moments later, Aunt Mona and two policemen walked into the yard.

We were all standing in the yard, taken aback, and the glow of the lamp fell on the two constables. Mother said, 'Mona, what's all this?'

'The sarge send these two fellers to make a search. He said you wanted a search.'

Mother seemed too shaken to speak. Auntie said, 'To search here? In this house? It couldn't be in this house. The gold chain's not in this house.'

'Well which house?' Uncle said. Auntie was taken aback. The policemen did not say anything but seemed impatient to go up the steps. Uncle said, 'You said the gold was here. You reported it lost. Well, who could take it? It must be here in this house. So the sarge send two men to help you find it – he can't do nothing else.'

The two policemen did not wait for Uncle to finish speaking but were walking up the steps into the house. Mother, who just a short while ago was seized with shock, spotted this and ran up the steps to meet them, and then went round to the other side of the table. Then she looked at them questioningly.

Aunt Mona had run up the steps too. She said, 'Claris, they come to search. You just have to let them.'

'Have to let them? Just a minute, this is my place. Let me take things in hand.'

Aunt Mona said, casually: 'You went and made a report. It's out of your hands now, Clar. That's law. You just have to let the men search.'

Auntie asked, 'So Mona you are the law now?' She said this very bitterly and it was as if she was on the point of exploding with anger. The policemen were paying no attention to them but were looking all over the sitting room, and on the cabinet, and behind pictures as well. Auntie Roomeen was very annoyed that they had begun their search regardless of what Mother said.

Aunt Mona said, 'Roomeen, what they trying to do is what you want. You want to find the gold chain – not so? Well that's what these fellers trying to find. That gold chain cost plenty money – I didn't see it, but the way you describe it, I know. These fellers want to help you find it. You know something? I'd give anything in the world to see them pull out that chain.'

Mother said sharply, 'Pull out that chain from where? What you want to say is that we hid it? That's what you want to say?'

'Hid it?' Aunt Mona laughed. 'Who said that? How you all could hide it and report it lost? Don't be silly, girl.'

Auntie Roomeen said, 'No policeman has any right to be searching here without a warrant. And besides, the gold chain ain't here. They can't search this place better than we can.'

The two policemen were now standing up watching Aunt Mona. They were finished with the sitting room and this was their way of saying so. Aunt Mona said, 'Boys, go ahead. They sent you to search.'

The one who I had seen Aunt Mona with at the window of the Police Station seemed to be the chief one carrying out the search. I remembered him. He came up now to speak to Aunt Mona and I was as annoyed as Mother and Auntie, and I stood up right there beside him. He did not seem to care about anybody at all; he did not even look at us. He just seemed to be concerned with Aunt Mona and with the other policeman who came with him. Even when he wanted to ask questions about the layout of the house, instead of asking Mother or Auntie, he was asking Aunt Mona.

When he asked Aunt Mona where Mother's room was, I could not stop myself. 'Aunt Mona, look Ma right here. She – '

'Shut your mouth, little boy!'

This incensed both Mother and Auntie Roomeen and they both started talking at once. The policemen seemed amused and just stood up with their arms folded, looking on. Then Auntie Roomeen stopped for Mother to talk. Mother was far too calm for my liking. She was never really excitable, and she never flared up, even when there was cause, like now. She said quietly, but firmly, 'Mona don't talk nonsense, eh. Don't insult Horace, because he belongs here. This is his house. Don't speak to him like that.'

'Oh, it's his house. I didn't know,' and she began to giggle.

Her policeman friend spoke to Mother for the first time. He said, 'Where you really lost the chain?'

'Well the chain was here and somebody stole it.'

'You saw that?'

'No.' He looked towards the other policeman and then towards Aunt Mona. They smiled. Then he said, 'The gold chain was in this house?'

'Yes, in a trunk.'

'Okay, let's see the trunk.'

Mother and Auntie Roomeen were fuming as they led the two policemen to the trunk. I felt extremely annoyed, too, especially to see the way these two men walked in the house. They walked as if they owned the place, their heavy boots hitting against the floor like sledge hammers. Perhaps if I had thought they'd find the chain I would not have resented them so much. But I knew it wasn't here. I knew it was not in this house, and that they were not searching the right house. At that moment the one I hated even more than the policemen was Uncle Ulric. Because of what he had done we had to go through all this and he was standing there and watching us go through it with his face as grave as if he did not know anything about the gold chain. There was a feigned look of nervousness on his face, as though he cared. Bitterness welled up in my throat, almost choking me. Mother and Auntie Roomeen were far too soft for him, I thought. If I were a big man I'd kick him out of the house! I was so worked up that I left the bedroom and went to the next room to a window facing the sea. The night was as black as pitch and there were few stars over the sea. The wind was blowing gustily and there was the restless murmur of the waves. I leaned forward with my chin on the window sill. I could not take my mind off those policemen. I heard them inside the bedroom knocking things about. I wasn't at the window a minute before I left again and went back to be near Mother.

By the time I got back to the bedroom in searching for the gold chain they had already completely turned up the things in Auntie's trunk. Most of the clothes were rumpled on the bed, and when I came in, Auntie Roomeen and Mother were picking up the last pieces of clothes from the floor and putting them on the bed. My heart raged. It raged to see that Aunt Mona was there and she was letting the policemen search in that manner. She was close beside the Constable that I recognised, and all the time she was talking to him, and at times he flashed a smile at her. I heard her call him Cordner. Uncle was there and could see this but he seemed lost, looking into the trunk. Auntie Roomeen and Mother just had to watch what was going on – they could hardly do anything. It was the law. Now that Constable Cordner was finished with the trunk and the trunk was empty, he turned to the wardrobes, and he pulled at a door in such a violent way that Mother said, almost pleadingly: 'Constable, you see this? Please take it easy. And you see the clothes in there? Go easy for me, please. Try and treat them light.'

Auntie Roomeen appeared to be on the point of tears. In fact, it seemed to me that at this time it was Mother who was the strong one.

When Constable Cordner opened the door of the wardrobe, he spoke in a mock friendly tone, 'You have a lot of nice clothes here too?' he said. 'All these pass through the custom? Sure of that?' He said it as though he was making a statement and at the same time as though he was asking a question. I was flabbergasted.

When he heard no answer he looked round at Mother.

Mother said, 'Constable, you came here to search for a gold chain. That's what I understood.'

'I'm only asking,' the Constable said.

I was proud of Mother. She put the Constable in his place in a very gentle way. Aunt Mona did not say anything, and when Aunt Mona let such a thing pass then you could be sure there was nothing to say. But the Constable forgot the pleasant tone of voice and became more vicious now, the way he was taking things down from hangers and feeling in the pockets and throwing them on the bed. He had taken down a few of my deceased father's suits and after he had squeezed them up and put his hand into their pockets, he dashed them on to the bed.

Now Auntie Roomeen was standing up in a corner and looking fixedly at him, and across the room, so was Mother. The other policeman was not doing much. He was taking things from the wardrobe, too, but he was passing everything to Constable Cordner after he had searched it. He was far gentler. Uncle was looking at them and the way his face was, he gave the impression that he thought they would find it any minute now. Yet he knew that it was in *his* house – or at the bottom of the sea! I passed my hands over my eyes and shook off the horrible thought. I said to myself, 'Oh God, Uncle, I prefer if you throw it away in the bush – because somebody will find it – but not in the sea.' I was sitting on the other side of the bed, and after I wiped away the thought of the sea, my over-riding hope was for these two policemen to finish and go. And at last Constable Cordner told Aunt Mona: 'That gold chain ain't here. At least it ain't in this room.'

Mother said quickly, 'Well it won't be in any other room.'

Auntie Roomeen shook her head, 'It won't be anywhere else. We'll have to leave it like that, Constable.'

'Up to you,' Constable Cordner said. I felt so glad and relieved it was as if the cool waters of the ocean had broken over me.

❈ Eleven

I WAS SO HAPPY that the search was over that I almost did not notice when Constable Cordner beckoned to Uncle. They were not too far from me, and I heard Constable Cordner ask: 'You is the feller who riding that bicycle outside?'

Uncle said yes.

'Ain't you is the same fisherman feller that living on Plaisance Road – on the left hand?'

Uncle said yes for a second time. I could see he was irritated. He had told me that all the policemen up Quarters knew him, and maybe now he did not know why this one had to pretend.

Constable Cordner rested a hand on his shoulder and said, 'Well take your time and ride up. And when you get home, wait. We coming.'

It was as if a bee had stung Uncle Ulric. He looked at Constable Cordner sharply, his mouth wide open, and then he turned towards Aunt Mona. 'What is this, Mona?'

Aunt Mona said, 'Boy, like you hard of hearing or what! The sarge give these policemen a job. Which is, to search for the gold chain. How they could search here without searching your place? This gold business is between you and Claris and Roomeen.'

'Between *me* and Claris and Roomeen?' Uncle said sharply. 'Where I come in? Girl, don't talk up, eh!'

Aunt Mona said, 'Ulric, listen to me. Ulric, Ulric, listen. You and Claris and Roomeen made a report – '

'We made the report – you wasn't there? You ain't a sister too, from this same house?'

Although Auntie Roomeen and Mother were glad that the police would search Uncle's house, they did not like Aunt Mona's attitude, and now they were looking at her with a great deal of anger. She took no notice of them. She simply said to Uncle, 'Yes, I was there.' She was looking at him with her full eyes and although I hated her I had to admit to myself that she knew how to put on the style. She repeated, 'Yes, I was there. And yes, I'm a sister too.' She chuckled and made a side-long glance: 'Not a favourite sister, but a sister, anyway. But this is not the point,' and she chuckled again. Then, getting serious again, she said, 'The point is that I only heard about gold, I didn't see gold. You is the one who kept saying, "I see gold. I see gold. Bring gold for me." That sort of talk.'

Uncle looked up to the ceiling and cried, 'Ha, God!'

'You didn't say that? Tell me Ulric, you didn't say that? You didn't say you see gold?'

'I saw gold but I didn't talk like that.'

Aunt Mona swung round to Auntie Roomeen. 'He didn't say that?' She looked to Mother too.

Auntie Roomeen said, 'He said something like that.'

Aunt Mona looked triumphant, and at the same time I'd never seen Uncle look so bewildered and confused. He didn't seem to know what to say. Aunt Mona began speaking calmly again. She leaned on the bed-post and said, 'Anyway, there isn't need for all this. Cordner just has to carry out orders. He searched this house, he has to search yours.'

'I thief the gold chain?' Uncle cried.

'Nobody saying that.'

'You giving the police orders now? You is the sarge?'

'Me? Poor me.'

'Well nobody going to damn well search my house!' As Uncle said this he stormed out of the room.

I was alarmed. I didn't know what would happen next, and I didn't know what to think. I had never liked Aunt Mona and I didn't like her now, but one thing she made me feel sure about was that nobody but Uncle had stolen the gold chain. For why should he go on like this if he didn't steal it? Why should he be so much against the police searching his place? But although I was alarmed, in a way I was sorry for him. Especially when Mother and Auntie Roomeen rushed after him in order to calm him down.

I was hard on their heels. They reached him as he was pushing off his bicycle but in spite of what they said he paid no atention to them but just jumped on the saddle and rode off in the dark. Auntie Roomeen came back into the house and said to Aunt

Mona, 'Whatever you do, remember he's your brother.' Mother was standing behind Auntie and I could see Mother's eyes were red.

Aunt Mona said, 'Well Cordner has to search his place.'

'I agree, but remember he's your brother.'

'Who saying no? We only trying to find the gold.'

Auntie Roomeen cried, 'It's your gold?'

'Oh, you don't want to find the gold?'

'Course I want to find it. But you talking so much, Mona. And so – so threatening. You are Sergeant Peters?. In any case, you in the Police Force?'

Aunt Mona didn't say a word, but gave a little smile. Mother was standing beside Auntie Roomeen, her chest heaving.

Auntie Roomeen went on: 'These two policemen are the people to talk. And Claris too, because she is boss in this house. And even me, because it's I who brought the gold chain from Panama. We could talk. But instead it's you who doing all the talking and giving orders.'

In spite of all this Aunt Mona just chuckled quietly and shook her head. I was amazed because she could be really biting and insulting when she wanted to, and I knew it wasn't a question of respect, because Mother always said Mona respected neither God nor man. But at times she could be so different from what you bargained for.

Constable Cordner and the other policeman were there while all this was happening but had not said a word. Constable Cordner had taken out his little notebook and was pretending he was looking through it, and he had looked about him and had actually written down a few things in it. The other policeman had fidgeted about and was now at the window. Now that Auntie Roomeen had stopped talking, Constable Cordner put the notebook in his pocket and turned to Aunt Mona and raised an eyebrow. I suppose he meant it was time to go. He stepped out of the room and Aunt Mona and the other policeman followed him. I went out into the sitting room to watch them go down the steps. As they reached down on the sand I heard Aunt Mona whisper, 'If I know him he ain't gone home at all.' Then I heard Constable Cordner reply, 'We have a search warrant. We could break and enter.' My heart gave *booboodoops*! I felt weak. I looked round. Neither Auntie nor Mother had come out of the bedroom, they were so angry. I hurried back to them.

As I entered the bedroom I heard Mother say, 'Mona is a dog,' and when she saw me she said, 'Excuse me, son.'

Auntie Roomeen said, 'It's this thing – you know – about Cordner. That's why she's so stupid.'

Mother was silent. They were both sitting on the bed, beside the pile of rumpled clothes from the trunk.

Auntie turned to Mother, 'Who's this Cordner, anyway?'

'Don't know him from Adam. Fairly new in Mayaro.'

'Look how he handled these clothes. Have to wash the whole pile of them now. Talk about uncouth!'

Mother said nothing. I could see her thoughts were far. Auntie said despairingly, 'What in God's name's wrong with Ulric? It's he who bring this whole thing on us.'

Mother shook her head bitterly.

Auntie said, 'I want back the gold chain, it's true. I want it back bad. But I don't want to make Ulric feel shame.'

Mother mumbled, 'I only hope he ain't going home now at all. I hope they ain't find him home.'

'But I agree with the search, you know,' Auntie said to her. 'Let me tell you this – I agree with it. Because it's Ulric who stole the chain. We know that. I mean, remember how he slipped away from us that night we were talking out in the yard. And Mona saw him inside. And he was pretending he was hurrying her up. I agree with the search because Ulric ain't mean to admit nothing.'

Mother was only half listening to her. She said, 'I almost wish he wasn't going straight home, though. They might rough up his things. Especially as he talk so – well, so bold. Almost violent.'

'Once they don't rough him up,' Auntie said.

'They almost sure to.'

'No they can't. They can't. God forbid! I'll kill Mona!'

'The best thing for him is not to go straight home. So when they get there nobody there.'

I said, 'They'll break and enter.' My voice seemed to startle them. It was as if they had forgotten I was here. Then Mother said, 'What nonsense this boy talking. Break and enter!'

'Constable Cordner said so.'

Mother looked at me wide-eyed. Auntie said, 'When? When he said so?'

'When they was leaving. Aunt Mona told him Uncle mightn't be going home and he said they could break and enter.' I was looking at Auntie as I was saying this, and suddenly I heard a squeak. I looked and saw Mother breaking down in tears. Auntie said, 'What you crying for? They can't do that. If they do that we'll make hell roll.' Then she herself burst into tears.

✳ *Twelve*

THEY DIDN'T FIND Uncle that night and they didn't break into the house. I knew because I had left for shool early next morning and I went straight to Uncle's. Surprisingly, he was in a pleasant mood, and he seemed extremely glad to see me. He said, 'What happening, boy? What time those fellers left last night?'

'Not too long after you went, Uncle. They didn't come here?'

'Where? Here? I don't know.'

He saw that I looked puzzled and he said, 'I didn't come here direct. You think I'll let them turn this house upside down?'

I was glad they hadn't come, but there wasn't a lot to turn upside down. For one thing, Uncle did not have a wardrobe; he had his clothes hung up on nails in the bedroom. And not a lot of clothes either. Just a few shirts and trousers – most of them ragged. And there were a few vests, some with big holes; and there were some discoloured pairs of underpants hanging from the nails, too. I couldn't see these things now because I was sitting in the living room. Uncle's apartment had two rooms. Separating the bedroom from the living room was a wall that went half-way up to the ceiling, and the wall came as if to block off the bedroom completely but it left space for a door. But there was no door, and Uncle had a blue dusty-looking polka-dotted curtain hanging where the door should be. What the curtain blocked off, on the left, was a wooden bed with a fibre mattress and a pillow on top of the sheet. And in the corner on the right were the clothes, hanging from nails. And right there, on the floor, was a piece of tarred fishing net. There was a bare centre-table in the bedroom with a tiny lamp that didn't have a shade. While talking to Uncle, in a flash I pictured the whole bedroom because I knew it so well.

I said, 'We was worried that – that they'd come and – er – and ransack the house.' My tongue nearly slipped and said we were worried that they'd break into the house. Uncle would have been furious and upset if I had let him know what Cordner had told Aunt Mona.

He looked at me: 'Who was worried? You mean *you*, not them.'

'How you mean, Uncle?' Although deep down I was bitter with him for leading us into all this, there was still a tender spot for him somewhere inside me, and I did not like to hear him talk like that. I had never realised it before but I *did* like him and I could not explain why. Perhaps it was because he was my Uncle, or perhaps because he had sunken eyes and bushy eyebrows – I could not explain it. If he had not stolen the gold chain, or if there had never been a gold chain in our lives I would have –

'You see!' He threw his hands out and distracted me. He had been speaking.

'Eh?' I said. 'Oh, yes. But then, Uncle – '

I stopped. He said, 'Well you asked me to tell you so I tell you.'

'That's how you put it, Uncle?' I wish'd I had heard what he said.

'Course!' he cried. 'And it's true.'

From that statement I had an idea of what he had said. He was wearing a pair of brown trousers, threadbare and patched at the bottom, and he looked as though he had slept in them. Which is almost certainly what he had done. Because I had never seen a pair of pyjamas in this house. And he must have slept bare-backed, too, as he was now. I always admired the way his chest was hairy and developed, and the way his arms were muscular – which came from rowing every day. After moving around now, getting certain things together, he laughed a forcing laugh and said, 'He asking me if that's how I put it. That is exactly how I put it.' He looked at my face to see what my reaction was, then went into the bedroom with a brass hook and a round, hollow piece of lead.

I looked around where I was sitting although I was used to the place. The room was almost bare. There were only three chairs – one which I was occupying, and there was one that seemed only propped up. That one was a real trap and he never let anybody sit on it. There was a little table jammed against the wall and on it were all sorts of pieces of lead, and sea-cork, and driftwood, and pieces of net and sail cloth. Prominent on the wall before me was a picture of Jack Johnson, the bare-fisted boxer, and on the wall behind me was the picture of an Ethiopian king, and it simply said below, 'Lion of Judah'. I didn't even have to look behind to take note of that. From inside the bedroom Uncle began to talk and when I heard what he was saying about Mother and Auntie Roomeen I kept a stony silence. Perhaps that was the sort of thing he had said in the first place – which I had not heard. After he was finished he waited a little, and then he said, 'Ah lie?'

'I don't know. They don't really feel so at all.'

He came out of the bedroom now and said with emphasis, 'You telling me they don't feel so? You didn't hear what Mona said? And Roomeen was backing it up. You think these sisters of mine any good?'

'What Aunt Mona said?'

'Mona didn't say that I said I see gold?' He seemed all heated and worked up and I could not possibly tell him that she had spoken the truth. But then he himself said, 'Well if I see gold I see gold, but what the hell Mona mean? And to cap it all, Roomeen was backing it up.'

I said nothing. He had a ball of marling twine in his hands and I wanted to remember to ask him for a piece of that, as it was ideal for flying kites and even for spinning tops. He went into the bedroom with the twine in his hand and he brought out a piece of wood shaped like an X and I do not know what it was for but I knew it had to do with the seine. He went out on the steps and on to the sand and looked in the direction of the sun. The sun was still very low in the east and the sunbeams were filtering through palm leaves because the whole of the Plaisance Road was lined with coconut trees. He came in again and he said, 'Ay, ay, boy you well early. Not even half-past six yet. But I have to go now, you know. You bet Stanley out there already.'

I had hardly noticed that he had changed his clothes. He had on a pair of short blue-dock trousers, frayed at the hems and a vest which looked a little yellowish from sea-water stains. In the back of my mind I was wondering where he was keeping the gold chain, or if it was here at all, or if it was at the bottom of . . . I shook the thought out of my head. He saw me shake my head and he said, 'You still sleepy?' I said no. I felt sure this priceless chain was here. Would he give it up? It would be so nice of him and everybody would be friends again. And he too would benefit richly – I was sure – and besides, he would stop the agony we were all suffering. Why was Uncle doing that to us? I thought. He closed the window and latched it and he went in again and I supposed it was to close up. A heavy atmosphere of pain hung over me now. The birds were tweet-tweeting in the coconut branches. When he came back out he asked, 'Ready to go?'

'Yes, Uncle.'

'But you can't go to school now. It too early. Why you come so early?'

'To see you. I'll walk down to the beach.'

He grinned. 'You come down here just to see me? Boy, perhaps you like your Uncle! They send you?'

'Yes,' I said. It was true, too. But I had wanted to come, anyway.

He said, looking away, 'They send him!' And he laughed. 'Ha, ha!' It was a sort of dry, mocking laugh. 'They send you and they say I thief their gold chain!'

We went down the steps and he closed the front door.

We were already in the road when he stopped short, as if something had just occurred to him. He said, 'Wait. Oho. They send you to see if you see the gold chain here.'

'Oh, no, Uncle Ulric. Oh God no. It isn't true. I could kiss the cross.'

I had been so shocked and taken aback by what he had said that the words just jumped out of my mouth. And oddly, the way I replied seemed to take Uncle aback too, for he said, 'Okay, Horace, okay. I know you sincere. I beg pardon.'

We walked down in silence towards the beach. It was really like walking through a coconut grove, and there was the piece of bright blue sea straight ahead of us. It was not as much 'bright blue sea', as it was 'silvery dazzling sea'. The palm leaves were protecting our eyes from the sun but the waters of Plaisance were like a glare. There was the constant 'bashaw, bashaw', of the surf. We continued walking in silence, and then Uncle said, 'The breakers tumbling this morning, boy.'

'Yes, Uncle.'

'You ain't still vexed?'

'Vexed?' I looked up at him, seeming surprised.

'Because of what I said about the gold chain.'

'Oh, no, Uncle.'

He seemed relieved. But I still wished he would give up the gold.

When we got to the beach the sun was like a big dazzling wheel over the sea. Like a big silver coin – like a sixty-cents piece – only that it was about ten times bigger. And a thousand times brighter. After we reached Plaisance beach we turned right, then Uncle speeded up. I almost could not see, because of the glare of the sun, but when I shaded my eyes I saw that Stanley's men were ahead, half-way down the beach and pushing the boat to the water's edge. Stanley's boat-house was directly opposite to them amongst the coconut trees. I said, 'Uncle, look they're there already.'

'Aha,' he smiled. Uncle was so used to the glare he had seen them right away. I put on speed, too, making the sand go 'crunch, crunch'.

Uncle said, 'Don't kill yourself. They can't go without me.'

There wasn't a very wide beach, because the tide was coming up, but the boatmen still had some way to go. The wind was not very high, but the breakers were pounding. Every now and again the seine-men heaved and pushed and stopped to rest. From the time they spotted Uncle they seemed to just stand up and wait for him to come. When he got fairly near to them he stopped and he said, 'Look, Horace, I have something to tell you. Don't get upset, because I know you know I ain't thief the gold chain. But I feel I have to tell you this: I ain't thief it, and if you hear anybody say so they damn lie. But look, I'll tell you what. We'll find it. We'll find it, you know. Or at least we'll find out the thief. And I'll tell you this again – so help me God! – I'll tell you this, if I have to take night and make day I'll get to the bottom of this.'

I gave him a smile that was about three-quarters sincere. 'I too. Count on me, Uncle.'

His face brightened and he was going to speak when one of the men shouted, 'Ulric – come on nuh, man.'

He put a hand on my shoulder, 'We'll talk. But I have to go now because they're getting impatient.'

✳ Thirteen

I WAS THE FIRST PUPIL in school that morning, and teachers who came in early made fun and asked if I had slept in the school. Around eight o'clock there were a few children in the schoolyard. There was Leo Pierre, a boy from my class. He came in early, too, but not as early as I did. When he came in he saw some boys playing cricket on the sand pitch and he just dashed down his book-bag and scampered off to the field. He had said to me, 'You playing? Come on.' But I didn't bother to go.

I climbed the stairs and went to the far end of the bannister to look down at the children playing under the coconut trees. The first person I saw was Claudia, in a ring of girls playing bean-bag. Then she left the ring and went to play hop-scotch, and the rest who were playing bean-bag left and gradually joined her at playing hop-scotch. Even in class the others tended to follow Claudia.

I looked down on the children playing in the yard and all the while I was wondering about Uncle and about that gold chain. I said to myself, 'I'll get to be close friends with Uncle. Close, close. Uncle is swearing to God he ain't have the chain, but who have it?' And I said the same thing that Uncle told me: 'So help me God I'll get to the bottom of this.'

There were a lot of boys playing cricket now and the game looked exciting. There were about three or four more boys from my class. One of the boys who sat at the back of my class went in to bat and with the first ball the bowler threw down his wicket. The wicket was a tin drum and the noise must have sounded all over Mayaro. I laughed. I heard the boy protest, 'You stone that one!' He was smallish, but stubborn and did not want to leave the wicket, and they took away the bat from him and gave him a few taps round the head. I laughed even more. Claudia, who was still playing hop-scotch, went over and said, 'Leave the boy alone.'

The one who had been bowling was the biggest boy from our class. He wasn't *bowling*, really, but stoning. Pelting. His name was Cleophas John, and now he walked over to Claudia and said, 'You is a police?' He said this aggressively, and Claudia went up to his face because she wasn't afraid of him.

From the time he said, 'You is a police?' my thoughts fled back to what had happened last night. What happened last night had never left my mind completely, but now it came right up to the front. I had felt nervous and scared of Constable Cordner from the time he had said, 'We could break and enter.' I straightened up from the bannister and turned my eyes up the hill to the Police Station. I had been trying to avoid looking there but all of a sudden I did that. The low cream-and-red building with its sloping roof looked very harmless from here. My heart was thumping.

I turned my eyes back to the school-yard again but this time although I continued to look at the boys and girls playing games I was hardly thinking about them. I asked myself: 'What happened to those police fellers when they left last night? How come they didn't go to Uncle's place?' Perhaps they had to come back to the Police Station first – I thought – and perhaps Sergeant Peters told them it was too late. Despite his long, curling moustache, which made him look fierce, Sarge might be a person who would say that. Because that day, when I looked at his face from near up, he wasn't aggressive at all. In fact he resembled my teacher, and that was funny, because they were both Peters. Anyway, maybe he told them it was too late to break and enter. Or maybe he told them they shouldn't break and enter at all – at least I hoped so. He must have said, 'Go early in the morning.'

'Oh,' I said to myself, although my heart was already beating quicker. 'Maybe that's why Uncle left the house so early.' But Stanley was on the beach anyway, and the boatmen –

'Horace, hello. How are you?'

I swung round. It was Teacher Myra. She was wearing a bright, flowered, multi-coloured dress, and she looked as fresh as though it were Monday morning.

'Well, thank you, Miss.'

She came to where I was leaning up on the bannister. 'You are a little early?'

'I was a lot early, Miss. I was the first person in the school.'

'Jiffy!' she said. 'You were an early bird. Early bird catch the most worms.'

I smiled.

'But shouldn't that be *catches*? "Bird catches." I didn't say that to catch you,' she said, and we both laughed at that. Then she said, 'I find it easier to say "birds catch," though, in this case, don't you? "Early birds catch the most worms." I think that's better.' She was still smiling and looking at me. She said, 'I suggest it to you because you like words. What's the first thing this morning – geography?' she asked. But it was more as if she was reminding me. She looked at the school clock. 'Cricky!' she said. 'Have to go and prepare the blackboard. Haven't got much time.' She hurried to our class-room.

I went to our class-room too and when I got there I found about five or six pupils already sitting down. I was a little disappointed because I thought I would be the first boy Teacher Myra would have met down in the class. Claudia was there – I didn't even see when she came up. In a short while more began coming in and the class was nearly full before the bell rang. Teacher Myra began laughing to herself, and we were all looking at her. She said, 'Could you all guess what I'm laughing at?'

We said no.

'When I'm early so many of you are early and when I'm late so many are late.'

'We like to follow you,' a voice said.

'Is that that so Nashus, or is it flattery?' I looked around. Nashus didn't answer because he did not know what flattery was. And I was sure many of those who laughed at him didn't know either. Teacher Myra guessed, and she was talking about it when the bell rang.

At geography, the subject was 'The Five Great Oceans', and Teacher Myra began talking of the ocean right beside us – the Mayaro sea. A lot of pupils in the class were surprised to know it was part of the five great oceans.

'What ocean is it, Horace Lumpres?'

I looked at her and for a moment I was a little confused.

She said, 'Who has ever been on the Atlantic?'

Nobody answered.

She looked at me. Somebody at the back said, 'His uncle is a fisherman.'

She appeared to be surprised but I was sure she knew that. She said to me, 'You have an uncle that catches fish?'

'Yes,' I said, and everybody laughed. She had emphasized the word 'catches', and she and I knew what it was all about.

'And you yourself have never been out there, boy?' She looked as if amazed.

'No, Miss.' The class laughed again because I had never been out there.

'Well, that air out there is bracing and one shouldn't miss it. Besides that, it must be a great experience. Maybe one feels like Columbus – who knows.' She had a wistful look on her face as her eyes stared through the window towards the sea. Of course there were only coconut palms between. The tide must have been already right up because ever so faintly I was hearing the crash of the waves.

A girl's voice came from the back. 'Columbus, Miss? Why Columbus, Miss?'

Teacher Myra seemed surprised. 'Didn't we talk about Columbus last week? His voyages of discovery? Don't you know about Columbus, Mavis?'

'Yes, Miss.'

The whole class was silent. Mavis was puzzled because I could see it on her face. She could not see the connection, nor could I. Perhaps nobody in the class saw the connection and perhaps everybody was afraid Teacher Myra would ask what it was. I hoped she wouldn't ask *me* anything. Teacher Myra could be so vague sometimes.

She stood up in front of the class, looking from face to face, with everybody tense. Then she said slowly, 'Last week we spoke of Christopher Columbus and his discoveries. Then we spoke of the Spaniards that came after him. The first Spaniards were good. Remember Las Casas. The other scamps took all the gold from the Indies.'

The class laughed to hear her say that, but I did not laugh. At the mention of gold my heart was thumping. What was strange to me was that she had seemed to glance at me and quickly glance away again. Now she had her head turned to somebody else, and she said, 'I am not casting pearls before swine, am I?'

Claudia said, 'You mean gold before swine, Miss.' Everybody laughed. Claudia was very sharp-witted and Teacher Myra knew when to ignore her. She could not ignore her now because Claudia had her hand up.

'Miss, you think there is gold in – at – '

Teacher Myra said, 'Gold is where you find it.' Everyone recognised that sentence. She repeated, 'Gold is where you find it. That is too true.'

Claudia went on with what she had wanted to ask: 'At – at the bottom of the sea, Miss? You think there's gold at the bottom of the sea?'

Teacher Myra seemed very interested. 'Yes,' she said, 'Could be. Why not? Sure there's gold at the bottom of the sea. Don't forget galleons sank.'

Then she said hastily, 'But let's hurry back to geography. That is history, isn't it? Anyway,' she said, turning to me, 'Horace Lumpres, you must make the most of opportunities. If I had an uncle who worked on the deep, I would have known what it was like to be there. Okay, let's look at the five great oceans.' She unfurled a big coloured map of the world over the blackboard, and pinned it on.

I listened to her as she went on talking and pointing out the five great oceans. I wasn't particularly paying attention, but I was listening because Teacher Myra was always nice to listen to. She was the only person that I knew who spoke so nicely, and I could never tell how she managed to do it. I didn't wonder about that now. As she went on talking and asking questions, and as the class kept answering in chorus, I was thinking of Uncle Ulric and the gold chain, and I was wondering if the chain was now in the deep – at the bottom of the sea. But I said to myself, 'No, not really. Uncle's too smart for that.' I felt he wouldn't have stolen it unless he wanted to have riches. Then what was the use of dropping it to the bottom of the sea? I remembered reading a poem called 'Jewels of the Sea', and there was a line about 'playthings of the deep', but I knew it was only – what did Teacher Myra call it – fantasy? I knew it was only fantasy. But where did Uncle Ulric hide the gold chain? He could hardly have hidden it in his house. There was almost no place to hide it there. I wondered if he had hidden it *under* the house. Or in the sand. Or maybe it was in a pocket of one of those ragged trousers hanging up on nails in his bedroom. It couldn't be. It wouldn't be. I began to feel bitter against Uncle again and I couldn't help thinking it might have been helpful to everybody if the police had gone to his house last night. Perhaps Aunt Mona was not too bad after all. Mother and Auntie had said she was so interested because she wanted her 'share', but perhaps if her police friends had gone to search they would have found it, and now we'd have all been better off. In my mind I heard the class laughing but it was like voices far away. It started very distantly – the laughter – as if it were ripples of the sea, and then it was all over me like a crashing wave. A voice beside me cried 'Horace!' and I turned round to Cedric in a startled sort of way, and there was great merriment in class. I looked towards Teacher Myra at the blackboard and she was standing there looking calmly at me. She said, 'Did you hear my question, Horace?'

'No, Miss.'

'Because you are not too well, I suppose. Remember you were ill the day — '

'Just half-day, Miss. Came to school in the afternoon.'

'That's right. This morning you are day-dreaming because you are not very well yet.'

I did not say anything. She stood before the map and both herself and the map seemed to brighten the room. The pink on certain countries seemed to go with the pink roses of her dress. Just below her neck there was a large blue section looking soft and velvety, and that seemed to match the blue of the five great oceans. It was only when she raised her eyebrows that I realised I hadn't answered yet. I didn't even know what the question was. She smiled kindly and said, 'All right, Horace Lumpres, take a rest.' Then noticing Claudia's hand up, she said, 'Yes?'

Claudia said, 'The coastal strip.'

'The coastal strip – that's right.'

The others looked at Claudia enviously. I did not know what to envy. I had not the least idea what the subject was about.

Throughout the geography lesson Teacher Myra treated me as though I was ill, and she spoke to me softly and kindly, and neither asked me questions nor gave me any work. Yet when

Frankie Fridal, in going to unpin the map and take down the blackboard whispered something about my being sick, she blurted out: 'Sick what! You believe that?' Just like that. I was surprised. At first I thought it was a joke, but she didn't laugh. In fact her face was filled with disgust. She didn't think that I had heard, especially as she turned away from me to say it. The pupils who heard laughed heartily and looked at me. She looked round, and when her eyes held me, she smiled softly and very kindly, as though nothing had happened. And she continued sparing me questions until Claudia, who must have been jealous, said, 'Miss, you forgetting Horace. He could talk because – . Teacher Myra, – '

'What is it?'

'Horace could talk.'

'He can probably talk but he's not feeling inclined to. And when you do I won't ask you either. Speech is silver but silence is gold.'

I didn't quite know what she meant by that, and I was sure no one in the class did. This was one of the occasions on which my teacher had us guessing. The mention of gold set my mind thinking of the gold chain and my thoughts wandered far. I said to myself: I wonder if it's possible Uncle didn't take it? I wonder if it wasn't best to look all over our place thoroughly – under the house, around the kitchen, in the yard, under the zecack tree – everywhere. My chest began to heave, and as Teacher Myra was dismissing the class, she looked at me concerned. 'Boy, like you getting the asthma too?' I said I didn't know. I didn't tell her that I didn't even know what asthma was. She said, 'Anyway, the next class is singing. The whole school, of course. Afterwards you must hurry home.'

At singing, the whole school gathered in the hall. The headmistress, big strapping Nessy Popwell, took the pupils in this subject. I sat at the very back of the class and Teacher Myra sat beside me. When the singing started up she whispered, 'Don't sing – it mightn't be good for you. Just listen.'

After listening for a while, she said in my ear, 'Aren't choral voices beautiful. Aren't children angels?'

I could have sworn she ended with the word 'sometimes', but

maybe it was the way she breathed. I said, 'Yes, Miss.'

'How old are you, Horace?'

'Nearly thirteen.'

She had asked the question, looking closely underneath my nostrils. She seemed very much amused. She said, 'Seems as if a moustache will start to grow soon.'

I looked at her. 'Mother said that last week.'

'Too true,' she said. 'I can see it starting up. You might have a huge moustache when you get big.'

'I'll shave,' I said, concerned.

'Why? Don't you like a bushy moustache? A long, curling, twisting one?'

'No, Miss.' I was thinking of the sergeant at the Police Station. When she was speaking to me now, she whispered very, very softly, and I tried to copy this but I always seemed to be making noise. So I didn't want to talk too much now – for fear of disturbing – else I would have told her I didn't want to have a moustache like the sergeant.

She whispered, 'My father has a nice one.'

Looking sidelong at her I could see there was a pleased smile on her face. She saw me looking at her and she put her hand on my neck and said, 'Feeling good now?'

'Yes, Miss.'

But the next song started me day-dreaming again, and it made my chest heave, as if I was getting what Miss called the asthma. But, oddly enough, now was when she seemed suddenly enthusiastic. She said, 'This is really a beautiful one. Come on – let's sing: *Rocked in the Cradle of the Deep*.'

Rocked in the cradle of the deep! I thought to myself alarmed. She didn't look at me now, but I felt I was going to faint.

❋ Fourteen

WHEN I GOT HOME Mother was in the smoky kitchen. When she heard me she came out and I said, 'Uncle okay – they didn't break into the house.'

'I know.'

I was surprised to hear that. 'You went up Quarters?'

'No, but Mona was here. She said they never went down there at all.'

I was silent. Then I said, 'Uncle didn't go home either. Not right away.'

'No? Where he went? Where he slept?'

'Don't know. Think he stayed out until late. Because of them.'

'Mona, that hypocrite. Saying how she was sorry for him.'

'Ma, don't talk about Aunt Mona.' I was upset and I went up the steps and to my room to rest down my book-bag. The house felt very empty. I had realised Auntie Roomeen was not there, of course. That was one of the first things I had realised. I didn't know why, but it was always different when Auntie Roomeen was there. You always knew she was there. I rested the book-bag on the table in my room and I came back down the steps. Mother was again inside the kitchen and there was the delicious smell of pumpkin talcurrie. I called to her, 'Where's Auntie Roomeen?'

The pot was shee-sheeing a great deal, and in her reply I heard only the word 'beach', and then I heard, 'Clunis'. My heart began to thump a little. I walked out to the beach.

When I got to the beach I looked right, then left, and then I saw them. Auntie was sitting on a coconut log, and Mr Clunis had one foot on the log and he was leaning up on a coconut tree close to her. They were not very far away, and in the direction of Point Radix. Here there were no houses and the coconut trees were closer and denser. When I looked it appeared that Auntie Roomeen saw me, but she did not call out to me. I began walking towards them but my head was turned towards Point Radix,

102

although I was not thinking of it. I was feeling confused and silly and annoyed. The fact that Point Radix was full of mist this evening, and that mottled clouds had settled over it, hardly registered in my mind.

I walked slowly, not looking the way of Auntie and Mr Clunis, and I was feeling extremely embarrassed, for now she *must* have seen me and yet she did not call to me. I was feeling so confused that if I could have turned back easily, I would have done so. When I was near up I looked towards her and I saw she was looking at me and smiling.

She said, 'Come from school, boy?'

'Yes, Auntie.'

'How was it? Good?'

'Yes, Auntie. Last night, you know, they didn't – ' I stopped. She said, 'I know. Mona was here today.'

I was looking at her and trying to avoid Mr Clunis' gaze, but now he said, with emphasis, '*Evening*, Horace.'

'Evening, Mr Clunis.' I was very shame-faced.

Auntie chuckled. 'He forgot.'

I did not bother about that very much because I was overwhelmed with a resentful feeling as I stood there. Resentful of Mr Clunis. I felt a little embarrassment for my Auntie, but mostly it was anger and – and what Teacher Myra said was a crime. Because before Mr Clunis looked for his own friends he was taking my best friend from me. And it was not only that he liked her but I could see that she liked him also. It was true that she would always be there, in my mind, and she would always be my Auntie, but it looked as though all the attention would be going to Mr Clunis. In fact she had seen me coming all the way, but instead of calling out to me she had sat there chattering with Mr Clunis. And with all that, Mr Clunis was always smelling of sweat and coconut husk! And Auntie was always perfumed. There was always a bottle marked 'Orange Blossom', or 'Limacol', or 'Cologne', on the dressing table now.

I saw her looking at my face and she probably thought I was still worrying about Mr Clunis, for she said, 'You mustn't mind Clunis. You scared of him?'

'No, Auntie.'

'Well you look so uncomfortable.'

Mr Clunis said, 'Oh, so you ain't scared of me?' and he laughed out. I didn't know what to say. Auntie turned to him, 'Why should he be scared of you – you are some tiger or something?'

He grinned. By the way she looked at him to say this I could tell there was a great closeness between them. Mr Clunis kept looking at her with a big grin on his face as he leaned against the coconut tree. He was not in his usual working clothes, but it was old clothes anyway.

At length Auntie moved her eyes from his and she said to me, 'So tell me – school went okay? I hear you are a bright boy.'

That took me aback. 'Not so bright.'

'Don't worry. I know. Isn't your teacher Myra Peters?'

'Teacher Myra – oh yes.'

'From Rio Claro. Haven't seen that girl in ages.'

I didn't even know that Auntie knew her. Maybe they were at school together. But Teacher Myra was much younger. I wondered how Auntie knew she was my teacher, but I didn't ask her. In fact, with Mr Clunis there, I wasn't feeling free at all. Nor welcome. I was feeling odd and I was feeling that perhaps he wanted me to go. I said, 'Auntie, Ma will be ready in a while.'

'You mean with the dinner? Oh good. Boy, am I hungry!'

Mr Clunis looked at me and said, 'You really don't like us talking, eh? Always something about Claris and kitchen. You want her to go in and that's that.'

'I only – '

He was still smiling, and it was clear he was making fun. He said, 'Anyway, while ago you said you ain't frighten for me.'

I had to smile. My eyes wandered to Point Radix. Mr Clunis looked there too. He said, 'Rain bound to come. Sure as day. Rain falling on La Point now.'

The sky had grown very dark over Point Radix and the sea there was choppy and slate-grey. The whole place looked desolate and the wind had risen and there was a chilly edge to it. Auntie said something which I didn't hear, and Mr Clunis answered, 'That is nonsense, Room. That is stupidness. After all, Radix is down there, past Plaisance. How the hell this could be Point Radix then?'

She answered him in what seemed like quiet rage. I wasn't looking. She told him, 'You helling in front the boy. What respect is that?'

He said, 'Okay, okay. But for me this is *La Point*.'

I heard her chuckle.

He said, 'And you grow up right here calling it *La Point*. What is this sudden Point Radix?'

'Because that is the right name. Besides, Radix down there is Radix Estate. This here is different.'

'Roomeen, I know you have education, but sense make before book. You feel I'm a damn fool?'

She laughed. She said, 'You damning now, not helling. You going good.' They both laughed. My eyes were still on *La Point* but I was wondering how an intelligent person like Auntie Roomeen could find pleasure in the company of Mr Clunis.

As I was standing there, looking, the thick mist completely obscured Point Radix now, and it was clear that rain was falling on the sea over there. I turned to tell Auntie and I was just in time to see her knocking Mr Clunis' hand away from her face. I was so astonished that I felt weak, but then I told myself, suddenly and finally, that that was the way Auntie and Mr Clunis wanted it, and that nothing in the world would change them. Still, I was bitterly disappointed with my Auntie making that kind of fun with a silly old coconut-picker. Although I was glad she was here I would be more than thankful when she left. And all because of him! When I had turned, and she had seen me, she had said, 'Yes, Hory? You saying something?' I had been so taken aback I had forgotten all about the rain on the sea. My heart was going 'voom, voom, voom, voom!' But she was smiling softly. Before I could stutter out something a few drops of rain must have fallen on Mr Clunis' head, for he cried, 'Rain, girl, let's go.' They got up and we began to walk fast along the beach. We heard the rain coming. He looked back and then he said, 'Run!' Putting on speed I overtook them. The rain was approaching very fast, and as I ran I heard the roar growing louder and louder. We only just reached the yard when the water came crashing down upon us.

Mother had the table all ready for dinner but when the rains came they caught her in the kitchen. I had run pell-mell into the yard and up the steps, not looking back for Auntie or Mr Clunis, but when I got inside the house, panting, and I went back to the front door and looked around, they were not there. 'Auntie,' I

105

called, looking at the kitchen door and feeling a little frantic in case she wasn't there. The rain was blasting down in big drops, and with the noise it was making on the galvanized roof of the house, and on the thatched roof of the kitchen, and on the sand, and with the noise of the wind in the coconut trees, together with the roar of the sea, it was impossible for me to hear anyone or for anyone to hear me. But now the kitchen door was pushed open a bit, but the wind slammed it shut again.

I did not bother to call again nor did I feel any fury because it was Auntie's hand that had tried to push the door open. So she was in the kitchen. I was sure that Mr Clunis was there, too, and I wished he had gone home, but he could not molest Auntie because Mother was there too. I went and took a towel and dried my head and changed my clothes.

When I had finished changing into dry clothes, I lay back on my bed, with my head facing up to the ceiling. In my thoughts there was Mr Clunis in the kitchen pretending he was listening to Mother, and smiling and nodding his head, but deep in his heart only liking Auntie. Yet Auntie could not really care so much about him because she did not bring him any Panama gold. At least, she did not like him as much as she liked us, my mind said. And then a distant voice seemed to tell me, 'And what was the good of bringing any Panama gold?' I suddenly began to feel anxious. We had lost the gold, lost it completely, and there was no sign that we would ever find it. Whatever had become of it? I wondered. Where did Uncle put it? In my wandering mind Uncle and Mr Clunis became as one, and I was thinking it was Uncle in the kitchen. And then it was as if a voice from far away began reciting:

In the bottom of the sea buried deep so deep
A dear little chain lay fast asleep!

I opened my eyes and shook the thoughts from my head. I said to myself, 'What's wrong with you, boy – you sleepy?' And although I smiled at myself I drifted again into the same state. And this time it was as if Teacher Myra's voice came to me distinctly: 'My father has a nice one. Curling. Why don't you want it?' And then it was as if we were on the beach and Mr Clunis, with Uncle's voice, was beckoning Auntie into a boat. In the delirium I kept crying, 'No, Auntie. No!' And I seemed to feel the singing of the school filling my mind, and Teacher Myra whispering, 'You have to watch it. All that glitters is not gold . . . All that glitters . . . '

When I opened my eyes it was already dark and there were noises in the living-room. I sat up on the bed and rubbed my eyes and tried to figure out who was there. I heard Aunt Mona's voice and my heart began thumping. I listened to hear if there was a man's voice and if so, if that voice was Constable Cordner's. I heard Auntie Roomeen talking, then Mother, and then I heard Uncle say, 'Honest to God, Roomeen and I'll tell you this now. I'll talk frankoment. If you and Claris could look at me and think I'd do that sort of thing, you all ain't *nothing*.' Uncle said the word 'nothing' with great force and vexation and the rest kept quiet. He said, 'If the police did break down my door, is then you was going to see ruction. Man turning beast.' There was silence again and then he said, 'When it comes to bringing police for your family – '

Aunt Mona interrupted: 'It's not a matter of bringing police for your family. The police there to help. That is their job. If you all report the gold chain lost, what you expect?'

Auntie Roomeen said sharply, 'You all?' Aunt Mona went on talking. 'If the chain's reported lost, it's the police who'll have to find it – or help find it. They have to search, that's all.'

Uncle said, 'Yes, but why my house, when the chain bound to be here.'

This roused both Mother and Auntie who tried to speak together. All I heard was Aunt Mona saying, 'Well they searched this one, too.' Then Mother's voice broke through: 'No, no, Ulric; wait. What you mean by saying it bound to be in this house? What you talking about?'

'The gold chain,' Uncle said drily.

'So it's in this house? So me and Roomeen are liars!'

Auntie tried to talk, too, and there was a confusion of voices, but Uncle's voice rose above all. He was saying, 'I know. I know. I know you ain't that. But you couldn't in any case because I saw it with my own two eyes.'

'Oh, you saw it?' That was Aunt Mona, and she said this so meaningfully that Uncle stared at her and said, 'What you mean?

I was saying that from the start.'

Aunt Mona did not answer. In fact, nobody spoke, and the silence fell so heavily, you could have cut it with a knife. That was Teacher Myra's phrase, 'you could cut it with a knife', referring to silence. If she were sitting here now that was exactly what she would have said. I tried to think of silence being cut with a knife. As I was thinking of it, I was jolted by Uncle's gruff voice. He said, 'Look, ah saying this, and you could mark my word. We'll find out what happen to this gold chain. If I have to take night and make day, I'll find out.'

Aunt Mona said, 'Well, boy, I'll be with you. I'll be with you because I myself badly want to know. I too old to believe in mysteries. Ulric, I'll be with you hook, line and sinker.'

I listened to hear if she would chuckle when she said 'hook, line, and sinker', but she said it seriously, and not just to sound cute because Uncle was a fisherman.

Uncle said, 'But you going Tobago – not so? – you was just saying something – '

'Just a minute,' Aunt Mona said, 'Something just crossed me mind. But I wonder. You know you can't trust little children. Now suppose – wait, where's Horace. I can't talk if – '

I didn't hear what Mother started to say because Auntie Roomeen cried, 'What in the name of heaven you trying to say!' She spoke loudly and I could tell from the tone of her voice that she was breathing fire. That was Teacher Myra's phrase again, *breathing fire*. I didn't keep thinking of Teacher Myra now though. My head felt hot. Somebody said that I was in my room sleeping and before I could throw myself back on the bed and close my eyes Aunt Mona pushed open the door of my room. I immediately began rubbing my eyes. She said, 'Boy, you there? You wake up?'

'Yes, Aunt Mona,' I said and I yawned.

She said to them, 'He's in here listening.'

'What nonsense Mona talking,' Mother cried, and Auntie Roomeen joined in, with her voice raised. Mother was very disturbed and agitated and I could hear it from her voice. She was always cool and calm until I was accused of something. She was very angry now and telling Aunt Mona the things I would do and the things I would never do, and one of the things I would never do was to stay quiet and listen to them. Against the background of talking I heard Auntie Roomeen call: 'Horace.'

'Yes, Auntie.'

'You'd better go out on the beach now and take a walk.'

Mother said hastily, 'He wasn't listening. Don't bother with Mona. Perhaps the boy just wake up.'

Aunt Mona said, 'How you know?'

'Because I know my child. He wouldn't stay in there and listen. If he was up he would come right out.'

Aunt Mona laughed derisively.

Auntie Roomeen said, 'I want him to go on the beach for a walk. I know he wasn't listening, but I can't answer Mona if the boy's in here.'

While she was saying this I had already brushed past Uncle and was now going down the steps.

When I came back I saw that their tempers had died down and that they were all sitting around the table talking. Their voices were normal, although subdued, and were sounding a little strained. I had never thought of Auntie as pretensive but she had me wondering when I heard her say, 'But Mona, I mean, do you *have* to live in Tobago. You think you'll like the place?'

'What's wrong with Tobago – anything wrong with Tobago? Besides, you think I'll sit down in Moriah and get cobweb? Girl, you bet I'll see Port-of-Spain more often than Claris.' She gave a little cackle of a laugh and without seeing her I could tell exactly what her antics were. She said, 'In any case I have to go wherever they transfer him.'

Of course I had already started wondering what was going on, but hearing Aunt Mona now I didn't have to wonder anymore. 'Oh, so that's what!' I thought. I had never realised that so much was happening, but nothing would surprise me when it had to do with Aunt Mona. I thought, 'That's what it is. Aunt Mona going to Tobago with Cordner!' I was feeling uneasy sitting here and listening, but at least they could all see me. I began wondering if I should go back on the beach.

Uncle said, 'So you'll fix up over here, Mona, before you go?'

'No, it's next week we leaving, man. We'll fix that up over there.'

Auntie Roomeen asked, 'Next week?' She looked shocked.

'It's next week you said? What's all the hurry?' None of us expected Aunt Mona to be leaving for Tobago so suddenly. Even I was surprised – though not sorry.

Aunt Mona did not answer right away, and then she spoke softly – so softly I had to lean back slightly to hear her. She was almost whispering. She said, 'It's that new sergeant from Rio Claro. Peters. I told you all about that girl. Well Peters putting pressure on him. He want to force his hand. But he prefer me so he decide to break away.'

Someone said, 'Oh.' I wasn't sure who said that. I was feeling uneasy in case Aunt Mona thought I was listening, and so I slipped down from the steps and was now out in the yard. From this distance I heard them talking freely now but of course I could not hear what they were saying.

I walked about in the yard, with my eyes on the coconut trees and on *La Point*, but with my mind trying to make sense out of what Aunt Mona had said. To be honest, it made no sense to me. Which girl was it? And whose hand was Sarge trying to force? And why? And what did that have to do with Cordner and Aunt Mona going to live in Tobago? I couldn't figure it out at all. But when Aunt Mona and Uncle Ulric spoke about 'fix up', I knew what that 'fix up' meant, and I thought a little wickedly that when Aunt Mona married the terrible Cordner she would be getting the husband she deserved. Not that I liked it. She was my aunt, however awful she was.

I walked around depressed, and after a while, when I thought that they had finished talking about it I came back and sat on the steps. In a sense they *had* finished talking about it, for they mentioned a lot of little domestic things, but then Uncle asked: 'What part of Tobago you going, Mona?'

'Mount Moriah.'

'You leaving so suddenly but I'll come over there to see you. Spend a day or two in Tobago. Tell me exactly where you'll be.'

Mother said, 'Day or two,' and she and Auntie laughed. Aunt Mona laughed too, and she said, 'He frighten to leave Stanley for long.' But then she started to explain in the finest detail. Uncle asked for a piece of paper and he was writing down, and he even made Aunt Mona draw. Aunt Mona laughed and drew something, and inside her she must have said the same thing that I said to myself: 'You think Uncle going anywhere?' Anyway, in the end

Uncle said, 'All right. Thank you, girl.' I felt a little strange because at that time he had a smile that was looking both sweet and sour. And as if he, too, was saying something to himself. Then he said, 'All right, you bound to see me over there.'

'Don't worry with you,' Aunt Mona said.

Mother and Auntie chuckled.

It was already somewhat late when Aunt Mona and Uncle got up to go. Aunt Mona had not seen me from where she was sitting, and as she passed down the steps she said, 'You was here all the time?'

'Not all the time.'

'You just come back from the beach?' Glancing around I saw the rest of them talking. 'Yes,' I said quietly.

'Good boy.' She went out into the yard.

Seeing her, Uncle came to the front door and called, 'Mona, you ain't waiting for me? You walking up to Quarters?'

'And that is something?' she said. 'You bound to meet me in riding up.'

I could see Uncle was uneasy. I heard him say, 'You see how Mona like to have everything her way? When she wanted to come here she came by me and I had to bring her. Now she want to go she can't wait.'

'Well let her go,' replied Auntie Roomeen.

'To walk all that way to Quarters?'

Mother looked at him and laughed. She said, 'But that's good exercise. In any case Horace walks that every single day. Twice a day.' She came and leant out of the front door and saw Aunt Mona across the track, leaning up near to Uncle's bicycle, waiting. She laughed again. Then she said, more quietly, 'Ulric you mean you don't know Mona yet? You think Mona walking up to any Quarters? I could excuse Roomeen, because she's away for years, but don't tell me you don't know Mona.'

Auntie Roomeen came to the front door and looked, then pulled her head inside.

I smiled. I was watching across stealthily at Aunt Mona – at the way she was fidgeting and looking impatient. Uncle, who was talking to Mother and Auntie on some other subject, stopped and said, 'She there? Let her stay there – that old schemer!'

111

In spite of that, though, he seemed anxious to get away, and in a short while he was easing towards the steps.

Mother said to him, softly, 'You could tell me what Mona see in that policeman? And so all of a sudden?'

Auntie Roomeen said, 'You bet something wrong somewhere.'

Uncle said, 'Something definitely wrong – although we talking about two different things. You all will see what I mean. But I'll tell you what – talking about sleight-of-hand? I too old to believe in mystery, too.' He said this and laughed a groaning laugh and nodded his head. He said, 'I have me own ideas, you girls will see what I mean.' Then he glanced at Aunt Mona standing by the bicycle, and he said, 'Anyway, look, I have to go. That girl make me feel so uncomfortable I'd better take her up.' I looked across at Aunt Mona. Although she was impatient to go she stood up there so stylishly that she reminded me of Teacher Myra's term: 'Statue of poise and charm'. I couldn't even remember what had prompted Teacher Myra to say that. Uncle had nearly reached his bicycle when he came hurrying back, and he called to Mother, 'I leave me pump up there?' Mother said no. As he came up the steps he whispered to Mother and Auntie, 'Don't bother with no pump. I have to go now but we have to meet and talk soon. I feel I'm on the right track.' Then he whispered 'What cause tide?' and he laughed, 'Heh, heh.'

Aunt Mona called from where she was, 'Ulric, you coming or not?'

He ran down the steps again and across the yard.

Mother said, 'I wonder if Ulric's all right. I mean, I wonder if he's sound in his head. He suddenly behaving so – '

She couldn't find the word and Auntie looked at her and chuckled. 'Ulric's all right,' Auntie said. 'Not a thing is wrong with him.'

'But what's he trying to say?'

'It's that gold chain. Something's up. I feel we'll get this chain right back in this house.'

I ran to the back of the house in the darkness, and I jumped for joy.

✻ *Fifteen*

THE NEXT MORNING in class Teacher Myra came to me, and it seemed as though she was going to ask me something, but instead she checked herself and put her hands to her mouth. Since she was right next to me, I said, 'Yes, Teacher Myra?'

She made a nervous little laugh, and then she said, 'How are you? Any fever or so?'

'No.'

She hesitated a little, as though she hadn't said yet what she wanted to say. Now she whispered, 'I find you look so – you know – so worried.'

I stared through the window at the big sapodilla tree outside. I didn't know what to say, so I just said, 'It's all right, Teacher Myra.'

'You are sure. Sure everything's all right?'

'Yes.'

Teacher Myra looked at me closely for a little while before going back to the blackboard. I could not help feeling that she looked as though she wanted to find out something. My classmates were looking at me but I did not pay any attention to them.

I looked at Teacher Myra writing on the blackboard. She was so graceful, quiet and gentle. Her hair was always combed so nicely. She had a pretty oval face, smooth and black, and she was so soft-spoken – and most times beautifully spoken. She was so unruffled and serene – although lately, like now, she looked uncomfortable. She was writing on the blackboard, and with a few strokes of the chalk she drew a leaf, and continued writing. And this was another thing about Teacher Myra. She was so talented that she could draw a leaf and continue writing as if nothing had happened. The subject was Nature Study. After she was finished writing she turned to the class and she began talking about a seed and its growth. Then, as if she wasn't doing anything at all, she drew a seed that was beginning to grow. Then she chuckled to herself without turning round, and when the class began to laugh too, she turned around and said, 'Class, every time I draw a seed I always remember – who is it, Tennyson?' Someone at the back of the class said, 'Yes.' Everybody laughed.

'Yes, what?' she challenged. 'What am I going to say about Tennyson?' There was silence and then the class laughed again.

'Everytime I draw a seed I remember these lines – ' And she spoke softly, almost whispering:

> "In the heart of a seed buried deep so deep,
> A dear little germ lay fast asleep."

As she recited that I became very alert. 'It's not so,' I thought. I almost said aloud, 'Teacher Myra, it's not so, it's "*In the bottom of the sea, lying deep so deep, A dear little –*" ' My thoughts halted in confusion. It could not be *chain*. It could not be *A dear little chain lay fast asleep*. Could it be? Maybe it was *worm. Worm* could be wrong, but otherwise I felt sure I was saying it right. Only, I did not want to risk it and find myself wrong, because then the whole class would laugh. At the moment I did not know where I had learnt those lines. This was a Fourth Standard class and we may have learned those lines way back in First Standard. Or perhaps in Introductory. Teacher Myra went on talking and I was calming my mind well enough to listen to her. She was asking Effy Thorpe about the growth of a seed. 'Isn't that the way?' She was saying. 'Doesn't it burst and sprout?' Effy looked confused. Effy said, 'Germ, Miss? You said germ, Miss.'

'It's the same thing,' Teacher Myra said. 'It germinates.' Then Teacher Myra pointed to another girl and said, 'Tell the class what *germinate* means.'

'Disease.'

'Disease! So this is hygiene?' Her voice was drowned by laughter.

She looked skywards and said, 'My God! And I tell people I have a bright class!' Seeing her look towards me I put up my hand.

'What's it?'

I did not hesitate. I said anxiously, 'To grow.'

The pupils were all set to burst out laughing, but she said,

'That's right. How many times have I not said that. *Germ* here means life. Very good, Horace Lumpres.'

Everybody's eyes were on me and although I wasn't looking at them, I felt their glances. And I was feeling embarrassed in a strange way because I had answered correctly. The teacher went on talking and I could see everyone was remembering what had just happened and now for certain I would not tell her about *In the bottom of the sea* because if I was wrong it was sure to take my fame away. At length she made her way to her table, put down the chalk, dusted her hands, and she said, 'All right, class. Dismiss for recess.'

As the pupils rushed and tumbled out of the class, pushing aside desks and benches and making a deafening noise in their eagerness to get outside, Teacher Myra caught my eye and signalled me to stop. I waited. As the last of the pupils cleared the class-room, she took up the duster, handed it to me and pointed to the blackboard. As I went to wipe the blackboard she sighed and said, 'Heavens! Aren't boys boisterous.' She was thinking of the boys who were bullying their way out of the class. I looked at her and we smiled and I quietly wondered if it was only boys that could be boisterous. I told myself I was so silly. Could one expect girls to be boisterous? As I wiped the blackboard trying to think whether I had ever heard the word 'girlsterous', Teacher Myra's voice interrupted me.

'What's the next lesson, Lumpres.'

'Hygiene, Miss.' I was surprised she had to ask that question. As I looked at her I noticed the same tense look on her face that I had seen earlier. I couldn't help thinking again that she wanted to know something.

When I was finished cleaning the blackboard she said, ¦You don't like hygiene?'

I did not. And she herself knew it was my weak subject. I did not answer her but went to put the duster on her table.

Now she was smiling. 'Your compositions are charming.' I felt as if a cool, heavenly wind had rushed through my body. I felt as though my chest swelled.

'Don't you find so?' She was talking about the compositions.

'No, Miss.'

'You are only trying to be modest.'

I smiled sheepishly.

'Do you want to do a composition for me next period?'

'But it's hygiene.'

'Down with hygiene,' she said. 'You and I don't like it.' Then she said quickly, 'But we have to know it, mind you. And we have to keep the body clean. That's true, isn't it? Anyway, take the hygiene period to write a composition. Make it colourful and vivid and – true.' Her eyes seemed to burn as she watched me and I felt proud because I felt she really liked my compositions. And when the rest of the class came back she made me feel very special and privileged. Because she put me at a little table nearby – and the class was jealous. Although nobody knew that I was writing a composition – for her. Teacher Myra said, 'Class, *now* we are going to talk about germs.' Everybody laughed loudly, and I stopped and laughed too.

❋ Sixteen

I WROTE in the composition about what I had heard about Aunt Mona and the policeman, Constable Cordner, and about how Constable Cordner was being transferred to Tobago and that Aunt Mona was going with him and that they were going to get married. I don't know if I said they were going to Tobago and getting married or getting married and going to Tobago. All I know is that when I got back my book the order in which I had said it was changed. While I was writing the composition I wrote feverishly and like one in a dream world. I took no account of the class nor of Teacher Myra. The more I wrote, the more the thoughts flowed in my head and I wrote frantically and it was as if my hand could not go fast enough. I just forgot about everybody and everything.

I wrote that we did not know where the gold chain was, if it was in the bottom of the sea lying deep so deep. I said that Uncle swore he would find out who took it and that everybody else swore that it was Uncle who took it. I said I intended to go with Uncle one day in the boat, because he had invited me, and because one day I felt he would talk about the gold chain and then we would know. I said we would have to remain poor until we found that gold chain. And I said we were accustomed to being poor.

I wrote that now made one week since Auntie Roomeen came here (although when I was writing I so wanted to get the words down that I did not stop to count). I said she loved us very much and I loved her more than anybody else in the world. And I wrote of Mr Clunis and at once it was like gall that came up to my chest. I said that I did not like him at all and I said that he would like Auntie Roomeen to marry him. I said that she had been under the coconut tree talking to him, and smiling and chuckling, and I said it looked very much as if she liked him. I wrote that I would find out even if I had to ask her.

Then I wrote about what St Joseph was like these days, with the factory always smoking, and with the evening still very bright when I got home from school, and with the sea clear on the horizon, and that Mother said the days were so long because it was now June. But there was a cigale, with its long wailing whistle, only the day before yesterday. I heard it. The cigale meant the rains were close.

'And weren't the rain close?' I asked in my composition. Although I hadn't been thinking of Teacher Myra directly, I knew she would like that. (She liked very much when you asked a question inside a composition. And she liked you to use words like 'weren't', and 'aren't'.) I stopped and looked at the question: 'And weren't the rains close?' Then I described how some days ago the rains came sweeping in from the sea and how Auntie Roomeen, Mr Clunis and I ran for the yard and I dashed inside and I slept. And then, as I wrote a vision of Mr Reid came to me – Mr Reid, whom I had not seen for so long – and I asked another question: 'What about the old man?' And I felt a deep longing pain for Mr Reid, although we were not close.

I had not noticed the buggy for a few days now and I said so. I said I missed Mr Reid – the narrow face, the slightly crushed mouth, the sleepy-looking eyes, and the white fluffy hair. Although I did not think of Teacher Myra directly, as I wrote that, I knew she would like that, because she always praised descriptions. I wrote that the buggy itself was black, with four huge, narrow wheels, and that the horse was brown. I had wanted to say it was a bay mare, but it did not look very *bay,* like the one in the reading-book picture, *Shoeing the Bay Mare*. So I just said the horse was brown, and that the way the buggy was, the seat was just behind the tail of the horse. I said Mr Reid always wore sandals, and a baggy pair of grey-flannel trousers – she liked the word 'trousers' – and a white shirt which was missing buttons.

And then I talked again about the look of the village, with bushy clumps of zecack trees under the coconut palms, and a few houses, and the factory piping smoke. Not too far away was the beautiful Point Radix. And then with my heart excited and racing I wrote the words: 'Wild nature, itself, was luxuriantly beautiful'. I could have cried out for happiness when those words came to my mind. I had read them in the lesson on Charles

Kingsley's visit to the Kaiteur Falls in British Guiana, and they rose to my mind now. I thought: 'Oh God, I'll kill them with composition!' When I raised my head in feverish gladness I saw Teacher Myra's eyes on me. She quickly glanced away. I felt a bit embarrassed and I looked around the class. My class-mates were engaged in their hygiene lesson, drawing germs and hookworms from the blackboard. I turned back to my composition but it was a little while before I started going on again. Because when I looked down at the page I had to see the trees and I had to see the sun and I had to see the whole village of St Joseph because I was writing about it. I closed my eyes a little and thought of the broad white beach with the tide coming up, and with the breakers rising and crashing, throwing up foam and spray. But although the breakers were rising and crashing, and although it was windy, there was sun on the sea and over Point Radix there was nothing but a blue cloudless sky. And there was no mist. And you could see the trees thick and green on the slopes, and towards the tip you could see how the Point dipped suddenly, and then there was a little space of sea, before you came to the 'Rock of Ages'. My chest and my head were filled with thoughts but as soon as I began to pour them out the bell rang for midday.

There was the pulling and pushing aside of desks and benches as the pupils made a wild rush to get out of the class-room, but I sat there, disappointed. The whole school was filled with noises and with children running to and fro. I was only half aware of the din. I had put my pen down but I felt as though I was still seeing Point Radix.

I felt a hand on my shoulder and I turned around to say, 'Stop playing up, Silly!' But as I opened my mouth I remained with it wide open.

'Finished writing?'

'No, Teacher Myra.'

She smiled. She turned back the pages of my book and when she saw how much I had written, she said, 'Gee whiz!' I didn't even know she knew that slang, and I was surprised.

She said, 'When will you finish that?'

'Now, Miss.'

She looked thrilled and anxious. She said, 'Okay, but if you don't have lunch don't say it's me. Right? It looks like a lovely composition. Very well, Lumpres – carry on. Keep it up.'

119

❀ Seventeen

I CARRIED ON WRITING my composition right through to one o'clock, without having any lunch. I carried on until my classmates came running, and stumbling, and crashing in, knocking down the chairs and picking them up again. They were so clumsy, they nearly swept me away in the rush. A few of them stopped beside me to see what I was doing. I crossed my arms over my book and leant over them. Claudia said, 'He didn't go to lunch,' and looked around for support. Everybody became curious about me and began gathering around my table. Teacher Myra said, 'Silence. And please go to your places. Please go and sit down.'

Claudia said, 'But Miss – ' She pointed to me.

'Isn't he sitting?'

'At a special table.'

'Because he has special hard work.'

Everybody laughed, and Teacher Myra said, 'Class!' And she struck the desk with the duster because she did not have any whip. Then, looking at the class, she pointed to the motto above the stage at the other end of the room. It was in big black letters and it said, 'Manners Maketh Man'. She did not say a word, but just pointed to the motto and the laughter died down. Then she said, 'Yes, Horace Lumpres is at a special table. I hate to make any distinctions between my pupils – I mean, among my pupils – but this is for Horace's good. He needs to work hard. Suffer it to be so.' She looked so earnest in saying this, and so pious, and so humble at the end of it, that the class looked sorry for me. I glanced at Claudia and she even hung her head. Then I looked at Teacher Myra who had already turned to the blackboard. I wondered what she really meant by saying I needed to work harder. Because it gave the impression I could not cope with the class. Which was fibs. I was far from being the dullest boy in the class. I looked at Teacher Myra at the blackboard. I wasn't at all pleased. Because the fact of the matter was that I was writing a composition for her and she didn't want the class to know it. Need to work harder, my foot! I said to myself. All that glittered really wasn't gold. Teacher Myra was damn good for herself!

I wasn't looking at her now – I was looking at the floor and thinking and fuming. I was even breathing hard. But in looking at the floor, with her image there, the long cucumber sleeves of the white herring-boned bodice, the black belt, and the flared pink skirt, as I saw her image there in my mind, while watching the floor, slowly the form faded, for my body was growing warm again with the composition I was writing. As her image faded, the living picture of St Joseph came back to my mind.

It was near the end of my composition and I wanted to round off the end nicely. I wanted the composition to end on a tempestuous note – just like the sea at Point Radix when the tide was high and the wind was strong. I wanted to give the impression of mist and spray and the dusk creeping over everything, but with the sky stained red, as if with blood, and with the sun setting in a blaze of glory.

As I began to write I felt as if the words were coming alive under my hand. It was a fine composition, even though I said so myself. I felt embarrassed to say this and it was a good thing I was saying it only to myself. I felt thrilled. As I looked to tell Teacher Myra I was finished, she was coming hurriedly to me. As soon as I lifted my head she must have known and she started walking towards me. Maybe she feared I was going to say I had finished my composition, and so let everybody know. I wasn't so annoyed with her now. She must have been looking at me all the time, for as she came up to me there was an anxiety in her eyes that I had not seen before. She took up my book without saying anything, and then said, turning away: 'What's that? You want to go outside? Sure.' And she whispered, 'Please go and have something to eat.'

I hadn't breathed a word.

The class was looking at us and the way Claudia watched it was as though she was saying it wasn't fair.

✳ Eighteen

IT MUST HAVE BEEN two or three days afterwards when Uncle came up to St Joseph to bring some fish for us. Or, rather, to bring some fish for Auntie Roomeen. I know it was evening because I was already home from school, and in fact Auntie and I were on the beach when I saw the person coming from far up, looking as though he was walking in the water.

'That's Uncle,' I said to Auntie.

She stopped and shaded her eyes with her right hand, and looked up the beach. She said nothing, but as she looked, slightly squinting in the evening light, it suddenly occurred to me that she looked as stylish as Aunt Mona. Among the three sisters Mother was the least stylish, and it was Aunt Mona who, as they said, 'took the cake'. And it was true. Sometimes Aunt Mona got on my nerves, just to watch her. She was naturally stylish and graceful, but no, that wasn't enough for Aunt Mona. She had to be always putting on. She had to be always over-doing it.

As I watched Auntie Roomeen squinting and looking down the beach I thought to myself of the big difference between herself and Aunt Mona. Of course they looked alike, but I was thinking of their ways now. It was simply that everything my Auntie Roomeen did – whatever it was – it looked so natural and graceful, while with Aunt Mona it might look even more graceful but I always knew it was thought up before. Auntie broke into my thoughts when she said, 'Yes, that's him. That Ulric all right.'

'But only now you see that, Auntie?' I almost couldn't believe it. I thought she had already seen him but was still looking down the beach.

She said, 'Boy, your eyes are young and bright. Wait till you get like me.'

I was taken aback. Auntie looked so healthy and charming and

122

wonderful I could not believe her sight wasn't better than mine.

I said, 'But Auntie, you ain't old.'

She laughed. 'I'm not young.' And seeing me look hurt, she said, 'Life's like that, don't worry. After one time it's two. You'll be like old Reid one day.'

I looked at her wistfully. She said, 'Hear this one: when bull's young it bursts the chain, okay, you tell me what happens when it grows old.'

I smiled sadly and said nothing. She said, 'It messes up it's own tail. That's life. Look what's in Ulric's hand.'

I looked towards him. He was a great deal nearer. 'Fish,' I said.

We stood up and watched him approach. Tide was going down and the shore waves were running on the sand and whispering. Auntie said, 'Boy, how come you made out Ulric from so far?'

'I just know Uncle from any distance,' I said. She smiled softly, but I was still a little sad about what she had said about the bull.

Uncle was near up now. The fish were small jacks strung on a cocoyea flex, and he had this in one hand, while in the other he was holding a bag. He was walking in the water, letting the small waves bathe his feet.

Auntie said to me, 'I find he was looking like a little boy, walking down there. He hasn't grown up very much, you know.'

We laughed. Uncle was not tall, but although Auntie looked so big and strapping she wasn't much taller than him. It always seemed to me that ladies looked taller than they really are. Take Mother – Mother wasn't all that much taller than me now, and yet you couldn't call her short. But if I put on long pants – long trousers – could I be taken for a man? And take Mr Clunis – he was tall, although not very tall, yet, as he himself always said, he could drink soup on Auntie's head. But Auntie –

'Aye,' Uncle Ulric said, 'What's up?' His voice brought me back to the moment. He came right up, leaving the water. Auntie must have thought of a joke as she watched him, for she burst out laughing – which made Uncle laugh too. He left the sea completely – his feet glistening with water – and he turned up towards us on dry sand.

'Tell me the joke,' he said to Auntie.

'What joke?'

'Well I see you laughing. You laughing at me?'

'At you? Why? Nothing's wrong with you. No, it's Horace

here who just gave me a joke. About his school.'

'About Peters' daughter? I bring a string of jacks for you, girl. And two anchores.'

Auntie said, 'What came over you, Ulric? You not well? Because weeks now I'm here and you never bring fish for me.'

I listened to Auntie and I couldn't help thinking how in this short time her accent had changed. When she came she had a strange, pleasant accent – a little drawl, but nice to listen to. And her grammar was perfect. Now she was falling almost completely into the way we spoke at Mayaro, and she was even getting the sing-song voice which sounded funny whenever I listened to anyone – except myself. At least it was very funny to what Auntie sounded like when she had just come. She still spoke better than everybody else around – except Teacher Myra – and her ways were still nice and charming. And I was sure this part of her would not change. Just that her speech and accent were not as refined as when she had first arrived from Panama. I kept telling myself: 'You know why she changed so much? It's that Mr Clunis.' Of course it was because of Mr Clunis.

Uncle stood up in front of us and he rested the bag on the sand. That had the two achores, I guessed. He gave me a friendly tap on the shoulder, and he said to Auntie, 'Girl, you was talking about time the other day. I spend nearly all my time in the sea. It's sea from morning to night.'

'And where you find time now?'

'Well –' he stopped and thought and tilted his head to the sky, and he said, 'Well, I had to make time. Something I want to tell you and Claris. But keep it, you know. Keep it – you know how.'

He glanced at me so quickly that I hardly saw when he did it. But I saw the response in Auntie's face and I knew. I wondered what was the new secret that brought him here so unexpectedly. The new secret that made him take time off although he was so busy with Mr Stanley's boat. Especially as he was captain – or nearly captain. I remembered how Auntie laughed when he came up, because he looked so funny, and how to pass it off she told him a fib about me giving her a joke about school. And how he had mentioned 'Peters' daughter'. I had promptly forgotten about that but it came to mind again as I wondered what the secret might be. I wondered if it had anything to do with Teacher Myra, but of course I laughed it off. Although she was Myrra

Peters, and was therefore 'Peters' daughter', Uncle could hardly come with any joke about her. 'But – ' I said to myself and my eyes caught Auntie's. She said, 'When you finish.'

'When I finish what, Auntie?'

'Day-dreaming, and talking to yourself.'

Uncle Ulric laughed out. I was embarrassed. I couldn't say anything.

Auntie said pleasantly, 'Well if you finish, let's go.'

Uncle said, 'I hope Claris there.'

'Oh yes,' Auntie said.

We moved off walking, Auntie on the side of the coconut trees, I on the side of the sea, and Uncle Ulric in the middle. I knew Uncle wanted to talk to Auntie without my being close at hand, so I walked down the sand, close to the water's edge. I was looking at the way the sea was quiet this evening and how a few seagulls were resting on the water far out. As I was looking at this, Uncle's voice made me jump. 'You want to go out in the sea with me this Saturday?'

I was so thrilled I could hardly believe my ears. I cried out, 'Oh, yes Uncle. Please.'

'Matter fixed,' he said.

Auntie Roomeen said, 'And what about me?' She had moved down the sand too, and was close to us.

'You?' Uncle looked at her from head to toe. He said, 'Oh God, Roomeen, man, you want to sink the boat?'

There were peals of laughter from both of them, and I laughed too. But I was wondering what was the news Uncle had that put him in that cheery mood. I was on tenterhooks to know.

❋ Nineteen

UNCLE ULRIC and Auntie went into the kitchen with the fish and I sat down on the steps. I heard Uncle talking in a normal voice, and Mother, glad for the fish, saying she'd clean them now, and so on, but suddenly all three of them lowered their voices and instead of lively chatter coming from the kitchen there were whispers and low murmurings. Shortly afterwards, Uncle opened the kitchen door and came out. He said, in his normal voice, 'Girl, I don't know about you, but I can't take this smoke, nah!' Auntie Roomeen came out after him, rubbing her eyes.

The two of them passed beside me on the step and went up into the house. I did not look back at them, but I could see from their manner that the smoke did not have half as much effect as the secret they were sharing. In fact, I took just one glance at Auntie Roomeen as she emerged from the kitchen and I could see her agitation and her surprise and shock. When they got inside they went into a far corner of the sitting-room. I didn't have to look back – I could tell by their voices. Auntie began saying something about sardines, and herrings, and jacks, and about anchore being in season, when, all of a sudden, she asked in a muffled voice: 'You know exactly *where* in Tobago? You have the piece of paper?'

There was silence, then rustling, and soon afterwards Auntie said in a normal tone, 'Ulric, tell me, how come they don't catch anchore all the year round?'

Right away I sat up. Because I was sure a lot was happening. Then in the silence I began feeling uncomfortable, and I said, 'Going on the beach, Auntie.'

'On the beach? Okay dear.'

I slid down from the steps and walked out a little in the direction of the beach, then, looking back and making sure no one was looking, I wheeled round and came out beside the house, by the back. My heart was thumping. I bent down and looked under the house towards the kitchen and I saw that the kitchen door was still closed. I walked along the back, passing under the side windows. I had glanced at the side windows but nobody was at them. I went back, past the side windows, and stooped down, keeping my eyes on the kitchen door. I was almost underneath the house, and from here I could hear them so plainly inside, it was as if the sound was coming through the floor-boards. I heard Uncle say, 'The man came to me, I didn't send to call him, he came down to the boat-house first thing and that's what he said.'

Auntie Roomeen said, 'But I find this so hard to believe. I mean, *how*? Ask yourself how. Only if Mona – I really can't believe that.'

'It damn hard to believe, I know that. But otherwise, what happen? It's a mystery. I tell you the man came down – we didn't touch the boat yet. Sarge came down first thing this morning and tell me that.'

Auntie said, 'But how come he suddenly get so vicious against this Cordner. Because a little glitter – You said he said he saw it? The actual thing?'

'No, he didn't say that. But he saw this glitter and he said it couldn't be anything else. And what made it more suspicious is that Cordner was packing up to go away. You see, they at daggers drawn.'

Auntie said, 'But we have to be sure what is that, though. Look, even a galvanized roof could glitter in the morning. Not everything that's glittering is gold. Listen, we went up in the station when? And he and Cordner fell out the next day, you said, because the sarge saw his move? Anyway, if you say that he and Cordner was so thick because of that girl of his, and Mona –'

Uncle interrupted her but this time I did not make out what he said. Then there was a sudden silence, and after a moment Auntie's voice called: 'Claris, Claris, come and hear this.'

Before Mother could open the door of the kitchen I dashed out from under the house and made for the beach.

After Mother had joined them inside and it was safe enough for me to ease back, I found myself in the same place, and I began – to use Mother's term – to pick sense out of nonsense. The sarge had gone down to the beach to see Uncle, Uncle didn't send to call him. And he had told Uncle that he suspected

Cordner of taking the gold. My heart raced. The sarge had seen a glitter, and he wasn't sure what it was, but he had seen a glitter which burned his eye. And it burned my thoughts, too, now. But then it was so unlikely that Cordner had found the gold that night. He and Cordner had had a quarrel and they were at daggers drawn and maybe Sarge was anxious to pin the theft on him. Or was it a real dagger that was drawn in the quarrel? Because if it was, that could glisten in the morning, too, as well as galvanize. That could fool Sarge. But the question that was circling in my mind was: how did they fall out, and why? They must have fallen out very badly for Cordner to resign straight away – although Aunt Mona had said they had transferred him. It was Aunt Mona who was foremost in my thoughts right now. She was involved in all this and I was trying to understand how. Sarge and Cordner had a quarrel because there had been some promise – I didn't understand this very well. And they had used the word 'breach' which I did not understand very well, and I must ask Teacher Myra about it. But what I did gather was that there was some letter in the dispute and that Aunt Mona was mixed up in all this. Thinking about all these things and trying to pick sense out of nonsense I figured maybe the argument had got so hot that Cordner had pulled the dagger at Sarge and Sarge had dismissed him right away. But also it looked as if something else was the matter and the reason why I didn't get it clearly was because at times all three of them spoke together. Anyhow, by the way Uncle was talking he seemed confident and jubilant. Auntie and Mother seemed puzzled and I could tell, from their voices, that they were far from convinced. In fact, at one time I heard Auntie say, 'All that fire-rage is because Cordner double-crossed that girl. Well Mona is my sister but I ain't have nothing to do with that. That is life.'

Uncle replied, 'Roomeen, you so silly. You can't see it's more than that? This man quitting so suddenly? Okay, you wait. I'll get to the bottom of this.'

I left them arguing and I walked out to the beach again, wondering if Uncle's suspicion was right. At times I thought it was, and at times, like Auntie Roomeen, I saw it as far-fetched. The only thing that kept throbbing in my mind was when, in the conversation, Auntie said to Uncle: 'But how come this sergeant could know all about me? When I'm going back, and all that.

128

How he's so sure I'm going back?'

That was what thrilled my mind, those last words. I did not stop to wonder how the Sergeant came to know all about Auntie, and when she was going back – although that was strange in itself, for I was the only one who had mentioned those things and that was when I was writing my compositions. Anyway, I didn't think about that a great deal because I was so thrilled. Oh how I wished Auntie meant she wasn't going back.

I stayed on the beach for about half-an-hour thinking about the big issue that was developing over the gold chain, and then about what Auntie had said, and then I thought about Sarge again and how he went down to the beach early this morning to tell Uncle about Constable Cordner. And I thought about Constable Cordner who had left the Police Force suddenly and was now home and dry in Tobago. Home and dry? I had meant to say 'High and dry', but my tongue had slipped. I chuckled nervously. Home and dry in Tobago. I wonder if, really . . . I wonder if –

'Horace!' Mother's voice shattered my thoughts. I looked and saw her standing on the steps of the house. Mother was not big, and she did not talk very much, but when she wanted to throw her voice it reached all right – even if, like now, it was against the wind.

'Yes,' I cried.

She made me a sign which meant it was time for tea.

❋ Twenty

AT TEA, Uncle seemed quietly excited, but Auntie Roomeen looked thoughtful, and puzzled, and, on the whole, not at all composed. Mother was calm, as always, and she seemed the only one who was at ease. I could see that none of them wanted to raise the conversation, and Uncle kept glancing at me and at my plate to see how I was getting on. I supposed he wanted me to finish and go. That made me relax and eat even more leisurely. I was sitting opposite him, with Mother on the left, near the window, and as I glanced towards her, through the window there was a glimpse of deep dusk and frothy sea. I suddenly remembered something and leant towards Mother.

'Ma, Uncle want me to go in the sea with him Saturday morning.'

'Go where?'

'In the sea. In the boat with him.'

Uncle looked at her and nodded. He said, 'Yes, yes. Saturday morning he going with me.'

He said it as if it was a matter settled. But it was no matter settled with Mother. She looked at him without saying anything.

Uncle said, 'Nothing to worry about. Horace wouldn't drown, you know. He'd be in the boat with all of us. No danger.' And he gave a quick little laugh.

Mother still did not say anything, and I looked at her pleadingly but she did not take her eyes off Uncle. He spoke now as if surprised at her. 'Look, we ain't making him work, you know. I only taking him out for the joy-ride. He wouldn't have to throw out any net, or row, or bail out water – so don't 'fraid for him. Matter fix?'

It certainly didn't seem a case of 'matter fix', for she turned to see what was Auntie's opinion. To my relief, Auntie made a flick of the hand, as if to say Mother was making a fuss for nothing. But then Auntie turned to Uncle: 'What you mean by saying he wouldn't have to bail out. The boat sinking?'

Uncle laughed so loudly you could have heard him from the beach. Auntie Roomeen laughed, too, but Mother was not at all amused. In fact, it was Auntie Roomeen herself who had to say: 'Claris, don't be silly. You ever hear a boat sink just like that? It's only because Ulric talked about bailing out water I cracked a little joke.'

Uncle laughed again. He said, 'Tell her – she doesn't know. These boats could go as far as Tobago and they wouldn't sink.'

Mother turned to him, and although she was smiling she looked half-serious: 'I hope you ain't planning to go to Tobago on Saturday.'

'Tobago for what? You mean, to see Mona?'

They smiled. Auntie said, 'That's the idea.'

'Well, when you going across don't take my son.'

The mention of Tobago and of Aunt Mona set me thinking of the gold chain again, and it set me thinking of Sarge and his view that Constable Cordner was the thief. It was clear that he had come to hate the Constable and I wondered what was really the matter between them – what had the Constable done to him. Mind you, it was not that I so liked Constable Cordner nor that I had already forgotten how rough he was to us. I just did not feel Sarge should use the gold chain to make a fool of Uncle. And to make us suspect Cordner just because he, Sarge, didn't like the man. Glancing at Mother I saw that she looked completely at ease now, and I was happy that I could go on Saturday. But I was still not completely sure. Although we lived beside the sea Mother never liked that big, restless, blue Atlantic Ocean. She never trusted it, and whenever I went for a swim she always said, 'Don't go far out, eh. Remember the sea ain't have branches.' I liked that phrase so much I even put it in a composition.

Auntie's voice made me jump. She said, 'Ulric, it's this Saturday Horace going with you?'

'Aha.'

'And Saturday I have to be in Port-of-Spain.'

I turned to her, surprised. Uncle said, 'What for?' Mother got up at that moment and started to take away the cups and the dishes. As I looked towards her I noticed that dusk had fallen heavily now and in fact she came directly back and lit the lamp. Funny how it was always lighter over the sea. Looking out through the window was one thing, but it was only now, watching Mother go down the front steps, that I noticed the coconut trees were gathering the night. I turned back to the room now, and pretended I was looking at the big *Home Sweet Home* reflected on the wall, but my ears were itching to hear why Auntie had to go to Port-of-Spain. And why couldn't I go with her on Saturday? I was thinking. Why couldn't I go in the sea some other time?

Auntie was hesitating to answer Uncle Ulric and he said again, 'What for, Roomeen – if I'm not asking you your private business?'

Auntie laughed heartily, and she called to Mother, 'Claris, come. Come and hear this.' Mother came in from the kitchen and stood on the steps. Auntie said, 'He asking why I'm going to Port-of-Spain. And he asking me if it's me own private business.'

Mother smiled. She said, 'Well, I don't know – it's for you to say. You alone know.' And seeing Mother laugh, Auntie threw her head back and laughed heartily.

I was very curious now. Looking at Mother's face I knew that Auntie alone did not know. When Mother was an accomplice I knew it.

Auntie turned to Uncle, the brightness of the lamplight on her face. She said, 'Yes, I have to go to Port-of-Spain to see about me own little business. How you know? You hit the nail on the head, boy.'

'How?'

'You remember what I told you on the beach?'

'No. When?'

'This evening – when you were bringing the fish.'

'You mean now there? While ago when I met you and Horace on the beach?'

She chuckled. 'Well not *now*. Now is night.'

And she was right, too. Although it didn't seem a long while ago since we had watched Uncle walking towards us with the bag and the string of jacks and his feet playing in the water, the sun had still been bright then. Now it was thick dusk outside. These things only flashed through my mind and I dismissed them quickly because I wanted to hear what Auntie was saying.

It was Uncle who spoke: 'Roomeen don't confuse me. What you say you told me?'

'I just said I wanted to see you.'

'Oh yes. And what you wanted to see me about?'

Auntie called: 'Claris, come. Come for one minute.'

Uncle looked puzzled and I was puzzled too. I wondered what was all this mystery about. Mother came hurrying up the steps and she too had a puzzled look on her face, but this look was so pronounced I knew it wasn't genuine. She held her two hands away from her dress as her fingers were covered with soap lather.

She said, 'You call me, Roomeen?'

'Tell Ulric what I'm going to town for. Tell him what's coming up.'

Mother made up her face as though she was taken aback but she seemed ready enough to burst out laughing. She cried, 'Me? I must tell him? That concern you and it's your business. You tell him.'

'Well, I mean – ' Auntie was looking at her.

'Well, tell him,' Mother said. 'He'll be glad to know. Girl, I washing up dishes and you call me in here for nonsense? Tell him. Sure Horace will be glad to know too.'

By this time my heart was thumping and when Mother called my name my heart made a heave inside and I wondered what in the name of heaven was really happening. Then Auntie said right off: 'I'm going to marry Clunis. Going to town Saturday to buy up me wedding things.'

I hardly heard her last words. My head seemed to reel and my mind seemed to go blank. For an instant I thought I might have been dreaming, so I pinched myself and I felt pain. I wasn't dreaming. My heart was thumping so violently it seemed to be shaking me on the chair. I turned around to see Mother's face but Mother was gone. I looked at my Uncle. He didn't look particularly shocked. When Auntie had spoken, he had just said, 'You serious?' And now he listened calmly as she prattled to him about what a kind man Mr Clunis was, and what a lonely man, and how she was sorry for him, and how she had grown to appreciate him, and how she felt she could make a life with him. And at this point she asked Uncle how he felt – if he thought she was taking the right step.

'It's for you to know,' Uncle said. He looked amused. He said, 'You make up your mind already and now you asking me for advice?'

'No. I only ask you how you feel about it?'

'Well, what is the position with Braff – you two divorced?'

'No, but he ain't coming back.'

'How you so sure?'

'Because – because,' and she looked at him and whispered something quickly with her lips.

He said, 'Oh, somebody else.'

I wanted to go outside but at this point I felt it more embarrassing to get up and leave, than to stay. Uncle said, 'But tell me something, you talking about you so sorry about Clunis and you appreciate him, but I would say you should like him too.'

She smiled.

'You have to have that here,' Uncle said, and pointed to his heart.

'Boy, that there from school-days. And you know that too.'

Uncle chuckled and grunted: 'And I know he have it too.' Then he said, 'So all this going back to Panama – that's squashed? Where will you and he be staying – here in this place?'

'Right here in Mayaro. In St Joseph. That's life boy. Funny eh?'

'Damn funny,' he said, 'Because everything started right here.'

Despite the storm of desolation that had broken over me, I was thrilled to hear Auntie say she was remaining here, in Mayaro. They went on talking but I wasn't listening, but I just wanted to get up and go outside so that they could feel free to talk. I looked at Uncle and he glanced at me, chuckling to himself all the while, and he said to Auntie, 'You see when you like someone from childhood? It's like hell, you know. So Horace better watch out.'

Auntie giggled, and embarrassed, I looked at her for an explanation.

She said, 'Take heed! Sure he has his little girl-friend already.' They laughed, and when I laughed they laughed even more.

'When you getting married, Auntie?' I said, to pass it off.

'Not sure yet. Could be next month.'

'Don't leave it too long,' Uncle said, and they looked at each other as if this was a special joke. I didn't know what they were talking about.

I let them go on talking and I sat there thinking about how all this had developed right around me and I had no idea about it until now. Perhaps that was what Mr Clunis had been asking Auntie to decide on? They had dealt with things very quietly, and it was clear they were aided and abetted by Mother. But of course this new turn of things should be no surprise to me, for didn't I meet them talking together, twice, Auntie sitting on the stump of a coconut tree? I thought of Mr Clunis. Although I did not like him at all – not at all – the fact was that through him Auntie would be here for all times. A thrill of joy ran through me and I turned and looked at her face. She smiled. She was paying attention to Uncle, who was talking as though he, too, was thrilled that she wasn't going back.

He said now: 'To tell you the honest truth, girl, I never liked this Panama too much. All my mind was on that bush and those big mosquitoes, and the Panama Canal that we always hearing about. I never liked this Panama business, and it was even worse when Claris talked about what happen to you and Braff. At least you in Trinidad now – you in Mayaro – and if the worse come to the worse, you have us here. And the fact is, Clunis is not a bad feller.' He smiled, and his teeth glittered like – well like gold. That was the right word, although I did not want to think it. That was the right word because his teeth were yellow. If they were white I would have said: 'His teeth glittered like ivory.' I saw his smiling mouth and I could not bear to look inside it, so I looked at the reflection of the lamp-shade on the wall: *Home Sweet Home*. Yes, it was home sweet home for Auntie. It was almost as if she was saying it loud and clear: *Home Sweet Home*. I turned to her. She said, 'Horace, I know you're upset as I didn't tell you all the time. But I meant to – okay?' She was looking at me softly and her eyes were pleading. Uncle was looking towards me, too.

I said, 'Yes, Auntie, it's okay.' I was so touched, I was almost overcome.

❋ Twenty-One

THAT SATURDAY MORNING bright and early I was down Plaisance Road at Uncle's place, and it wasn't long before Uncle took his strong coffee and we two were walking down the beach towards Mr Stanley's boat-house. It was not completely clear yet, and although you could see the dawn breaking, you could still see stars in the sky. It was the time of day we called 'fore-day morning', and this was the first 'fore-day morning' I had seen at Plaisance. My heart was pounding because I was going out in the sea.

Uncle said, 'The breeze blowing cool and nice, eh – Oh gosh!' Although he was not a tall man – not much taller than I was – in the faint light I could not see his face very plainly. As we walked down the Plaisance Road, straight towards the sea, the wind was whipping strongly, in gusts, and it felt a little chilly, although Uncle said it was cool. He said to me, 'Boy, I still thinking about you. I tell you to be here early but you know I didn't expect to see you here this hour!'

'How, Uncle? Why?'

He shook his head and chuckled. He said, 'You is a brave man to walk down that road from St Joseph in darkness.'

I looked up at him puzzled. It was amazing how fast the day was breaking; I was seeing him a little plainer now. I didn't say anything and he said, 'What time you leave home?'

Now it must have been about half-past five. I said, 'About five.'

He laughed to himself. He said, 'And you walked through that coconut, and all down the road here to Plaisance by yourself? You meet anybody?'

'No.'

'You wasn't 'fraid?'

' 'Fraid what, Uncle?'

'Boy, you is a man,' he said. 'Brave. You know, people always talking all kind of talk about soucouyant, and la jablesse, and spirit – you know; ghosts, dead people. I meself never meet up nothing yet. But it have evil.'

I was surprised about Uncle. I never believed that he had given any thought to this sort of thing. At school we called it folklore, although a few of the pupils said they had seen spirits. Most of them were afraid of the dark, too. The girls, especially, were afraid of the dark.

I didn't know what to say to Uncle so I just said, 'I didn't think about that.'

He said, 'Brave boy. They say Mayaro have a lot of soucouyant. I meself never see none.'

We reached the path under the palms near the sea. I was surprised to see that the day was almost completely cleared up now – in that short while. The coconut trees were no longer like shadows, but bright and distinct. There was a burst of cock-crow. We passed the little box-like house on which was scribbled the words: 'Harold Gill – Tailor', and after a few parlours and shops, we turned right, along the little sand path, then walked out towards the beach to Mr Stanley's boat-shed. When we got there Mr Stanley and all the men were at the shed. They were putting the oars into the boat and they were ready to start pushing the boat to the water's edge.

They were pleased when they saw Uncle. Mr Stanley said, 'Oh, you bring the boy.'

'Aha.'

The men looked at me, grinning, and one said, 'That's Claris' boy?'

Uncle said, 'Yes, that's Claris' boy.' And he murmured, but not for me to hear: 'Brave too bad.'

I pretended I didn't hear. The men were very friendly, but you could see they wanted to get on with the seining. A few of them raised a chant, and they all held on to the boat. Uncle held on to the boat, too, but he did not want me to help. At certain moments during the chant, someone said 'heave!' and they used all their strength to move the boat, but they did not move it very far at a time. But in this lively way they managed to be getting the boat down the beach. I kept beside them. At one point during their little rest Uncle looked at me and mentioned the word 'brave'. I began to feel that I had done something.

By the time we got to sea and were beyond the breakers it was clear daylight, and in the distance the sun was peeping over the horizon. At the back of the boat the net was piled up in a great black heap. Standing just in front of the heap was Uncle and sitting down in front of Uncle was me.

I was still thinking of how we had got here. After we had pushed the boat to the water's edge, and then to deep enough water to float it, we had jumped inside and the men had rowed frantically to get out of the big waves of the breakers. The breakers had tried to push the boat back, and the boat had begun riding high, and dipping, the bow plunging into the hollows and being pushed back up by the swells and curling breakers. And then the back of the boat – which Uncle was calling the stern – began rising up violently and then dropping down again, as if the whole boat was going to sink to the bottom of the sea. Uncle kept telling me, 'It's all right. Don't be afraid, it's all right. Nothing wouldn't happen.' I was holding on tightly to my seat and my heart was pounding. But I had to pretend that I was not afraid because on the beach Uncle had kept on saying how brave I was.

Sitting right in front of me and facing me was one called Taso. Like the rest, he was rowing with his back to the bow, and as the boat dipped and rose, with the sea-spray falling on us in showers, he grinned at me. He had two big teeth in front, and several missing, and he looked what Teacher Myra would have called: 'a curious picture'. Now as we cleared the breakers he relaxed on his oars and he said to me, 'You was 'fraid, eh? You still 'fraid?'

'I wasn't 'fraid.'

The other men looked at me admiringly, and at the back of me I heard Uncle say, 'Talking 'bout brave!' As a whole the rowers were taking it easy now, because here the sea was calm and they did not have to pull too much. Thinking of this my mind went to Teacher Myra right away and I smiled inside me, because she always said, 'Class, rally on. Don't rest on your oars!' That was exactly what the men were doing now – resting on their oars. And didn't they deserve the rest! As I watched the blue sheet of sea around me, I was thinking of telling Teacher Myra about this great experience. Not relating it to her, but in the way I loved best – through a composition. My eyes must have lit up, for Taso looked at me and laughed. He said, 'You enjoying it?'

'Yes, Mr Taso. A lot.'

The men laughed, and Uncle, behind me, said: 'This boy always like anything like this. Adventure and things like that.'

Taso said, 'He could swim?'

Uncle said, 'Yes, man. I sure. Horace, you could swim?'

'No, Uncle.'

'No?' I could see he felt let down.

Taso said, 'You can't swim and you in boat – and you saying you ain't 'fraid?' The other men laughed and looked at me in amazement.

Uncle said, 'I thought he could swim. Ha, Lord! Boy, you better pray she ain't go under.' The men laughed noisily.

I did not even think of the boat going under, and I myself did not want this sort of adventure now. I thought: these big muscular men came here to fish, no to go under. And then I said to myself: but they could swim, they wouldn't go down. It's you who would go down. They were all looking at me and being quietly amused about me. And they were amazed, too, because I didn't look as if I was worrying. I wasn't, really, at this time. These fishermen were all wearing torn-up, patched-up trousers, and although I wasn't afraid, if the depth below me were not part of my mind I would have been very much amused about that. Because they looked funny. They were bare-backed, too, and the wonderful thing about them was their big muscular chests and arms, and as I watched the black bodies, beautiful-looking and glistening in the sun, I wondered if I would develop such muscles if I grew up to pull oars too. Not that I so wanted to be a fisherman.

After we had gone a little way into the ocean, Uncle began giving orders and they all became businesslike.

As Uncle was standing behind me I couldn't see him but from the way he was muttering he seemed to be looking for fish all the time. The rest of the boatmen seemed obsessed about fish, too, for they were rowing and looking all around. I was feeling so excited that I was not thinking of fish at all. It was unbelievable, the vast Atlantic just below me, beside me, and all around me, and stretching away like a vast, wavy floor of blue. To the east, the sun had lifted off the horizon – it was big and round and silvery, and if I watched its dazzle and took my eyes off, then everything else was dark. The sky around the sun was silvery-blue, and the horizon itself was what Teacher Myra would have called 'breath-taking'. But it was when I looked to the other side and saw the coast that I gasped with wonder and surprise.

It did not seem to be the same place we had come from, but we could not have come from anywhere else. The coast seemed very far away and I was seeing, for the first time in my life, the entire stretch of beach that was the Mayaro shore. Far away to the left was the hazy Guayaguayare Point, and the beach swept from it in a semi-circle, and came right around until it ended, far away to the right, in my own Point Radix. My heart raced with excitement. Although we had turned and were now rowing southward, Plaisance seemed straight ahead of us. The coconut palms along the shore looked cloudy and feathery, and the wide beach we had left now seemed just a white curving line. Towards the shore there was just the stretch of wavy blue sea, and where the turbulent breakers crashed, I could see only white foam.

Uncle's voice made me jump. He must have been watching me look, for now he said, 'Nice, eh?'

I grinned. Taso and some of the other men grinned too.

'You like it?'

'Uncle, this is so great. So – so . . . ' I didn't know what to say.

He said proudly, 'And we see this every day. And we don't think nothing about it.'

Taso said, 'But this same sea. It could get terrible. For instance, if we see it making up for a storm, we have to run, yes.'

One of the rowers near the bow said, 'Taso, don't frighten the boy. It nice now. If it nice it nice.'

I was going to ask Uncle something when all of a sudden he cried, 'Throw!' and two or three of the men, including Uncle himself, began to throw out the seine into the water. I, too, turned around and started to help. As I started to throw out the net one of the men beside me took up part of the net with an end of rope and held it, and I saw Uncle nod at him approvingly, and said, 'Right, because you know what would happen!' The man, who was standing beside the heap of net just laughed. I did not know what he was laughing at, but I smiled. I had taken off my shirt and put it under one of the seats of the boat and I thought he might have been laughing at that. Or perhaps he was laughing because I had no muscles.

The others did not pay much attention to me now. A

businesslike attitude seemed to have taken over. On Uncle's direction they had turned the boat in a semi-circle – I could not tell our movement unless I watched the shore. And they seemed to change again and now they were going directly towards the shore. By the time they reached the breakers they had cast out the great part of the net, and now they brought the boat almost to a standstill next to the turbulent waves. The man who had taken up the end of the rope still had it in his hand and now he went and stood up on the edge of the stern, and the boat turned around, and to my astonishment the man plunged into the sea. When he rose again he was quite a little distance from the boat, and then he was lashing his way through the breakers and before long he was with a group of men on the beach.

I watched in awe, hardly realising Uncle was looking at my face. Then Uncle said, 'You say you like to write story. This is life – this ain't story. Write about that!'

My heart was racing. The boat left the breakers and went again into the blue and then made a huge semi-circle and headed for the shore. I watched this, not understanding what was going on. The black bodies were glistening and as they leaned back and pulled on the oars I felt I had never seen anything so graceful, and so much in – what was the word Teacher Myra liked to say? *Unison*. I had never seen things so much in unison. The wind was blowing gustily about us, and in flapping and fluttering about the boat, it seemed to be reminding me of what Uncle said, 'This is life . . . Write about that.' My heart was still racing. In fact it raced a little more when he said that because I was wondering how he knew I liked writing. That was odd, for I had never told him. I looked at him now. I couldn't ask him anything for he was busy talking to the men and looking as if into the water at what he said was a school of fish. I saw nothing. The boat raced towards the breakers – the men pulling hard on their oars – and then we were amidst the breakers, with the waves crashing against the boat, and with the boat heaving and riding high and plunging, and with spray raining down on us. I couldn't help being terror-stricken and holding on with both hands. One of the men was bailing out water with a bucket, and seeing me holding on, he said, 'You 'fraid and we reach the beach already? Look the beach right there.' And he laughed.

Looking round I saw the boat was rushing in to the beach – the same wide beach, lined with coconut palms that were right there in front of me, and were not hazy. Before the boat touched the bottom almost all the men jumped out, leaving me alone with Taso. Uncle himself was waist-deep in the water with the other end of the rope in his hand. I watched him. Taso worked the boat backwards towards the beach, until the boat stuck in shallow water. Uncle and the other boatmen were already on the beach pulling their end of the seine.

Taso said to me: 'You could jump out now or you still 'fraid? It ain't deep. Only your pants will get wet.'

I went to the edge of the stern ready to jump out. 'I ain't fraid,' I said. My eyes caught Uncle's line of men, near to us on the beach, and there was another line, a little way down, where the fellow had swum ashore with the end of rope. They were all leaning against the rope and pulling. They were now pulling in the net after capturing the school of fish in it. I understood. The word 'school' made me think of Teacher Myra, and right away a picture like the one before me came to mind. For she had drawn such a picture on the blackboard once, and had written below it: 'Toilers of the Sea.' How beautiful, I thought. How great! Then I was roused by the voice behind me, 'Jump!' Taso cried. I was so taken aback that I lost my balance, and the next moment I made a big splash down in the water, and I was on my bottom, with my trousers all wet. I heard Taso roaring with laughter. I couldn't help laughing too.

❋ Twenty-Two

AFTER THE TWO lines of seine-pullers had almost met – which meant the net had almost closed in – and after we saw the beating, captive fish beyond the breakers, Uncle nudged me and said, 'You tired pulling? You want to go up by the boat-house?'

'No, it's all right, Uncle.'

'Look who's up there.'

I turned and looked and to my astonishment the sergeant with the curling moustache was up there. He was leaning against the boat-house and talking to Mr Stanley. Uncle whispered to me, his face glistening with sweat, 'It's me he want to see, you know. All of a sudden he nice to me.'

'Why?'

'Why? Take it cool, I'll tell you why. You'll see why.'

I was a little frightened on Uncle's account. Right away I thought of the gold chain. I wondered if the sergeant had positive information that Uncle had taken it and was now trying to trap him. I was sorry the matter had reached the police because I felt at this stage that if it was Uncle who had stolen it he would give it up some time.'

I said, 'Uncle, you *have* to go up to see him?' It was a useless question. There wasn't any way Uncle could avoid him, unless he stayed in the sea! In any case, Sarge knew where Uncle lived.

Uncle did not seem very worried. He said, 'What you mean? After we bring the seine right in I'll go up and talk to him.' And he chuckled and said, 'Perhaps he only want a few anchore.'

I was surprised and relieved. I looked at Uncle's face. We had both taken a little respite from pulling, as the end of the seine was near. Beads of sweat were running down Uncle's temples right down his cheeks and dropping down his chin. The same thing was happening to me, too. Uncle said, 'All that old talk he giving me these days! But he on a good trail.'

I was puzzled. The seine was now right in shallow waters and

Uncle was beginning to pay full attention to it, and he stopped talking to me. Crowds of people appeared on the beach as if from nowhere, and corbeaux, too, were swooping down on to the beach from the coconut trees. We pulled in the net on to dry beach. As we pulled, with the net alive and throbbing with fish, all the rope and net we had pulled in were piled up behind us, and the remainder was lighter now because it was almost out of the water, but still it was heavy with the beating, frantic fish. We pulled this right up on the beach, with carite, cavali, and anchore, baychine, cocoro, and moonshine, and all sorts of fish leaping about the sand and with the fishermen suddenly fierce and surrounding the net, and grunting, and driving the crowds back. Mr Stanley came down from the boat-house, and as he took charge of the catch, Uncle came and tugged at my sleeve and he said, 'Let's go up to see Sarge.' We walked up to the police sergeant.

Sergeant Peters had a big smile on his face as Uncle and I reached him. He said, 'This is your nephew? The bright boy?'

Uncle said, 'Yes.' I was flabbergasted that the sergeant should say that. Maybe Uncle had been boasting.

Sergeant Peters said to Uncle, 'You thought of the thing I told you?'

'Yes, Sarge, but we so sure about it? I don't want to go there and let him make me a damn fool.'

The sergeant looked irritated. 'He'll make you a damn fool if you want him to. Throw the facts at him. You could handle things – I don't have to tell you what to do. I just give you a tip. But with what we already talked, you could throw the net over him. Let the man know that you sift things already and you could see through him. Take the boy with you – he's a bright boy. You bound to find out.'

'But you see, Sarge, you saying throw the facts at him but we ain't have facts. We ain't have real hard facts, and if the man want to hide behind – '

'Hide behind what! He could run but he can't hide. I know what you calling facts – eye-witness. Okay, but what's in the darkness must come to light. And you know how it will come? Remember this, you know how it will come?' And he smiled. 'Circumstantial evidence,' he said, as if playing a trump card.

'Circumstantial evidence can't fix him.'

'What! Ho, ho! Haw, haw, haw! When you find out those details about where he was on such and such a day, and what he did. And who he talked to, and who he was with. When you find out, just throw him over to me. I'll nail him to the cross.'

I was completely bewildered. I looked at Uncle, but although he saw me looking at him he was so worked up by the sergeant that he didn't say anything to me at all. In fact, in spite of what he had said, this was not old talk to him at all. He had only made me feel that way. I wondered now what trail Uncle and this sergeant were on.

While I was thinking about it the sergeant said something which escaped me, and Uncle said, 'Look, Sarge, I'm a busy man. I mean, you see what sort of life I lead. Look down there – you see?' The people had crowded round the fish like vultures, and the real vultures were waiting a little way off. Mr Stanley was selling both wholesale and retail. From the way the crowd was now, I could see that the heap of fish had dwindled right down. The men were gathering the seine and ropes in the boat again, perhaps to go out a second time. I was watching this and at the same time I heard Uncle saying to him, 'You see? This is the sort of life I have. It's all the time; all, all the time. Every day. So I don't want to go over there and spend two, three days for nothing. And I might even end up by – ' Uncle stopped.

'I know what you was going to say,' the sergeant said.

'How you mean?'

'You going to say you might end up by breaking up your sister's life.'

Uncle did not reply.

'I know all about that. I know blood thicker than water.' Then the sergeant looked all around him and even back into the boat-house. Then he said, 'I know blood thicker than water. But if he could do that he's a criminal. You have to save your sister from that scamp.'

'But suppose she – ?'

'Suppose she in it? That's what you was going to say?'

Uncle just looked at him.

'Ulric, don't make yourself scared to talk. We is we.'

Uncle said, 'Suppose she's mixed up in it, and suppose all this come out in the court-house, what you expect will happen – she wouldn't take a jail?'

'Jail? Who say that! Oh, that's what you frighten for? Well look, I'll tell you this – I name Peters. As long as I here she can't take no jail.'

He said this in a big, forceful way, and beat his chest. Uncle just stood there quietly, and I stood beside Uncle. To them it was as if I wasn't there.

Sergeant Peters said, 'Mona ain't have no business with any jail. It's this criminal who is a damn thief.' The sergeant looked very worked up and he was about to speak again when Uncle said, 'Sarge, one thing. If we decide on anything the boy have to know. I mean it's he and me who will – '

The sergeant interrupted with a belch, and then he looked up at the sky, then twirled his moustache, and after this he said, chuckling, 'You mean the boy don't know? And all that ruction pass?' He looked round at me and I turned and stared towards the few dead fish and the corbeaux. I thought he had completely forgotten that I was there.

When the sergeant had chuckled and said, 'You mean the boy don't know? And all that ruction pass?' Uncle had put his hand under his chin, as if he didn't want to talk. Then he said, 'Well, he know. He know what happen. But he don't know the – the latest.'

But I guessed what the latest was. I was thrilled because Uncle wasn't in it – it seemed – and because we might get the gold chain back. From the time they had mentioned Aunt Mona and jail and the scamp, I knew what it was right away. At least I knew what trail they were on. I felt happy and hoped what they were saying was right, and that we could nail somebody to the cross.

Sergeant Peters had continued talking with Uncle and now he looked at me again. 'Sonny boy, you mean you don't know the latest?'

I had not been expecting the question. I blurted out, 'With the gold chain?'

Sergeant Peters laughed out. Then he turned to Uncle. 'This boy have more brains than you,' he said. 'You see that forehead, you see those bright, bright eyes – you bet he have more brains than me and you put together.' Then he laughed again and held his waist, his fingers astride his thick, broad, police belt. Then he turned to me and said, 'Yes, about the gold chain. We have our suspicion. Of course you know who it is.'

It could have been none other than Constable Cordner and that was what I said.

Uncle's face twisted with astonishment but the Sergeant did not look surprised. All he said was, 'I know this boy is a cinch.' And he told me, 'Yes. We have circumstantial evidence.'

Uncle said, 'But this Horace bright like a new penny!'

The sergeant said, 'In school too.' And just as I was wondering how could he know that, we heard a shout, and he turned to where the seine was. Only that there was nothing there now but a few people with fish and black net on the sand. There were lots of people walking away from the beach. Uncle told Sarge: 'It's me – ' Sarge looked puzzled. He said, 'Is me Stanley calling?'

Uncle said, 'No, it look like me.'

Mr Stanley was standing there beckoning to Uncle. I was sure it was to Uncle, because what would he be calling the sergeant down there for? Uncle pointed his finger to his chest to ask if Mr Stanley meant him, and the way Mr Stanley beckoned violently, I could almost hear him cry, 'Come nah, man!' Uncle walked down to the seine and I was left alone with the sergeant. The sergeant let a few moments pass and then he said calmly, 'Look at you. Bright young feller. Your teacher like you, your mother working so hard to mind you. And that – that vagabond trying to take bread from your mouth.'

I said nothing.

He said, 'You know how much that chain worth? Thousands.'

My heart leapt. 'Sarge, you saw it?'

The curling moustache flickered as the sergeant opened his mouth to speak, then he seemed to hold back, considering. He lifted his eyes over my head, looking as if over the horizon, and as I looked at his great round face, for a moment I thought I recognised . . . but it could not be. It could not possibly be . . . As my thoughts flitted back to the class-room the sergeant rested a hand on my shoulder and asked earnestly, 'He didn't tell you about it? Ulric?'

'You mean the latest? No Sarge.'

'You sure? It so funny. I talked to this who-cut-you-head only yesterday morning. How come he didn't tell you?'

He looked a bit irritated. But I was sure Uncle did not say anything. Or was I? Uncle did not say anything to *me* but I remembered now he had talked quite a bit to Mother and to

Auntie Roomeen, and I also remembered he had told them something about the sergeant meeting him on the beach. But it was true that I myself did not know anything about it. Before I mentioned that Uncle might have told Mother and Auntie, I said, 'Sarge, you saw the chain?'

Without answering me directly, he said, 'That chain Roomeen brought came from Panama.' He was not asking me this but was talking with the air of someone giving valuable information. But what he said was so obvious that I just kept looking at the sea.

The sergeant continued, 'She brought this chain for the use of Claris. And for you.' He nudged me. 'She arrived here on the twenty-first and on the twenty-second Roomeen and Mona and Ulric missed the chain. But it was on the night of the twenty-third that Cordner went to search. Don't think that funny,' he looked at me and chuckled. 'The chain was missing long before that. Anyway, forget that. We know that Cordner responsible for the missing gold chain. We sure about that.'

At once I saw that there was something odd, but without stopping to work it out I seized on his last words and I said, 'You saw it, Sarge?'

'You mean the gold chain? That scamp was . . . Wait – Ulric didn't say what happen?'

'He was talking to Mother and Auntie. Think he told them.'

Sarge looked relieved. He said, 'Oh, so they know the position.' I was sorry I had told him that because I, too, wanted to know the position. He seemed agitated and happy. He put his weight on one foot, then on the other. I saw him turn his head to where Uncle and the fishermen were pulling up the nets. Corbeaux were about the beach, pecking at dead fish. There were a few dead sharks and cutlass-fish and sapatey about – fish the people did not want. But the corbeaux wanted those, though, and were pecking away. The fishermen were busily pulling the net back towards the boat, and they were looking towards them. Although the men were not pulling the seine now, the words came to my head: 'Toilers of the Sea.' Uncle was talking to Mr Stanley and they moved further up the beach now, for the tide was coming up. At last they started walking up the beach towards us.

The sergeant said to me, 'I could make that arrest. Sure as day I could make that arrest. But Ulric too damn slow.'

I looked up at Sergeant Peters. He said to me, 'Ha, boy, you don't know. The amount of things that vagabond say he'll buy for Mona!' His eyes were open wide, and his arms were outstretched as if to show the number of things. His face looked pained. 'The amount of nice things he said he'd give her when they go to Tobago. But Cordner never had money – I know. I should know. I always lending him a little shilling, two-shillings.' He grunted bitterly. 'This man never never had money. They was out in the gallery and I was inside the Charge Room. They didn't see me because I was bending looking for something under the counter. And I was killing meself laughing because I say hear this son of a who-cut-you-head two-timer. I say hear this nincompoop worthless good-for-nothing, making joke. But when I hear the word "gold", and then "pawn". I remain quiet, quiet, like a little mouse. I find what I looking for but I still keep bending down. Waiting to hear a little more. Then I hear only quietness. You know when I raise me head they already gone down the hill?'

My heart was thumping wildly. I said nothing but just watched Uncle and Mr Stanley walking slowly towards us and wishing they could walk a little slower. But they were near up now.

Sarge seemed very worked up and annoyed. Under his breath he blurted out, 'Gold. Pawn. But how I could arrest a man on two words?'

Just after this Mr Stanley walked up and Mr Stanley took the sergeant's right hand in both his own and shook it saying, 'Long time no see.'

Sarge said, 'Long time no see and you in the sea every day?' The two of them laughed, but I didn't, because that was what we called a stale joke at school. Uncle did not laugh either, and in fact he looked as though he did not understand. Maybe it was true that I had more brains that the two of them – Uncle and Sarge. Maybe the three of them, if you counted Mr Stanley, too. The sergeant began to tell Mr Stanley something about Rio Claro, but I could see that after a few moments Mr Stanley was not interested – perhaps because Rio Claro had no sea! I smiled. Mr Stanley then asked, 'What about the girl?'

'Still there teaching,' the sergeant said.

'That's a nice girl,' Mr Stanley said. 'Refined. And she getting to look more and more like you.'

Sarge said, 'Yes, but the vag – ' And he stopped. Mr Stanley said, 'The last time I used to see her – when I used to be in Rio Claro regular – she was a little girl. Now I could see her in your face.' He said this wistfully, not paying attention to Sarge.

I wanted to hear what Sarge was going to say. He looked at Mr Stanley now and he just smiled. But you could see he was upset about something. I realised too that Mr Stanley had known him in Rio Claro. That was why they were so cordial. Because Sarge was still new on the Mayaro scene.

Uncle had left us for a moment, and I watched him pointing to the boatmen and talking, and directing, and they were still pulling up the net, most of it covered with sea-weed and with dry sand. The sea was reaching half-way up the beach. When Uncle came back, Mr Stanley said, 'Give the sarge a few anchore.'

'Okay.'

Once more Mr Stanley took the sergeant's big hand in both his own, and then he left him and he went down the beach to the boat. As he walked down I marvelled at how high the tide had already come up. When Uncle and I had arrived here this morning there was such a broad beach. In the grey half-light the boatmen had to push the boat a long way to the sea. Now, from where we were standing at the boat-house the water's edge was just there. Just about three boat-lengths away. In fact, the boat itself was brought up not too far from us. Watching Uncle now I noticed there was a heap of fish in the boat. He took up three big anchores and came back to the sergeant. As he walked back the sergeant laughed and nudged me.

He said, 'You know why I'm laughing? Bet you don't know. Well, everytime I come here they think I come for anchore.'

I smiled and tried to look surprised.

When Uncle reached, the sergeant took the fish and said, 'Like you bribing me, boy. You don't have to bribe me because I ain't have nothing against you.' He was chuckling. 'I ain't have nothing against you – just your brother-in-law.'

'He ain't me brother-in-law yet. And that depend on you, Sarge.'

'You getting smart!'

'You like these fish?'

'But it have bigger fish in the sea!' The sergeant's eyes were opened widely.

'You talking in parables.'

'For you to unfold,' the sergeant said, and laughed loudly. Then he said, 'To be serious, let me take home these three fish now, eh. While they fresh. And clean them nice.'

Uncle said, 'Clean? You? What you talking about clean, Sarge? Ain't you have a big daughter in your house?'

The moustache twitched again, as if the sergeant was going to speak. Then he stopped. Then he said, 'She ain't proud, you know. She ain't proud – this boy could tell you.' My heart gave me voom, voom, voodoom voom. I looked up in his face. But although I was sure, there was just a ray of doubt. Because only the faces were similar, but –

I stopped my train of thought as the sergeant went on speaking. He said, 'That's one thing I could say. She have a clean job but she ain't proud. I ain't saying she proud.' And he took a deep breath and he said, 'But she hate to clean fish.' Uncle laughed at that.

Sarge said, 'But *I* like to clean fish, so what? And when I was in Rio Claro who used to clean fish for me – the mother ain't there and she down here. Boy I going home because I off now.'

'Well, wait for me, Sarge, because I'm off too. Saturdays we only go out once.' Then he dropped his voice, 'Sarge I want to talk to you.'

'You mean about that Tobago thing? That's what I come here for, man. To see you.'

'You think he really have that chain?'

'I ain't think – I sure. Sure, sure. Sure as day.'

❊ Twenty-Three

ON THE MONDAY MORNING when I went to school Teacher Myra seemed so excited to see me. The subject was geography and she always said I was good in that and I felt that this was why she was so friendly – even nervous – about me. In the class before this we had used the manual *Homes Far Away*, and now in this class we were using *People Far Away*, but to tell the truth Teacher Myra never liked these books. She always said, 'Far away from where?' She said this as a joke, just to make us laugh, but I knew that what Teacher Myra meant was that we lived here and should learn about here first. In fact she always pointed to one of the mottos on the ledges inside the school. It said, 'Charity Begins At Home.' She said she believed in that.

Now Teacher Myra just wrote 'Geography', on the blackboard, and she shifted the board from in front of the class so that we could see the map of Trinidad and Tobago on the wall. I wasn't sitting at any special desk now but was back in my old seat. Teacher Myra said to us: 'Look at the map carefully and look at the relative positions of Trinidad and of Tobago.' Then she cried, 'Sarah, you know the term "relative position", I don't mean to ask if you have any relatives in Tobago!' The whole class roared with laughter.

Teacher Myra was like that. She always called such jokes 'corny', but when she was in a good mood she made them herself. Not that it was so corny in Sarah's case. Sarah's parents came from Tobago and everyone knew she had a lot of relatives in Tobago. But Teacher Myra called all jokes like that, 'corny'. Like the one the sergeant made last Saturday, when he said 'Long time no see'. Oh, yes, the sergeant – I thought. I wanted to ask – . But no. But . . . As I was thinking of it, the laughter died away, and she was talking again, between chuckles:

'First, look at the position of Tobago in relation – in relation to Trinidad. The distance between – is it far?' She wasn't chuckling now, but earnest. 'If so, how far?' She was looking around for somebody to point to, but Frank Fridal put up his hand, and when she turned to him he said it was near. The class laughed, and she said, 'Yes, it is near, relatively.' We were convulsed in laughter and she turned her face away, chuckling. Then she said, 'By the way, there's another word – but this is not an English lesson. There is the word, *compar-'*

'*-atively*,' Claudia said, causing Teacher Myra to rock back in astonishment.

'Well, welll!' she said. 'That's a good one. You are very sharp this morning, Claudia. That's right.'

The class was silent with shock. She turned to me, 'Bet you didn't know that one.'

'Yes,' I said, and I was almost hurt. I was almost hurt because I had used that word several times in my compositions. Only that it had not occurred to me a while ago.

She turned to Frank again: 'All right, Frank, you said it is near. It *is* – comparatively speaking. We won't talk about miles now. Okay, that's Tobago. Sarah could you come out here and point out Mayaro on the map?'

She always picked on Sarah for things like that because Sarah was not very bright. But we had pointed out Mayaro several times, and talked about it, and in any case the word *Mayaro* was written as – as big as the world – to quote what Teacher Myra always said. She always added, 'almost'. Sarah came out and pointed correctly to where Mayaro was, and Teacher Myra pointed to me and said, 'Would you say that's far, Horace Lumpres?' She looked at me fixedly. My heart pounded.

I said, 'Yes, Miss.'

'Comparatively,' she said. 'If we think of the places in *Homes Far Away,* and *Peoples Far Away*, Mayaro is just a stone's throw from Tobago. Just a slice of sea between.' And she made another corny joke that again had the class rolling with laughter. She said, 'Tobago is just a stone's throw – I wonder which of the boys can throw that stone?'

Then amidst chuckles she said, 'All right. All right, class. Attention. So far as we are concerned Tobago is far away. That's Horace Lumpres. So let's talk about places far away – in Tobago. And about those people far away. Tobagonians. Okay, class?'

Everybody said, 'Yes, Miss.'

We talked about the island of Tobago and about its people in such great detail it was as if we were all going to live there. And certainly we talked as if we were all going there right away because Teacher Myra mentioned the name of the steamer and where it docked in Port-of-Spain and what time it left Port-of-Spain, and what time it arrived in Tobago. I was surprised she knew so many things about it. I felt very uncomfortable as she was saying this because she was looking at me more than at any one else. I was afraid she'd ask me some question on Tobago. She left off talking about the ship and it seemed that we had all arrived there already for she began saying how you crossed a bridge when the steamer docked in the chief town, and how you went straight up a hill. She did not dwell too much on the chief town because we all knew it was Scarborough, but she talked of a place which none of the others seemed to have heard of before – which was Mount Moriah. I was amazed when she said Mount Moriah because that was the place my Aunt Mona had said she was going to. Teacher Myra talked about the way to get there from Scarborough, and it was as though the class was in Tobago and on its way to Mount Moriah, such fine details she gave. What astonished me was that she was talking about this place as if it was the most important place in the whole of Tobago. She said now: 'Class, if ever any one of you has to go to Tobago at any time do not fail to go to this beautiful place on the hill – Mount Moriah. I told you how to get there from Scarborough.'

My heart was beating fast, and so much faster now because she was talking and looking at me. She went on talking and I went on listening to her and looking at the map of Tobago, which seemed to take new life and vividness on the wall. I knew she was from Rio Claro and I wanted to ask her how come she knew Tobago so well, and how come she loved Mount Moriah so much. I was almost jealous for I felt Mayaro was the nicest place in the world – and it was Teacher Myra herself who had made me feel so. *Charity Begins At Home,* but she was talking of the beautiful place on the hill. And her home was Rio Claro. I sat there dreaming and drifting in my thoughts, and so far were they travelling, in fact, that I did not realise she had dismissed the class. The tumbling, the pushing and pulling of desks, the screeches they made, and the scurrying past me, and the bouncing, soon jolted me to what was happening. I looked around at the din and at the same time I saw Teacher Myra walking towards me.

She came up and said, 'What a wonderful composition – that last one you wrote!'

I was pleased and embarrassed. 'The last one?'

She said, 'Well, I like all the ones you write, but that one you did on Friday – it was, shall I say, exceptional?' I took my eyes away from her face and looked outside. She continued, 'But you know that, of course, because you saw I gave you full marks. I don't throw away marks you know,' she said. 'You have to earn them.' She said this laughingly, and she sat on the bench in the next row, half-turned to me. I was thrilled about the composition and what she had said, but when I looked at her sitting on the bench, and with her hands on the desk, I could not help laughing. She looked like an overgrown pupil.

She said, 'What are you laughing at?'

'Look like you in class again, Miss.'

'God forbid! My bones are too hard for that. You think I look so youthful?'

I laughed even more. Her legs were so much too long that they could not get in under the bench, and she had to sit sideways, with them outside.

She must have guessed exactly what I was thinking because she said, 'I just have to grow down a little bit – that's all. It wouldn't be too hard for me to get to be a child again.' We laughed. She said, 'Sometimes I actually feel like a child. True. That's how I feel so often when I read your compositions. I know I'm your teacher, and you wouldn't believe this, but I often ask myself: Could I write one like that? I really don't know. I think when you grow up you lose something. Don't you think so? But it's more than that. Sometimes I ask myself: Can you bring things to life? That's the point. *You* do that, and that is the crux. You see, it's not just writing words, it's bringing things to life. I can teach you to write words, and grammar, and so on, but – '

'Miss, you speak good grammar.'

'I always try. It is one of the only things I have. Usually I'm modest, and when people praise me for it I tell them that isn't anything. But it *is* something, and between you and me I am proud of it.'

And I was proud of her too, for it, but I did not tell her that.

She was proud of me and of my compositions, and that was what was in her eyes now, and I had been so embarrassed I had mentioned her grammar to see if she would stop talking about me.

But she went on, after a few moments of silence: 'Yes, as I was saying. The work you do for me. I like your Point Radix – your *La Point* – I thought I could hear the sea breaking against it. Sound and sight. You make these real.'

I felt so thrilled and yet I wished she would stop. I felt to cry out.

She said, 'Only you made me smile when you said: "Wild nature . . ." ' She broke off giggling and I felt so stung and hurt that I retorted, 'Miss, it's Kingsley who said – '

She put up her hand. 'Seaweed. That's seaweed,' she said in disgust. She said, 'Don't bother about Charles Kingsley. Sometimes his essays are all right, but he can't bring things to life. In any case he over-describes. Hear this,' and she mimicked: 'Here come home from the Convent two coloured young ladies, probably pretty, and possibly lovely, certainly gentle, modest, and well-dressed.' And she chuckled and asked, 'What does that mean?' I didn't know what to say. I hadn't read that part and I did not think Kingsley could ever be ridiculous. She said, 'Be yourself. When you write, forget Kingsley and everybody. Aren't you yourself when you write?'

'Most times, Miss.'

She said, 'I know, because I see you, and I see how you get worked up and involved, and it could only be so because you tell the truth.' I turned my head towards the window, sharply embarrassed. I was not sure about the word 'involved' here, but I had an idea of what Teacher Myra was saying.

She said, 'But don't bother, don't feel all shy and soppy, because it's not what you look like when writing – it's what you write. And what you write is good.' She said this softly, and I heard a click, and when I looked down towards the front stairs there was a group of girls from my class looking at me. I saw Effy Thorpe's face. I turned around to Teacher Myra. Although she did not turn her head, she said, 'I saw them. That's natural. They're jealous. It's only human. Maybe I shouldn't really be sitting down here talking with you.'

I looked at her and I felt badly. Although she had a watch she

156

glanced at the school clock. 'I took up so much of your recess time,' she said. 'I suppose I ought to let you go out and make up for this time now, but they'll be even more jealous.'

I saw she was concerned and I said quickly, 'That's nothing, Miss. I ain't bound to go outside.'

'Well I just won't keep you in next time,' she said, smiling. Then she said, 'Jealousy is such a terrible thing. *I* can tell you!' I smiled because I thought Teacher Myra was making fun, but when I looked at her face I saw it was crossed with fury and with something I could not describe. It frightened me. But as I looked again I wondered if I had seen right. Because she was smiling and cheerful now, and when the bell ended recess she playfully pulled back the children rushing in.

❋ *Twenty-four*

IT WAS HARDLY a week later, when, on going through the little coconut track to the factory, I heard a whistle, and when I looked up I saw Mr Clunis sliding down a coconut tree.

I waited, and when he reached down I walked towards him and said, 'She ain't come back yet.'

'I know,' he said. 'She might come back anytime now. What time you suppose to be going Rio Claro?'

'I have to wait till she come back. Going over to the factory now. Just want to tell Ma that Auntie ain't come yet.'

His face was bright, but I could see he was somewhat agitated as Auntie had not come. He said, 'I should really go with her, but you know how it is, with the expense these days. I didn't want to lose the day's pay.'

'Yes – ah – yes, Mr Clunis.'

I had fumbled and hesitated because I did not know what to call him. I had thought about it and knew that I should be addressing him in a different way, but it was hard to change just like that. He walked about in the low bush under the coconut tree, picking up all the dried nuts with the point of his gleaming cutlass and putting them in a heap – what we called 'slamblaying'. As I watched him I thought of him talking about not wanting to miss the day's pay, and I was wondering now whether he got paid by the coconut he picked or by the tree he climbed. As I watched, I saw him pull up a green coconut.

'You wouldn't mind this?' he said. 'You'll have it?'

'Yes – ah – yes, Mr Clunis.'

'Now this is Friday. You all set for Sunday?'

'Yes.'

He grinned nervously, and I grinned too. He said, 'I hope we meet the tailor feller. No point in going quite Rio Claro for nothing.'

I had not even thought that the tailor might not be there. He

158

couldn't be out all day, though.

Mr Clunis said proudly, 'We'll be wearing the same thing. Same cloth, same cut.'

I just grinned.

He had stopped trimming the coconut as he talked, the moistened, gleaming blade resting on the sliced-off top of the nut. Now all he had to do was cut a hole in the hard shell. He did so with one short chip, and handed it to me.

As I was drinking I was thinking of no other person but Mr Clunis standing there. I was thinking of how we got to be friends and how I had come to like him. I was thinking of how odd it was that I was no longer jealous, and was almost anxious for Auntie to marry him on Sunday. I could almost see myself then, near to him, wearing a suit of the same cloth as his, and of the same cut. And I was thinking how funny it was that with all this, I still could not decide to start calling him 'Uncle.' And every time I called him 'Mr' I could see as if his face – '

'Boy, you ain't finishing or what!' His voice interrupted my thoughts. I had stood there, my head thrown back, with the coconut on top of my lips, but I had almost forgotten that I was drinking. Now I started to drink in haste.

He laughed. 'What was happening while ago?' he said. 'Now all I hearing is glock, glock.'

I laughed. When I was finished he split the coconut in three with three strokes of the cutlass, and cut off a chip – which we called a 'spoon' – so I could scoop up the jelly in it.

I said, 'Thanks, Mr – ah – Mr Clunis.'

Again he seemed to shake off a little irritation, but he was bright soon afterwards and he said, 'When you go up Rio Claro–' He stopped. Then he said, 'The thing is, boy, I can't go to try on this suit. The man take me measurement, but when I go back the suit will be already made. I mean I couldn't go back to try it on.'

He said this as if he was complaining so I said, 'I neither.'

'But it's I who marrieding,' he said, and we were both convulsed in laughter.

He said, 'If *your* suit don't fit you, then you could fit it. But with me, I have to make sure I look nice.'

'I want to look nice too,' I said earnestly.

He said, 'But Horace, boy, you ain't seeing me point. I is the groom, boy.'

'Yes – er – yes, Mr Clunis.'

'But I know what you mean, you know. You couldn't go for a try on and I couldn't go for a try on. We in the same boat.'

That expression greatly amused me, because I had just begun to think of Uncle Ulric, who had made us go to the tailor in Rio Claro. And saying 'we in the same boat,' made me think of Uncle going out to fish.

Mr Clunis was looking at me. 'Why you laughing?'

'Because what you said made me remember Uncle.'

'Which Uncle you talking about?'

I just cut my eyes away from him and pretended I didn't hear. Teacher Myra had an expression: 'Every thing in due season.' I suppose after Sunday Mr Clunis could talk in that sort of style, but not now.

He must have guessed my thoughts for he passed it off saying, 'I didn't want to go quite Rio Claro to make me suit you know. If is wasn't for Ulric – '

'Well, that was just what I was thinking.'

'I wanted to go to Harold Gill in Plaisance.'

'Uncle doesn't think much of him.'

'Okay – Ulric keep saying Gill always making suit for fishermen. So what?'

I laughed. Uncle said Roomeen's bridegroom had to be turned out by a proper tailor. Mr Gill was too ordinary for Uncle because Uncle passed his tailor-shop every day! And because Uncle went to school with him. I had heard Uncle telling Mr Clunis, 'Who? Harold Gill? Harold Gill could sew for anybody? I was in same class with him – Harold Gill can't tell me nothing!'

I chuckled at that, too. Mr Clunis had been looking around for the coconuts he picked, and he saw my face. 'Boy you laughing with yourself?' He seemed very amused. Having collected all the dry nuts and having flung away the shells of the green one he had cut for me, he was walking around, looking up into the coconut trees. I supposed he was thinking about which one to climb next. I had been on my way to the factory to see Mother and I thought I'd better go on. But I was still thinking of Uncle. Just fancy Uncle despised Harold Gill because Gill sewed for fishermen. Now what was Uncle? I chuckled. Claudia had a way of saying, 'Thing to cry you laughing at!' This was really something to cry about. I couldn't believe Uncle could think so little of fishermen because in fact they were all in the same boat. In the truest sense of the word. I laughed so heartily that tears came to my eyes. I was laughing openly, and Mr Clunis looked round, astonished. 'But what happening here – this boy going mad? Horace, you all right?'

'I remember a joke,' I said.

'What the hell is this! I hope the joke isn't me.'

'Oh, no.'

By this time he was standing on the bulge of another laden coconut tree, and the cable-rope, which we called 'bicycle,' was in his hand, ready to be clasped round the trunk. He said suddenly, 'By the by, you know this Sergeant Peters?'

'Just by seeing him sometimes.'

'I wonder if he's a smart-man. I find he's very close to your Uncle. They close like finger and ring these days.'

I said nothing. Nothing at all.

He said, 'I was only wondering. That moustache, that twirling ... Something in that, you know.' Then he laughed it off and said, 'Anyway, don't bother with me, eh. I so stupid. But I was telling you: he is the man who pump the thing about the Rio Claro tailor in Ulric's head.'

'I know.'

'All this about bespoke tailor. We'll find out bespoke tailor if the suit can't fit. Sergeant or no sergeant I'll break his backside.' I almost choked with laughter. Mr Clunis clasped on his bicycle rope and all but walked up the tree.

After a while I walked off to the factory, taking the sand road that led to the barracks. Suddenly, before I had got very far, a short, shrill whistle pierced the air, and I turned back and looked up. It was Mr Clunis and he was pointing. My eyes caught the direction, and sure enough, at the junction of the coconut grove and the main road, there was something that looked like a horse and buggy. I cried to myself: 'Oh, Auntie!' I started to trot towards the buggy and I glanced to see if Mr Clunis was scurrying down the tree. He was not, and presently coconuts began to fall 'boop! boop!' I knew he was as excited as I was, to know she was back, because he had been looking out for her all the time, but he was already beginning to play cool and independent and as if he could do without Auntie. I trotted until I reached close to Mr Reid's buggy, which was already half-way down the sand road, and then Mr Reid brought the buggy to a stop. Auntie cried, 'Gosh, look Horace!' and she got out of the buggy and hugged me. She said, 'Reid, it's all right, you could go on. We ain't have far now. We'll walk the rest.' Mr Reid still stood the buggy up as if he was hoping we would both jump in. He was smiling as he looked at me. I was puffing and out of breath. I said, 'Morning, Mr Reid,' but I didn't pay him any more mind than that. Because there was Auntie with her big radiant face, looking like the morning star. She was wearing her wide sun-flower hat, and that frilly lilac dress she brought from Panama.

She said, 'Look at this boy, ready for Rio Claro and everything!'

Mr Reid said, 'Because it have a wedding.'

We laughed. Perhaps it was the first time I had heard Mr Reid say something that made anybody laugh. Auntie Roomeen had a parcel in her hand, which I took from her. She asked, 'Waiting for me a long time?'

'Long, long.'

'Good gracious,' she said, looking as though she was sorry. Then she said, 'Come on. We better jump in the buggy and get home quick. Mr Reid said he's taking us to Quarters to catch the bus. Claris home?' The time was just about half-past eleven and I told her Mother was still in the factory.

'Okay. When we get up there you run over and call her, and afterwards she could go back. Daddy Reid, how about half-an-hour? You'll be ready?'

Mr Reid's face crinkled up into a smile. He seemed to take it as an honour simply for Auntie to talk to him. He said, 'Sure, Roomeen. And I'll come right there home for you.'

We were in the buggy, sitting just behind him, and he was letting his horse take its time down the coconut grove.

In reply to him Auntie said, 'Oh, good. Thank you so much. It's really nice of you.'

'Don't mention it,' said old Mr Reid. 'The pleasure is mine.'

I was taken aback by the nice pleasant talk going on and I never knew Mr Reid could be so gallant and up to mark with a lady. I looked at the back of his head now, and though I admired him I was feeling a tinge of something else. Yes, I was jealous even of old Mr Reid!

❋ Twenty-five

MR REID was prompt and we were out of the house in a jiffy and were soon on the bus to Rio Claro. I could not help feeling glad that Uncle did not like Harold Gill as a tailor – even though I knew he did not like him for the simple reason that Mr Gill sewed for fishermen. I could not help feeling glad about this because I had not gone to Rio Claro since I was about five, and I could hardly remember that trip. In fact I had no recollection of the place at all – not even a vague recollection of people and houses, or of simple things like laughter or ice-cream. All I remembered was the big, droning bus.

'How you so quiet?' Auntie said.

'Oh – nothing, Auntie.'

'You know Rio Claro?'

'I went there once. With Aunt Mona.'

She looked at me. 'Since that time? You were almost a baby. You haven't been there since I went to Panama?'

'No, Auntie.'

'Well, well!' She eased up near to me. I was sitting on the inside, at the window, and she had her left arm around my neck. She was smelling sweet, and the scent was of her favourite perfume *orange blossom*. Although she had changed the frilly mauve dress to a blue one, I still thought of her in it, for when she was wearing it she looked something between the sunset and the ripe zecacks. I had always wanted to tell her this, or something like it, and now, because of the silence – apart from the drone of the bus – I said: 'Auntie, your mauve dress. Looks like zecack.'

She looked at me in a puzzled way, and laughed. She said, 'Zecack? Which dress you mean, the lilac one?'

'Yes, that one with frills that you was wearing today.'

'That's lilac washed in lavender.'

'Looks like ripe zecack.'

She pursed her lips and thought, and there was a whimsical smile on her face. She said, 'I see what you mean. Yes, somewhat. Although the mauve in zecack is not so mauve as lilac.'

'No, Auntie, but when the zecack really ripe and the mauve fading down to white, I find it looks like that dress.'

'You are right,' she said. 'Sometimes the sky – '

'The sunset,' I interrupted.

'The sunset – that's what I was going to say. Sometimes it makes me think of sunset, and – and sadness,' she said.

'But Auntie, you going to get married. It should make you think of happiness.'

She laughed heartily, but what she had said had made me sad in a strange way. She put her hand on my head now and said, 'Boy, you so smart. I said sadness because, well, because after joy is sorrow. You ever hear that? So they say – after joy is sorrow. But really, I feel so happy.'

Looking at her beaming face I began to feel happy too. I said, 'Mr Clunis happy too. He cut a green coconut jelly for me. You saw him, Auntie?'

'I only heard the coconuts falling boo-doop boop, but I didn't look up. I'll see him when I get back. And then I'll see him all the time – not so?'

I grinned. She realised I liked him now but she did not realise I liked him so much because of her.

We were silent again and I listened to the bus droning along. The forests were thick on either side and there were houses in clearings here and there. I was thinking about this and I was thinking about how nice my Auntie Roomeen was. And I was thinking of how many treasures she had – apart from the lost gold chain – the number of dresses and shoes and hats – and yet she was neither pompous nor vain. Outside of my thoughts I heard her voice asking the conductor what was the distance from Mayaro to Rio Claro, and the answer was exactly what Teacher Myra had said in class – fourteen miles. Auntie was glad to know. Then she said to me, 'You saw Clunis early?'

'No. Just before the buggy came up.'

'And you mean he didn't even come down from the tree?'

'Mr Clunis getting accustomed to you and you getting accustomed to him.'

164

She looked at me as if surprised to hear me say that. She said, 'Words of wisdom. You sure right, Horace. Clunis and I have a long way to go in married life. And we ain't start yet.'

I giggled.

'Of course you know I'll be moving over to his house. Right there in St Joseph.'

'I'll still miss you, Auntie.' I smiled but she must have still seen the pain, for she said, 'You'll still be my right-hand man, and my chum, and favourite. And I ain't going far from you – as you see.'

'Yes, Auntie.'

As she leaned over to me I turned my face to her sleeve so she wouldn't see my eyes. I began feeling her sleeve wet against my face.

She said, 'Boy, ain't I proud of my nephew. I hear he could write so well.'

I was surprised and shocked to hear her say that and directly I would have asked from whom she heard it but my heart was still full to overflowing. She murmured something vague about the sarge boasting about me, but I could not believe that, except he was talking about the time we chatted in the boat-house. The only other thing was if Uncle had told the sarge about me – but what did Uncle know about my writing? I was trying to compose myself to ask her about this when she turned to me: 'Come on, Horace, tell me, I want to hear what you really feel.' She did not speak for a while, and then she said, 'You think I'm doing the right thing?'

I was taken aback. 'But Auntie you can't do anything else now!' My voice was tremulous.

'Who told you so?' She was laughing. She said, 'So if I see I'm going off a precipice, I can't turn back? I ain't sign any paper yet, you know. And I ain't see the priest.' Her face was radiant, and there was no doubt at all that she wanted to marry Mr Clunis. In any case she was on her way for his wedding suit. Also, I knew in my mind that she had forgotten all about Panama and was looking forward to a new life here with us. One good proof of it was what she just said. When she had said 'I ain't sign any paper yet,' it was the first time I had noticed her saying 'ain't.'

'Auntie, you will be happy and everything will be nice.'

'You really feel so? I hope you just ain't trying to make me feel good. To be serious, I really like Clunis. But marriage is a big thing. I tried it once before, and well – you know. And your Auntie isn't a little girl anymore,' she laughed. 'You think things will work out? *I* think so.'

'And I *know* so. It bound to work out.'

'Why?'

'Because you so nice. And so good to everybody. And you so cheerful.'

She laughed. 'Don't forget it takes two.'

'He is such a good person.'

Her face lit up. 'Who?'

'Mr Clunis.'

'You realise that?' She looked at me in wonderment, then she hugged me and kissed me. Where her face touched me, my face felt wet. She said, 'I'm so glad to hear you say that.'

I said nothing.

'He'll be your uncle. A real uncle to you.'

'Yes, Auntie.'

There was silence, and I said to myself, 'Uncle Clunis', and I was surprised how easily the words came. I felt happy. I looked at her and remembered how easy it was, too, for her to say, 'Daddy Reid.'

She leaned back in the seat now, contented, as the bus droned on. Her eyes were still a little red. She was looking outside now. Here there were many more roadside houses, and the high woods had fallen right back. She whispered, 'We getting to Rio Claro. This is part of the outskirts. Won't be long now.'

I suddenly grew anxious to arrive at Rio Claro. I looked at her and she must have seen the keenness on my face.

She said, 'Thinking about the suit?'

'Yes, Auntie. I'll see how it will fit.'

'It will fit great,' she said. 'He is a bespoke tailor.'

'And I'm thinking about the wedding.'

'It will be a big time,' she said.

✳ Twenty-six

AUNTIE ROOMEEN'S WEDDING was such a big bright occasion that had my Uncle Ulric not come in the late evening and whispered to me what we had to do, I would have gone to bed that night more enchanted than I had ever been in my whole life. For it was otherwise a happy, happy day. The first thrill had come to me in the morning when Auntie Roomeen had appeared dressed all in white, and with a bouquet of white roses, looking as beautiful as a goddess. Yes, that was the phrase Teacher Myra used to me afterwards: beautiful as a goddess. I was thrilled to see Mr Clunis, too, and perhaps a little bit shocked. For I had not seen him in anything else but torn-up trousers and shirt; sweaty, bare-foot, and with cutlass in hand. And now he was in his smartly-cut coal-grey suit, clean-shaven, with his shoes shining and his hair well-trimmed, and looking so wonderful and strange.

When he had finished dressing and he had called me to see him, I had run to him and we threw our arms around each other, and I said, 'Mr – I mean, Uncle Clunis, the suit looking so good. You ain't looking like you!'

He had laughed and said, 'Fisherman could ever make suit? That's why I went to Rio Claro.'

There was a crowd there at the wedding house, and I looked around quickly, embarrassed, for I knew there were several fishermen around. I knew that Mr Stanley, for instance, was close by, somewhere. Then I heard raucous laughter and looked round, and I saw it was Taso. I was a little surprised because it was laughter you would hear on the beach when the seine was in – not in a wedding house. I asked myself: 'Do fishermen care?'

I quickly forgot what Uncle Clunis had said about Harold Gill. In any case Harold Gill wasn't a fisherman; he only sewed for them. I felt perhaps Uncle Clunis wasn't being fair to him, although, to be honest, I was glad he didn't sew my suit.

I looked around at the people in the room. Even though it was early morning and there was a crowd, it was just a crowd of friends that had come to see Uncle Clunis off to the church. Uncle Clunis said to me, 'You better go and get ready now. Don't do no more work.'

'Ma want me to help around the house and in the kitchen. She said when it's time to go to church I'll dress.'

He had stood there looking at me and really it was as if I had been standing in front of a different person. The barber must have taken all day on his head, for it was so well-groomed, with the hair even, the razor-line sharp and clear-cut, the 'sheek' neatly blocked off, and with a wisp of moustache on his upper-lip. His face, too, seemed unusually smooth, as if he had rubbed fine sand-paper on it. He had a white rose in the lapel of his jacket – and the jacket itself was unbuttoned, showing frills on his white shirt. His bow-tie was of the most delicate grey.

When I told him what Mother had said, he called towards the kitchen, 'Claris!' and when Mother came, he said, 'Look, the wedding is at eleven o'clock, you know. Let Horace go and get dressed.'

I noticed that Mother was smiling as he was talking. When he was finished she said, 'You could tell me where Mr Clunis is? The coconut-picker? I ain't see him this morning. You could help me, Mr Gentleman?'

Uncle Clunis laughed but pretended he was not laughing and then he said, 'You making joke, but I serious. Look, it's ten o'clock already. Just now guests starting to come. Horace said he bringing his teacher and school-friends early. I mean – ' He stopped, and I supposed he was confused by the way Mother was looking at him and laughing. Now she said, 'Clunis, you getting cold-sweat or what? You getting *gigiri?* Mister, all you have to do is to get married. Leave everything else to me. I running this fête!'

He stood up there and she laughed and turned back to go into the kitchen. He looked agitated. He said, 'And Claris, just one more thing. I want this little boy to realise that I ain't any "Mr Clunis" now. I is his Uncle.'

Mother laughed but I turned away because my heart became full. Mr Clunis must have been very agitated for he did not see that I had realised this already. Mother said to me, 'You better go over and dress now, Horace. You better go now because your

Uncle Clunis want to see you getting ready.'

I hurried away to our house.

This was the time I had seen Auntie Roomeen in white, and I was so thrilled. She was dressed and sitting on a chair now, with the bouquet of white roses, and there were several other ladies about her, preening her up to make her look better. She had no veil and this was the only little disappointment I had, because all brides wore veils – so far as I knew. When she saw me she beckoned and said, 'He dressed yet?'

'Yes, Auntie.'

'How he looking? The suit fit good?'

'Oh yes, Auntie. It's so nice. Beautiful. It have Uncle Clunis looking so strange.'

When I used the term 'Uncle Clunis' I saw her eyes flicker, and she threw her arms about me and kissed me. The ladies around were chattering and laughing. Auntie held me off and whispered, 'I'll see him just now, boy. Oh, Horace!'

'Auntie, where's the veil?'

'Veil?' She laughed heartily, and some of the women around her heard me and laughed too. 'Veil?' she said again. 'So this is the first time I'm getting married? I married before, boy, and I see everything to see – I don't want no veil over my eyes.'

There was so much laughter around me, it was just as if hens had burst out cackling. I really did not understand the joke, and in fact, what Auntie said just did not make sense. She saw my puzzlement and she said, 'Anyway, don't mind that. What about Claris – she over there still?'

'Yes, Auntie.'

'Guests starting to come? Who there?'

Just before I came into the yard of our house I had seen Teacher Myra coming through the coconut grove. I told her that. Claudia was with Teacher Myra, and there was also Effy and Frank Fridal. As Auntie did not know my school friends I did not mention them. But I mentioned that just behind Teacher Myra was the big ambling figure of Sergeant Peters. She said, 'Oh, they come already?' I did not quite follow. Who had come already – and I told her this, trying to suppress a smile – who had come already were some of the fishermen. Mr Stanley was there, looking dressed well enough to go to the church, and Taso was there, looking as though he was bound to go back home to change. Some others were there too, and ready to go to the church, but looking as though Harold Gill had fitted them out. A few of Uncle Clunis' friends were already there too. And of course old Mr Reid was there, with the buggy. I told her Mr Reid looked so special, he surprised me.

She was touched. She said, 'Daddy Reid there already? He's taking us to the church.' Then she got excited, 'Look! Look your Uncle Ulric!'

'I know,' I said. This made me want to see the time. She knew what I wanted and right away she said, 'Don't wait to see no time. It getting late. Just slip in and get ready fast. If Daddy Reid's here, it getting near to time.'

I turned to see Uncle Ulric walk in with a brown tweed suit, with hat, tie, and shoes to match, and with a big watch on his wrist. I gasped. Auntie Roomeen said to him, 'Oh God, boy, you'll kill them? You looking so sweet!' She wanted to kiss him but he didn't bend down.

He said, 'Good. Roomeen, you have to get busy. It's quarter-to-eleven now and the priest fixing up.'

I did not hear the rest of the conversation because I had dashed into my bedroom. I did not stay long and when I emerged from my room Auntie Roomeen was getting ready to go down the steps. When she saw me she gave a shriek of surprise and delight, and all the ladies gasped. I was really looking great!

❋ Twenty-seven

WHEN WE WERE coming back from the church, walking along the beach and then along the beach track under the coconut trees, something happened that almost spoilt this golden day. I was walking behind Mr Reid's buggy, which, apart from Mr Reid, had Uncle Clunis and Auntie Roomeen side by side; and just behind me were Auntie's close friends who had dressed her for the wedding, and who had decorated this ramshackle old buggy with roses and coconut leaves. The ladies were chattering all the time. I had not been thinking of them, but of how lucky we were to get such a cloudless day, and to find the tide so low, when all of a sudden I became aware of whispering and then bursts of laughter. The one who had seemed the closest friend of Auntie, putting the finishing touches on her hair and on her face and dress before she had left for the church – that one said, 'I wish the man could come back and see this. I mean, he ain't even dead. She left him in Panama and come back for this one.'

I felt stung and surprised. I looked back but they seemed to ignore me. Mother had stayed in the kitchen at Uncle Clunis' house, for she was in charge of the wedding banquet, but I had looked back to see if Uncle Ulric was near, and to know if he was hearing.

He was a little way behind, walking along with Sergeant Peters, and their conversation seemed so lively that even if he were near he might not have heard. I went along feeling uneasy and furious as the ladies went on chattering.

They were chattering softly, and I couldn't quieten my mind enough to listen, but I still heard one of them say: 'What's all the fuss, this big amount of food and drinks and banquet? She's no young girl.' And amidst giggling and laughter someone asked: 'And what about him? You know I ain't know him so good?'

I did not hear much of the reply but I heard the words 'coconut-picker', and I heard the person say, 'As you see, he's no

171

young boy either. You know how long he running life?'

I did not understand this last expression and I did not try to – I was so furious. We were nearing home now – the chimney of the St Joseph factory was not far away amongst the coconut leaves. I could hardly wait until I got home to tell Mother. I heard a burst of laughter again, and I wished I had been listening because directly afterwards I heard the words 'And Mona'. I started walking faster, trying to keep up with the buggy. The horse was stepping livelier because it was seeing its home. My head was feeling wild and my heart was thumping. Just before Mr Reid drove into the wedding yard, a hand touched me, and it was one of the very ladies who had been chattering about Auntie.

She said, 'You is Claris' son?'

'Yes.'

'I was noticing you. A big day like this and your face so vexed up? I thought you did like Roomeenia.'

I wanted to shout: 'I thought you did like her too!' But I said nothing.

She said, 'Brighten up, boy. It's your tanty wedding day. Look! Hear how those violins starting up as we coming. I so glad Roomeen get – ' And she paused a little and then she said, 'I so glad she get somebody good.'

I did not say a word. I saw Mother, and I just broke away from this lady and went to meet her. As Mr Reid's buggy rolled into the yard the little music band filled the air with serenade. They were playing *Here comes the Bride*. It was Al Timothy's band and even without seeing them I knew it was Pappy Timothy on the saxophone and St Hill Zavier on the banjo, and I was not sure who were playing the violins. I called Mother aside and in just about one or two breaths I told her everything.

When I thought she was going to be furious, she was so calm I was astonished. She just shrugged it off and said, 'What you worrying for, you don't know what jealousy is? Boy, you still young, you don't know nothing.'

'But Ma these people was with Auntie all the time this morning. Auntie's close friends. Laughing and talking.'

Mother smiled: 'You always talking about mottoes. You ever hear this motto: *All that glitters is not gold?*' 'When I was going to school it was up there on the ledge. But now it must be rubbed off. They must put it back.'

I looked at Mother in amazement. My heart was racing. I said, 'That motto still there on the ledge. Ma, that is true. All that glitters . . . Oh God, those ladies! They suppose to be Auntie's friends, you know.'

'But don't tell her. Don't tell Roomeen anything.'

'Why?'

Mother shrugged again. 'No reason why she should know. It will only upset her. These people ain't worth it. Think of your Auntie's happiness. She wouldn't be happy if she know about those sufferers.'

I looked at Mother and almost laughed aloud. Mother was really good for herself! She was calm and gentle, but as Teacher Myra would say, her tongue had a sharp cutting edge. Thinking of Teacher Myra I just glanced around for her, but I did not see her now. She had been a little way behind as we walked along the beach.

I thought of Mother calling the ladies 'sufferers', and of what she said about jealousy, and of Auntie's seemingly comfortable station in life. For example, her vast wardrobe of beautiful dresses, and even the fact – it came with a great rush to my head, I had almost forgotten it – even the fact of the gold chain. This made me remember the mention of Aunt Mona and I told Mother.

Mother said, 'Well of course they know Mona, and perhaps they could say a lot of things about her, but not about Roomeen.'

'What you mean?'

'Well, Horace even you know about Mona and Cordner. Don't talk about it now. In any case they quite in Tobago. Don't bother about that. Look, let me go in and prepare, eh! We'll talk later. Enjoy yourself, son.'

I left the kitchen door and standing at Uncle Clunis' steps the beautiful strains of music seemed to transport me. The violins were especially touching, and above all things, what could they be playing? They were playing *Home Sweet Home*, giving Auntie Roomeen a welcome in the place where she was going to live. Standing there by the steps and thinking of this, and thinking of everything, I felt like crying. Then, amidst the music and the chatter and the laughter, a familiar voice rang out: 'Miss, look Horace Lumpres – he's like a prince, Miss.'

173

That was Claudia. I was thrilled to hear what she said. And to see the faces of so many of my school friends. And there was Teacher Myra's face at the window. She was looking down at us and smiling and she seemed as comfortable as though she were in school. I had invited them all at the last moment when I had put into my composition that there was going to be a wedding. Teacher Myra had taken that as true and had said putting it into my composition was an invitation. She said she was going to be there in any case because her father had to be there. I was thrilled to see her face at the window now.

Most of my school friends were out in the yard. They felt freer to run about. Besides, Uncle Clunis' house was small, so while there was the music inside, and the crowd of guests, and the speech-making and the sticking of the cake, we out in the yard were playing games and having a wonderful time. I took most of them over to my home and Claudia liked the house very much, but what Frank Fridal and Lennox and even Effy – what they said they liked most of all was just being under the palms and near to *La Point*. After staying a little while over at our house so that they could see, as Effy Thorpe said, 'where I came to school from', we went back to Uncle Clunis' house, and this time I went up the steps. Inside, Auntie Roomeen and Uncle Clunis were sitting at the head of the banquet table, and Miss Wong was in the little group around the table, and a great number of people were around them. Between Miss Wong and Mr Reid was one of Auntie's friends, in the middle of singing *Bless this House*. As soon as she finished Auntie beckoned to me excitedly, and she said, 'So Horace, you wouldn't even come and kiss me?' All eyes were on me and I squeezed forward, embarrassed, passing between the table and chairs and people who laid kind hands on me, and when I reached Auntie Roomeen I put my arms about her neck. She threw her arms around my neck and she squeezed me to her and then she kissed me and when I looked at her I saw that her eyes were red. Mine were red, too. Then I held the hands of Uncle Clunis but he threw his arms around me too, and he kissed me, and then in this jovial way he held me off and he said, 'What, you mean you looking better than me, boy! Bespoke. *Caramba*!' And when he saw my face he said, 'Oh chuts. Big man like you have water in your eyes?'

All this while people were watching and laughing and talking, and some were saying 'poor thing!' and there were all sorts of comments. I hardly heard or listened. When I left them I had to squeeze through the crowd again, for the house was packed with guests. I was passing through towards the front steps this time, and I was quite close to the musicians, who had hardly stopped playing. They had been playing softly during the speeches, and they had accompanied the singing, and now they had waxed full again. Even if I had not known who Uncle Clunis had asked to come and play I could have told what band it was because it was Pappy Timothy and his group who could play so sweet. They were from Radix village – the same place Uncle Clunis had argued about. As they played they made everybody feel like dancing. Only it was hard for everybody to dance in there – the place was so small. Every time I stood up to get a space to pass my feet began tapping. By the time I reached down the steps I was almost all right again, but yet Claudia cried out, 'Miss, he's sniffing!'

She was pointing at me and looking up at Teacher Myra. She said, 'His eyes pink as your dress.'

Teacher Myra had on a pink dress with long, flaring sleeves. She had come outside because I suppose Claudia would not leave her alone at the window, and now she was standing at the root of a coconut tree, beside Uncle Clunis' kitchen, and what looked like slices of sun and shadow were splintering on her. She said to Claudia, 'That's the Aunt he loves best – the one from Panama who is the bride today. He's bound to sniff.'

'And when she goes back? She's going back, Miss?'

Teacher Myra said, 'Ah, Claudia. Then what's the sense in getting married? No, I should think not. The gentleman works on this estate and – '

Claudia interrupted: 'Miss, how come you know so much?'

Teacher Myra was confused for a moment. She stuttered a bit, then she said, smiling, 'Oh well, you see, I know lots of people.'

Teacher Myra did not look at me and I did not look at her. Yes, she knew lots of people, there was no doubt about that. And she had got to know lots more through my compositions. And so, while it surprised Claudia that she knew Uncle Clunis worked here, it was no surprise to me, and maybe, through my foolish pen, she knew a great deal about my family circle and about me.

As I was talking I was looking towards Point Radix. From here there was a clear view and the opening in the palms seemed to frame it as a picture. The afternoon sun brightened the headland and there seemed a glint of silver where it met the sea. That was because the waves breaking against the headland had left an edge of froth.

Teacher Myra roused me by saying, 'You'll say it's full now? The tide.'

I was a little self-conscious. 'No, Miss. It now coming up.'

'*La Point* looks picturesque.'

I was thrilled and embarrassed.

Claudia had slipped away to her friends and as I looked around, Teacher Myra said, 'You see that strapping man over there in the yard?' She was pointing to the other side of the house. 'That tall strapping man over there. In the tight suit.'

'That's Sergeant Peters, Miss. You mean that man talking to Uncle?'

She looked amazed, 'That's your Uncle over there? That's the Uncle Ulric?'

'Yes, Miss,' I said, looking away.

'I've seen him before, you know, but never in suit. And that confused me. It's the same way lots of people have never seen Daddy in civilian clothes.'

I laughed, but was a little puzzled.

'But you seem to make him out easy,' she said, 'I was trying to test you.'

I looked at her. I said, 'Miss, that's Sergeant Peters, Miss.' And then I remembered something. I remembered the resemblance – but of course it could not be. But she was laughing. I said, 'Miss, you mean Sarge – ' And I stopped.

'You didn't know that? Don't tell me you didn't know that.'

'I was thinking about it once. In the boat-house. But I didn't think – '

I couldn't go on. She said, 'You're are a fine one. You know he is Sergeant Peters and you know I am Myra Peters. True he is new here from Rio Claro. But you have imagination, you should have worked this one out. I thought you knew Daddy was my dad.'

I wondered if she really thought that. In a way I was flabbergasted but I thought I should have known. Only I didn't connect such a thing as the police with the refinement of

176

Teacher Myra. But I'd seen her going up to the Station once or twice.

I said, 'Oh, that's why you go up there sometimes?'

'Exactly. And there was I, calling you a sharp boy.'

'But Miss – ' I said, and stopped.

She smiled. 'Don't worry. But it is amazing the number of difficult things you know, and this simple, obvious one escaped you.' Then she looked round. 'Where's Claudia and Frank and the rest?'

'Claudia and Effy went out to the beach.'

'Without permission?' she cried. I had to smile. She sounded just as though we were in class, and I could not tell if she was in earnest or not. Then she said, with a faint, strange smile: 'I think I'd go out on that beach. I'd like to. To see the chip-chip just peeping out of the sand, and to see *La Point*, and to watch how the tide keeps coming up.' She wasn't looking at me at all while saying this, and this kept me from being self-conscious, and in a way I was glad that what I wrote was so much on her mind.

'I'd like to go,' she said, looking out through the palms.

'But why not, Miss?' I turned to her puzzled.

'Look at Daddy's suit,' she said.

Sarge was wearing a black suit and it was so tight it was as if it would burst any minute. I had noticed it before, of course, and laughed.

'It's tight,' I said.

'He had that suit when he was thin. Years and years ago. He's still wearing it and making people laugh at him. I feel so cut up.'

'But that ain't nothing.'

'That ain't nothing for you.' She frowned and twisted her face.

It was the first time I had seen Teacher Myra behaving like a silly big girl and not like Teacher Myra at all. The first, first time. And I didn't feel I liked her less for it. I just felt I knew her more. As we stood there talking I realised her father had spotted her for he kept on glancing towards her. She kept on talking to me about different things but she was very conscious of him there, for every now and again she kept on saying, 'Don't know why he didn't come in police uniform.'

After a while we heard 'Myra!' and as we looked, the Sarge put his hands to his mouth, like if making a funnel, and said, 'The boy.' At the same time I noticed Uncle Ulric was beckoning to me. She said, 'You better go on to your Uncle.'

Before I moved off I said, 'Miss, everybody having something. You wouldn't even have an ice-cream?'

She said, 'Thank you kindly, but I'm not feeling up to it.'

I wondered if it was the sergeant's suit that had so upset her. I myself was feeling too filled up to eat. But there was food and cakes and drink all around us. The sarge was holding a glass as I walked towards them.

It was at this time that the beautiful enjoyable wedding changed for me. Pappy Timothy was still playing as sweetly as only Pappy could play, and as I walked to Uncle Ulric and Sarge, people were beginning to dance, even outside. Even the coconut palms, which were singing, seemed to be dancing with the wind. There was Frank and Claudia dancing as a pair, and when Claudia tried to swing to the strains of 'Oh Rose Marie,' she fell flat on her bottom. Because she wanted to make style with her Carioca shoes. When she fell most people laughed, but I could not. There was an old man with a panama hat who was dancing with his stick but wasn't moving any place. Claudia got up and dusted the sand from her skirt, with Frank waiting, and when she saw the man with the panama hat, I saw her point to him and turn around looking for Miss. I only saw these things, for listening to what Uncle and Sarge were saying, I could not laugh – and indeed apart from the marriage itself, the wonderful joy of the wedding faded away. I broke in to the talk. 'But Uncle, *tomorrow*? It has to be tomorrow?'

'Tomorrow or never,' Sergeant Peters said, laying a hand on my shoulder. His face seemed nervous and it looked even more so as his moustache was twitching. The ends seemed more twisted and curled up than I ever saw them before, and every time he spoke they seemed to jump.

Uncle was silent, but the sarge said to me again, 'Now or never, Sonny boy. If you give Cordner five minutes more than tomorrow you'll never see him again.'

Uncle said, 'Only one thing, Sarge. You one hundred per cent sure it's him? Don't make me go to Tobago in vain, you know. Me and this boy.'

My heart pounded. I frantically looked at Uncle but his eyes were on Sergeant Peters. The sarge almost flared up with irritation. He said, 'Ulric, you know who you talking to? You see me with a glass in me hand but I ain't drunk, you know. In any case I in this game donkeys years, and when I talk to you as man, it's man talking to you.' He was gesticulating and his moustache kept on twitching, and he was moving from leg to leg very agitatedly in his tight-fitting black suit. He stopped now and he spoke with emphasis: 'Yes, I'm damn well sure Cordner thief the gold chain. And you know why I so sure? Because I saw the bleddy gold in his possession.'

Both Uncle and I became excited, and Uncle said, 'I thought you said – '

The sarge stopped him. 'Don't bother with no thought now – it's me, Peters, talking to you. I have evidence now to nail and be Christ I'll nail him. Don't know what the hell he think Myra is but I could guarantee he thief that gold and if you just do what I was telling you, and then contact Scarborough Police Station afterwards, we'll heave him across here like a rotten anchore.'

And then the sarge said the most puzzling thing. His voice was trailing and he said under his breath, 'Like to jilt good woman!' I could not understand it because I never knew another person was involved. And I thought it was the fact that Sarge saw him with the gold that made Sarge want to bring him to justice. Yet Sarge looked so furious when he said, 'Like to jilt good woman!' that I felt there must be something else. I really did not understand.

At the point when Sarge had said, 'Don't know what the hell he think Myra is', I was even more puzzled, because I could not imagine what part my teacher could be playing in this sort of thing. I wondered whether the glass of rum he had in his hand was not, in fact the explanation. Now I was thinking more than ever of Constable Cordner and that gold chain, and I did not want to waste any time because the gold was in Tobago and in his possession, and we had to make a bid for it, even if we just had to surround the house. But we had to move now, as the sarge said. We had to –

I felt the heavy hand on my shoulder, and I said, 'Yes Sarge? What you said?'

'You know what time you have to sail?'

'In the morning.'

'Early, early. I already gave your uncle all the instructions and it's you and he.' He looked at Uncle, 'Whatever happens, leave here early, so that you'll get there in time. And remember it's tomorrow or never. Just do what I say. When you come back you and your whole family will be rich, boy. You wouldn't have to fishen any more.'

When he said this last part Uncle looked at him with disdain. Uncle said, 'What? Don't go out with the seine to fishen? In the open sea? What you think a little bit of gold is? It will take more than that to keep me from going out there.'

Sergeant Peters laughed heartily. He was laughing all the while Uncle was talking, and afterwards he said, 'Right, man. Carry on, man. Hard work is nice. Isn't it? Eh? Isn't it? Catching hell nice too bad. Carry on, man – don't let Sarge stop you.' He laughed again and then the laughter and even the smile was suddenly gone. He said, 'I don't mean to insult you, but how you like living in that broken-down two-be-two ajoupa. A little hut with the galvanized roof leaking like strainer when rain come. You like that?'

Uncle did not answer. His head was turned away as if he didn't want to hear that. His head was turned towards Uncle Clunis' place where the wedding party was in full swing and where everyone seemed to be making merry. His eyes were staring vacantly at the window, and both his hands were in the pockets of the smart brown suit he was wearing.

Sarge said, 'Look, I'll tell you the honest truth. What you like is what I like – a little bit of luxury. We never had a chance to have that. If I could afford it I'd sit down on me bottom and pay people to work for me. But don't worry your head, the sarge could never pay people to do this kind of job. In any case I'll never be able to afford luxury. But you could jump high, you could jump low, or you could jump in the middle, that is exactly what will happen to you when you come back from Tobago. In any case if you don't like riches Claris could do with gold, and you could give you lovely sister what married today. And what about this little boy – your key man?' Then he said suddenly, 'Look, I like to know what I'm doing. To lay me trap straight. You going Tobago yes or no?'

'We going in the morning, Sarge.'

His face grew bright. 'Early, eh? First thing.'

'Aha,' Uncle said.

'I'll crucify that son-of-a-gun,' Sarge said.

Uncle had got worked up and now his eyes were bloodshot and fierce. I was feeling fierce, too. I had realised, of course, that Sarge wanted to disgrace Cordner, not so much because of the gold chain itself, but for a reason which I was not very clear about. Or was it really because of the gold chain and because of us? I did not know. Whatever the reason, though, that gold chain was not lost, but was there, in Tobago with Cordner, and we should soon hold it, glittering, in our very hands. My heart was thumping as I stood there. I could hardly wait for the dawn to break.

I jumped as I felt a weight, and it was the big hand of Sarge on my head this time. All he said was, 'I like this boy. And I know he real brave and clever.' He was glancing towards the front steps every now and again, and at this moment he whispered, looking uneasy, 'Look, I think I'd better beat a retreat from here. I better withdraw. She keep on looking and looking. She harrassing me. She want me to go home and change. Look, I think I'll go and put on me police clothes.'

❋ Twenty-eight

UNCLE AND I left by the four a.m. bus. We took the road to Rio Claro and we got there when the blackness of the night had thinned a little and there was a little grey in the sky. As we passed here the tailor came to mind, and I reminded Uncle of him, how he had made the two 'bespoke' suits for the wedding. Uncle, who had been sitting silent and grim beside me, did not say anything at first, and then he said suddenly:

'What you was saying about the tailor?'

'He's living here.'

'Where is here?' he said, looking out of the window.

'Rio Claro.'

'Don't tell me we in Rio Claro already. Thoughts far, boy.'

It was too dark to see the houses plainly but I knew we had just entered the village. When the bus reached the centre of the village, by the big junction, we had to change for the place called Princes Town.

It was high day-light when we reached Princes Town and there we changed for San Fernando. To me, Princes Town had seemed a giddy, throbbing mass, but when I arrived in San Fernando I thought it was the biggest whirlpool of people and streets and houses that I had ever seen.

We changed again, taking what seemed a road without end, and it was not until about eight o'clock that our bus rolled into the capital. And here again I felt overwhelmed by the sight of the place, and at first I felt that if I did not hold on to Uncle I would be lost forever. But when we reached the waterfront and saw the boats and launches on the water, I took courage from Uncle, for he became very composed. He saw some boats come in with fish and he said, 'They ain't fishening like we always fishen in Mayaro. But sea is sea and fisherman is fisherman. We could rest here. We have to wait for the Tobago boat, but we could ask anybody. Come, let's look for a place where we could get some eats. You ain't hungry?'

Uncle was talking so brave and bold that I felt sure he was scared. Because Teacher Myra had said something about this very way Uncle Ulric was now, and about whistling in the dark. Only that it wasn't dark and Uncle Ulric wasn't whistling. But everything else seemed to follow. Uncle Ulric and I found a parlour amongst the offices and merchandise on the wharf, and Uncle jauntily pulled out a two-dollar note and bought mauby and rock cakes and I ate and looked out on the water.

I was quietly taken aback by the blue sheet that stretched motionlessly into the distance. It was as if I was in class and hearing Teacher Myra's voice: 'Look at the map of Trinidad. Consider the western coast now. That is the Gulf of Paria. A quiet sea – not rough and unruly as Mayaro sea. Because it is? Yes, Claudia, because it is sheltered. This is a gulf, class. You know what a gulf is, Sarah? All right. Here in Mayaro the waters is the Atlantic Ocean.'

I could almost hear Claudia saying, 'How you could say "waters is," Miss?' and Teacher Myra saying, 'This is not an English lesson,' and explaining at the same time why she had said that. I was thinking about the class but at the same time it was easy to push Mayaro and class from my mind, for this was such a strange and different world.

I kept looking at the sea near the jetty and I couldn't help being amazed at how the launches and boats and the big ships with funnels came up alongside the row of houses. Teacher Myra had referred to such houses as 'Customs houses'. And where the beach should have been there was a big concrete wall dropping abruptly into the sea. The tall buildings at the waterfront and the long, slanting funnels of the ships made me feel very tiny. I looked at Uncle. His thoughts seemed again to have gone far, and I did not know whether they were in Tobago or in Mayaro. My thoughts went again and again to Teacher Myra, for she had described all these things before. Every time I thought of her now I saw her in my mind in that pink dress looking down into the wedding yard from the window in Uncle's house. Uncle Clunis, that is. And at her back the room full of dancing people. And the music. And Sergeant Peters with his curling moustache standing with Uncle and myself under the coconut tree. Teacher Myra's father. Hearing his voice now, in my mind, I began breathing hard again, and my thoughts completely switched from the past and I was thinking of Tobago.

Uncle tapped me on my shoulder when he was ready to leave the parlour, and we went directly to buy our tickets, and when it was time to board the Tobago ship he tapped me again, and all he said to me was: 'We going across to deal with the rascal. Make up your mind for anything. It's man to man.'

'It's one to two,' I said. 'It's two of us. Don't mind he is police.'

'It might be two against two. You think I trust Mona? She is me sister but she better not tangle with me.'

Good God! I thought. Strange how I had completely forgotten Aunt Mona. I had not reckoned with her at all. Somehow I did not see her as being involved in this. When we sat down amongst the crowds of passengers in the noisy, heaving ship, I whispered: 'Aunt Mona ain't in this, Uncle. It's Constable Cordner who took the gold chain.'

He swung round to me. 'Mona ain't in this? So what is she to him? You think she'll sit down there and see us break his – break his –' I could see him struggling to find a proper word. Finally he said, ' – and see us break his bam-balam.'

I laughed. And then something dawned on my mind. I said, 'Uncle, you ain't mean we hitting him?'

He said, 'That is not the plan. The Sarge tell me what to do and how to handle it. Things should be easy. Just a few questions and then a few contacts and on his admission we could topple him into the hands of the law. Because we have solid evidence. But don't forget we come from quite Mayaro and I missing a good day's work and so if I see the chain you think anything like Peters or the Tobago police or Mona or even Cordner could make me wait for law? If I see the gold chain and he resist me I'll beat him to a bleddy pulp. I'll cuff down that worthless rascal – '

'Uncle!' I cried, and elbowed him. He wasn't talking loudly but it was loud enough for the other people around him to be staring at him. He saw this and bent his head. He was still fuming. He looked at me sideways and he said, 'You think I good! You think these arms only make to pull oars. I never hit nobody yet but so help me God if I see the gold chain I ain't going to no law.' When he lifted his head again and looked at the passengers and saw they weren't paying him attention now, he turned to me and showed a clenched fist. He said, 'I'll use this bleddy hammer of death on him.'

'Then the police would hold you.'

He did not say anything.

'And what about Aunt Mona. You'll beat her?'

He looked at me and it was quite a few moments before he answered. I saw his face relax from the fury that had twisted it. When his voice came it was weakened and mild, as if he had the devil drained out of him. He said, 'Mona? Mona ain't nice, but she is the last one. She's a deceitful, no-good, so-and-so, but – but blood thicker than water.'

I was silent.

He said, 'You was there that night they ransacked the house?'

'Yes, Uncle.'

'So you know what your Aunt Mona is. A treacherous Jezebel. But she is me sister.' He shook his head. 'Look, I don't want to tangle with Mona. I don't even want the law to come in. All I want is for Cordner to hand up the gold chain.'

'That's what I was hoping for. You think he'll hand it up?'

'I don't know. But that is the main reason we going to Tobago. The gold chain. I don't want to come back without it. You think I bothering with Sarge and what Cordner did to –' He stopped, then he said, 'You think I bothering with Sarge? What he and Cordner have is their business. What I want is the gold chain, and if he saw Cordner with it then I know where to go and get it.' There was a pause and then Uncle said, 'And you think I bothering with all that riches talk he was talking– that Sarge? All that golden life? Riches is nice, and you could do with plenty of that. You so young and you have the world before you. And Claris could do with that, too. And Roomeen. And Mona, too – why not? Though not the lion's share, what she want. And to be honest, yes, I could do with some of that too. But the main thing is to clear me name. See? You with me?'

'One hundred per cent, Unc.'

'Even in this?' He clenched his fist again.

'Uncle!' I cried. He laughed. I supposed he was teasing me now. But if it came to that, I was ready. It was man to man. Or perhaps two against two.

❈ Twenty-nine

WE ARRIVED IN Tobago early the next morning. During the whole of the journey Uncle Ulric had grown from tense to calm and calm to tense. And I had seen him laugh only once. That was deep in the night. I had lain beside him on a bunk and the boat was rocking and dipping, and once, dipping violently, it had pitched me in the corner, although when I rose from the floor and looked, Uncle was in the same spot. I said, amazed, 'Uncle, you all right?' That was when he laughed. He laughed until he nearly choked. He said, 'Boy, what wrong with you. Old sailor like me you asking me if I'm all right? This rocking is something too?'

'It pitched me down.'

He had chuckled, 'You pitched down yourself.'

He had then told me how to lie down so I wouldn't get thrown off. He had said, 'Lie down on your back and arch it. Curve the heels. The sea swelling and it choppy like hell but that ain't nothing. Try to get a little sleep.'

But he himself had not slept a wink. He told me so now, as we landed. He said he had lain with his eyes open all the time. Now as we crossed the harbour road in the dawn he mumbled: 'Stick close to me. Let's follow those people. The bus-stop should be over there. We could ask. It's Mount Moriah we going, eh? Remember Number Fifteen, Windward Road.'

I did not speak. I was close to him and we walked with the crowd across the bridge to the bus-stop. I hardly looked around me to see the famous Scarborough. That was Teacher Myra's term: *the famous Scarborough*, and she had described how it was now, and how it had been in the times when the British, French, and Dutch had made blood flow here. My mind was filled with Constable Cordner and the gold chain, but far in the back of my mind I was hearing the beating drums of those ruthless soldiers, and my blood tingled a little. Although when Teacher Myra had been describing the Scarborough of those times Claudia had made the class laugh at her, I felt it had been exactly as she said, because what I was seeing was so much like what she described. Claudia had said, 'But Miss, how you know what it was like then. You weren't there.' Teacher Myra had let the class have its good laugh, and when this was over she just said, 'Claudia, this is history.'

It seemed such a short while after landing that we were at Mount Moriah and in front of Fifteen Windward Road. Uncle and I stood gazing at the mansion in awe, and I said to him, 'Uncle you sure it's here?'

He just looked at me and said, with a blank face, 'Chain gone.'

My heart shook, 'What you mean, Uncle?' My head felt wild. It was clear he meant it had bought this splendour.

Surprisingly, he spoke without rancour or bitterness and without the pain of disappointment. He said, 'Gold gone, that's all. We just have to fight them in the courts. We'll just follow what Sarge said and topple them over to the law.'

'But Uncle you sure this is the house?'

He calmly took out a piece of paper from his back pocket. 'If here is Fifteen, Windward Road, it's here.'

There was a big number fifteen on the gate-post. On the gate, too, there was a button which said 'push'. When Uncle Ulric pushed it we heard a faint, distant ring. Shortly afterwards I cried to Uncle Ulric, my heart wild, 'Oh God, look Aunt Mona. That's Aunt Mona? Look, Uncle!'

Uncle Ulric showed no emotion when the draped figure came out to the front of the house. The person, dressed in a long flowing green gown, had opened the door with a flourish and had come out to the front of the Grecian steps. She was about to walk down, when, seeing us, she appeared as if seized, mouth open, her right hand to her lips.

Uncle Ulric shouted from the gate-post, 'Mona, it's only me. It's only me and Horace.'

She stood up for some moments looking at us. Between us and Aunt Mona there was the long gravelled walk, with a thick rose garden on either side. Aunt Mona said, with a weak voice, 'Push the gate.'

No sooner had she said this than Uncle pushed the gate and was hurrying to the front steps. I walked fast behind him, my heart pounding wildly. When he reached the foot of the steps he said, 'I could come in? And the boy?'

She looked at him, and apart from the green gown and the jewellery she was wearing, it was the same Aunt Mona. For there was the pretty face with the large oval eyes, with long curving eyebrows and with dark eyelashes that she had made even darker. Her hair, which she had never left alone, was now puffed right up, and a green bar-comb stuck in the middle. Her lips were pressed together. I said it was the same Aunt Mona, also, for as she did so often, she replied to Uncle Ulric with her eyes. When he asked if we could come in she gave him a sharp, blistering look and then she turned to lead the way inside. But with all that I could tell she was frightened and shocked.

Uncle stood up where he was. He said, 'I asked if I could come in.'

She said, 'You didn't come all the way here to stand up outside.'

He said, 'Well I didn't expect this. Perhaps it's too good for me.'

She said nothing.

He said, 'But I know nothing but the best is good enough for you.'

She said, 'Ulric – you coming in?'

This was the first chance I had to hear her voice properly, and if I had not been seeing her with my own two eyes I would not have felt it was Aunt Mona's voice. For despite the scathing reply she had made to Uncle Ulric, her voice was now unsteady and tremulous. She seemed to tremble a little as we walked in behind her.

She turned round and said, 'How you know I'm here?'

Uncle Ulric laughed. She had forgotten she had given the address to him herself. Uncle said, 'You don't bother with that.'

'Who sent you? Who you come from?'

Uncle said, 'Well let's sit down, nah. I come from a place they call Mayaro. Let's sit down and talk.'

We were now inside a big sitting room, and as Uncle was talking he was looking around and it was as if his eyes were popping out of his head. For the room was most resplendent with a bright red carpet on the floor, from wall-to-wall, with lovely antique furniture, and with huge paintings on the wall. I was staring too, amazed, because I had never seen such things before. Even Teacher Myra had not spoken of such beauty. The wall was of a delicate shade of sea-blue and there were decorated gold ridges running along the corners and up along the sides of the eaves. From the ceiling hung wonderful glittering chandeliers, such as I had seen only in books before. In fact, it was only now I knew such things were real. In the room itself there were several beautiful velvet-covered easy chairs – some the same colour as the carpet and some green and cream, and around a dark polished table there were wooden ones, the wood worked in fancy designs. And they must have been varnished, too, for they were gleaming like mirrors. As Uncle Ulric walked into the room he went to one of the loveliest of the velvet-covered chairs, and before Aunt Mona could say anything he sat right down into it, his clothes dusty and reeking of the boat and of sweat.

Aunt Mona opened her big eyes in horror, and then she turned away.

Uncle said, 'What's that?'

Aunt Mona said, 'What's what? I didn't say anything.'

'Oh, I thought you didn't want any fisherman sitting down in your luxurious room. On your luxurious chairs.'

Aunt Mona just stood there watching him.

Uncle Ulric said, 'Mona, I come to see you and Cordner. Call Cordner – but wait. I'll talk to you first.'

She looked at him questioningly. He said, 'You have a nice house here, man.'

She did not answer.

'When you bought it?'

'Bought it?'

'Look Mona, I ain't have time to waste. I might be a fisherman but I ain't no damn fool. When you bought this beautiful million-dollar house?'

She gave a sort of chuckle and she said, 'Well if it cost millions it ain't my millions because I ain't have that kind of money. Cordner resigned from the Police Force and with the money he got he bought it.'

'Right,' he said. He had brought pencil and a note-book and

now he took them out and started to write.

He said now, 'How much money?'

Aunt Mona shrank back. 'I don't know. I never asked him. That is the man's business.'

'That will be the court's business very soon now. He inside? I'll talk to him just now. But Mona, I'll tell you something. Blood thicker than water, and I wouldn't make you take a jail. But you all denying this little boy. I come to Tobago to just take back the gold chain from Cordner, and leave everything right there. I didn't want any court or anything. Look, Sarge waiting for Cordner, ready to drive a nail in his coffin. And you know what? It will have to be like that now. You all sold the blasted chain and bought this mansion and you talking about money from Police Force? One minute he transfer one minute he resign? Sarge will fix him good. Sarge will hang his jack upside down. Let me talk to him now. Call Cordner.'

Aunt Mona stayed silent and in the meantime Uncle Ulric looked round and saw me standing. 'Boy, you still standing up?' he said. 'Sit down somewhere, anywhere.'

'No, Uncle. It's all right.'

'Look here, boy!'

Aunt Mona said, 'Sit down, Horace.'

I sat down.

Uncle Ulric said to Aunt Mona, 'You calling Cordner?'

'What Sarge say he'll do to him? Sarge ain't have evidence.' Her manner seemed to have changed completely. She was looking at Uncle now as if she did not care.

'He blasted well have evidence. Sarge saw him with the chain. And Sarge is determined because – '

'Because of that stupid what's-her-name. She is the first girl to get jilt?'

I sat down looking at them. Aunt Mona was a tigress once more. I wondered who this girl was and why Sarge cared so much. I was sure it couldn't be my teacher so I didn't bother about that.

Uncle said, 'You won't call Cordner? Well I ain't talking no more. All I could say is that Sarge want his head and Sarge will get it. But if he anywhere near and hearing me,' Uncle raised his voice, 'If he just there in the bedroom I want him to know that I is the only man to save him from years in the calaboose. Years and years in jail. All you have to do is – if you pawned the gold chain, mortgage or sell this mansion and get back the chain for me. Else Sarge will get you, boy. The vengeance of mocow will fall on you. We'll fry you in your own fat!'

Aunt Mona said, 'You could talk to the wall, he ain't here.'

Uncle looked stunned. 'Oh, he ain't here. Sarge will *still* get him.'

'Sarge get him already.'

'What you mean?'

'Cordner is in Trinidad. He gone to Mayaro. Only last night he left by the boat. I know it sounding odd but it's true. He got a letter from Sarge.'

'When he got this letter?'

'Friday. He didn't want to go because he said the Sarge was talking nonsense. But I said go and face him and tell him you with me now and that's that. It was some breach-of-promise talk Sarge had in the letter, and Cordner said so far as he know the girl all right so what the hell. I tell him leave by the first boat – and that was last night.'

'You read the letter?'

'Yes, he showed me.'

'Why Sarge wanted him to come? You sure it was only because of the girl?'

'The letter didn't say anything else. It said Cordner must come and they would do some deal. The letter said something like, "I only have one daughter and nothing could compensate because you break her heart. But I know you well off now and you could fix me up".'

'I see,' said Uncle Ulric. 'Oh, I see. And Cordner went to fix him up?'

'No. Because he ain't have nothing left. But the letter said, "One hand can't clap, remember that". And it said something like what you said a while ago. It said, "And you better come now. I have evidence and I could nail you to the cross".'

'That sounds like Sarge.'

All the time they were talking I was wondering what other daughter Sarge had, and if she was in Rio Claro. And I was wondering why Sarge didn't talk the truth instead of saying he had one daughter. Because of course this daughter in question could not be my teacher.

Aunt Mona went on talking. 'Cordner couldn't sleep. He didn't sleep Friday night, and Saturday night. So on Sunday I said well go to the man. He said he wasn't going nowhere. But yesterday morning when he got up he said, "Look, I better go to Sarge once and for all. He ain't have no damn evidence. I'll have to go and see him else he'll never leave me alone. I'll be back tomorrow". That's what he said and he just went by the late boat.'

'And you believe Cordner that the Sarge ain't have any evidence?'

'He ain't have a scrap of evidence against Cordner.'

'But he saw the gold chain. He said one night when Cordner was packing up he saw something glittering.'

'So everything that glittering is gold?'

'You want me to prove that Cordner thief the gold chain?'

'You could never prove that.' She seemed to be getting overwrought.

'You want me to prove Sarge saw him with the gold chain?' She paused for a moment. 'That doesn't mean he stole it.'

'Well how he came by it? Somebody give it to him?'

'Oh God, Ulric, Cordner ain't steal any chain.' She started to tremble and the next moment she burst out crying. She all but collapsed into a chair behind her.

I was astonished. I had never guessed it would end like this, and so easily.

Uncle Ulric said, 'Oh, I see. So Mona, that was what it was. Well, well, well. It took all this, and me and Horace coming to Tobago to find out.'

He shook his head and looked at me. I stared at him, bewildered.

He turned to Aunt Mona, 'I could make you go to jail, Mona,' he said. 'But you know I would never do that. All the same, when you finish crying tell me everything that happen to that chain. You all sold it to buy this house?'

There was a weak 'Yes.'

'Well all right, just tell me how the chain disappeared from Claris place. That's the first thing. Otherwise Claris and Roomeen will never believe. They still blaming me.'

She was still crying hysterically, and he walked over and patted her on the head. His own eyes were filled with tears.

❊ Thirty

IT MUST HAVE BEEN quite late on Wednesday night when a burst
of laughter from Auntie Roomeen woke me up. So much had
happened that at first I was confused and did not know where I
was, but moments later I realised that I was at home and in my
own bed. The voices were out in the hall, and I could distinguish
Uncle Ulric's jerky voice very clearly, and then Mother's voice
every now and again, then Auntie Roomeen's cries in surprise,
and Uncle Clunis' remarks – the chief cause of the laughter.

I lay in bed listening to them, and then I sat up to hear more
clearly. I heard Mother say, 'But Ulric, you know, this whole
thing sounds like a fairy-tale. I know the magicians say: "the
swiftness of the hand deceives the eye", but oh God, my sister
could thief neat!' Auntie Roomeen sounded convulsed with
laughter.

Mother said again, 'No, it's true. I ain't see better magic than
that. When it was again, boy? You know I just can't remember
that time. You say we was outside?'

Uncle was beginning to explain when Auntie Roomeen
interrupted. 'You can't remember that night – I think it was the
second night after we lost the chain. We stood up there in the
yard –right outside there – and I was telling you all about
Panama. And then while I was talking she cut across me to ask
Horace what cause tide? You can't remember?'

Mother said, 'Oh, yes. Of course.'

'So Ulric was saying she and Horace went up the steps because
she wanted Horace to show her something in his book.'

Uncle said, 'And this time poor Horace don't know what she
up to. But I wanted to leave, you see. I wanted to leave and I find
she was staying too damn long. So when I went up the steps she
and Horace was looking for something in books. In Horace
room. But that was the trap. Because when I knocked on the
door and she came out with the book in her hand, she said

193

"Ulric, what you doing here?" '

I could hardly hear Uncle for the laughter which broke out. Auntie Roomeen kept on saying, 'Oh Lord, don't kill me!'

Uncle was going on, 'This time your trunk was on the table half-open, because – '

'Because I knocked off your hand and it didn't close properly,' Auntie Roomeen said, amidst her slices of laughter.

Uncle said, 'Anyway, Roomeen's trunk was open but I wasn't thinking about that because that is not my business, but now you know, it's the gold chain Mona was after not what causing tide.'

Peals of laughter rose up again and I could hear Mr Clunis' deep voice against Mother's and Auntie's.

'And she herself told me when I was questioning her in Tobago, that even before that – before I came up the steps – she had already grabbed the chain and put it down her back.'

His voice was very indistinct now, drowned as it was by the din.

'She herself said so,' Uncle said. 'She said that time she went out in the hall with book telling Horace there have more light. But she made sure Horace stayed in his room, looking up the other books. And this girl could thief like a cat. Horace ain't hear nothing. By the time he came out to the table, gold gone.' A chorus of laughter went up, and even I, sitting up on the bed, laughed too, and shook my head. I agreed with Mother then. Auntie was really the neatest thief in the whole world.

Uncle went on talking and you could tell he was in a happy, jovial frame of mind, overjoyed that he had solved what to everybody else was a mystery. Everybody that is, besides Mona and Cordner. They went on talking about the gold chain and I heard Mother say, 'And you say they sell it and bought that mansion? The boy was telling me. Well, well, just fancy that. What? But of course. And what with big flower garden, and luxury furniture and plush red carpet, if you please. Ulric you sure you wasn't dreaming, boy? Sounds like Arabian Nights.'

I had lain back down on the bed again and I muttered to myself, 'You mean Tobago nights.'

Uncle laughed, 'Ha, ha!' when Mother said that and he replied, 'You damn right, girl. When I was in that house I had to pinch meself because I thought I was dreaming.'

I then heard Uncle Ulric trying to describe the wonderful

things that Aunt Mona had inside the house, and then he stopped and said, 'But you all looking at me as if I is a madman. Well ask Horace. Chandeliers. It's big chandeliers like this I'm talking about. Ask Horace. Go and wake him up and ask him.'

Mother said, 'What? Wake up Horace this hour? You must be crazy. In any case Horace sleeping like a log, you could ask him anything?'

'Well ask him tomorrow.'

I had just sat up again, but hearing Mother I was already lying down, with my eyes shut, and trying to look like a log. I couldn't hear them so well now but I could tell Uncle Ulric was trying to convince them, and I could hardly wait for the dawn. Because everything he was saying was true. When we came in I was so tired I was only able to give Mother a hint, but as I lay there now, I was bursting to tell them of the mansion at Fifteen Windward Road. And then, too, I could imagine the colourful composition I would write about it. They were talking about Aunt Mona again but I was only half-hearing them. I only said to myself, 'It's a good thing it was *our* gold she took!'

I was thinking of the composition I was going to write – where I was going to start and how I was going to round off, when I heard Auntie Roomeen say, 'It was the same day Ulric. Not long after you all left here. Boy, that was a big sensation in Mayaro – a policeman in the cells.'

Uncle Ulric said, 'Sarge out to get that man. And it's not so much for the gold, you know.'

They all started to talk, including Uncle Clunis, and I realised everybody had known what was happening except me. And my own Aunt was involved! It really stunned me to know what was happening, and even more so when they mentioned the name 'Myra Peters'. In spite of all they were saying, I kept asking myself, 'You sure? You sure? Could it be *my* Teacher Myra?'

My thoughts were drifting and I began to think of my Teacher Myra, who, I felt convinced, had really nothing to do with the thieving Constable, and I felt sure it was either a big trick or a big mistake. With my head on the pillow I was seeing her in the class-room reading my compositions. She always read them avidly, as though she was devouring them, and it struck me again how she liked my descriptions of Point Radix, with the mist and the spray and the froth against what she called 'a backcloth of blue sky'. And I thought of how she also liked the description of the rainstorms when they were coming to the beach from over the sea, and how at that time the sea became choppy and the whole horizon became what she called 'a backcloth of grey'. And she always liked my description of boats casting their nets – especially when I wrote about that day when I went seining with Uncle Ulric, and when I wrote about the people whom I usually saw afar in the boats, but whom I said were then just beside me, their glistening bodies almost touching me. I had used one of her favourite phrases when I had described their rowing: 'A poem of grace'. She liked that, and I could have seen how she relished it while she was reading it, her eyes shining with eagerness and delight. I had talked about the men rowing, the black limbs moving forward, then backward, and the oars pushing back the blue water with hardly a ripple in their wake, and how the man on the bow were casting out the nets, and how Uncle Ulric – the captain – was helping him and directing how to surround the school of fish. I lay thinking of Teacher Myra sitting at her desk reading my composition and then quietly asking me about Auntie Roomeen and Aunt Mona. For a long time I lay thinking about Teacher Myra at the table in school, and then it was as if my thoughts shifted.

It came to me that I was not in the class-room at all but as if I was still in Tobago and seeing Aunt Mona in that flowing green gown and confusing it with a figure in pink at Uncle Clunis' house on his wedding day. I could swear I was hearing Pappy Timothy's band playing and seeing coconut trees swaying, and my Uncle Ulric and Sergeant Peters chatting softly by the side of the house in the yard. And having thought of Uncle Clunis I thought of Auntie Roomeen, and oddly enough, no other vision would flash to my mind but the vision of the day when, after they had left the Police Station, Uncle Clunis had brought old Mr Reid and his buggy, and had taken up Mother and Auntie from Miss Wong's store.

'Old Mr Reid,' I said to myself. A strange, sharp feeling came over me. I must have been between sleep and wakefulness but I was sure I was not dreaming. 'Old Mr Reid,' I whispered to myself again. 'I wonder how he's going. I must pass in and see him sometime.' My thoughts drifted further and further away and I did not know what took place afterwards. All I knew was that the sun was bright on the coconut trees when I opened my eyes.

✳ Thirty-one

IT WAS THURSDAY MORNING, but it was not an ordinary Thursday morning as always. Uncle, who was going out in Mr Stanley's seine, as expected, was to come to the school at lunch-time to meet me, and together we were to go over to the Police Station to see Sergeant Peters. But as soon as I got into class, Teacher Myra came to me nervously and took me out to the verandah. School was about to start and children were running up and down. My class-mates, who were curious because I had missed yesterday, followed to peep. Teacher Myra waved them back. She seemed grave. When we reached the end of the verandah she said, 'Sarge want to see you. The person is here, you know. Whom you went to Tobago to see. He's in the –' She stopped. Then she whispered, 'Sarge want to see you; why don't you go up?'

'Have to wait for Uncle Ulric. Uncle Ulric coming to meet me at twelve for us to go up.'

'No, the sarge wouldn't wait. He told me to send you.'

I said nothing.

'There isn't anything to be afraid of. *To thine own self be true* – that's Shakespeare. Remember that always. So therefore you'll tell him exactly what's what.'

I did not speak.

'And if you have to go to court. God forbid – but if you have to go to court, it's a question of the whole truth and nothing but the truth.'

My heart shook violently and I trembled somewhat. She said, maybe to calm me: 'It will never get that far.'

She was leading me off slowly, and I was putting my finger to my forehead to ask permission, when she said, 'The place nice? Where you went.'

'It's a mansion,' I said, and all my fury over Aunt Mona swept over me. I felt weak, and held on to the bannister rails. I felt

197

giddy. Why did she do that? Just for the love of luxury she stole the gold chain, went and sold it, and bought a vast mansion in Tobago, and now she had us all in a mess. We might never get back the gold chain – in spite of all Uncle was planning – and in the long run I might have to go to court. I didn't know what Sarge would tell me. Teacher Myra saw the anger that swept over my face, for she put an arm around my neck and whispered, 'Think kindly.'

I could not answer her. She added, 'Don't let rage consume you.'

I stood there for quite a few moments, breathing hard, and although my anger towards Aunt Mona welled up to such a pitch, I wanted to assure Teacher Myra that whatever happened, even if Aunt Mona took some years in jail – as she deserved – I would still like her, Teacher Myra, and that I would always know that what they were saying about her was a big mistake, and that in time it would clear up, and I myself would clear her name. I was thinking about all this, and hoping she would never hear what they said about her, but as she watched me and saw that I was going to speak she put a finger to her lips and said, 'Sh-h.' And then she whispered, 'You remember the lines on rashness, don't you?

> *And many a word at random spoken,*
> *May soothe or wound a heart that's broken.*

You remember it?'

'Yes, Miss.'

'I don't know what you were going to say but I thought it was best not to speak. Not that someone's heart is broken.' And it was odd, but as she looked away I was sure I heard her whisper, 'Not anymore.'

As she turned back to me I looked at her and she was the same old sweet Teacher Myra. She said, 'You look puzzled. You are wondering about the lines? They come from "Many an Arrow", and you read them in "Choice Quotations".'

'I know, Miss.'

'You going up the hill now? He said you must come.'

'I'll go, but – don't know what to do, Miss. Uncle Ulric said – '

'Okay, if you want to, you can go down and meet your Uncle Ulric. I'm only passing on what the sarge told me.'

'You call him Sarge too, Miss?'

'Yes, Why not? Sometimes I do.' Then she said, 'I went up there to him this morning and I saw the man through the hole.' As I looked at her, for a moment I thought I saw a flash of hate and anger in her, but it could not be, for when she spoke again she was the same soft Teacher Myra. She said, 'Okay, hear what I said, think kindly, and speak nothing but the truth.'

'Yes, Miss,' I said. I put my finger up to my forehead: 'Permission, Miss.'

'You may go, Horace Lumpres.'

I walked down the stairs of the school. I did not go to the beach. I went up to Sarge.

❊ *Thirty-two*

'OH ME LITTLE MAN!' Sergeant Peters said, as I walked timidly into the Charge Room. He was beaming, and his face was big and round and shining, and his moustache seemed to curl up more than I remembered it. He got up and put a hand on my shoulder. He said, 'So you went to Tobago and all!'

I looked around because I did not feel Sergeant Peters should be speaking so loudly. His voice was big and booming. He was alone in the Charge Room, and I could see an open window in the other room behind.

I said, 'You sent to call me, Sarge?'

'Yes, naturally, I want to talk to you a little bit. About Tobago. If I have to press a charge – '

'But it's Uncle. I only went with Uncle.'

He laughed. 'Of course it's Ulric. I didn't say you did anything. You getting frighten? I didn't say you did nothing, Sonny boy. The man who did something we have him in good charge. You know that round hole behind there?' And he laughed, 'Haw, haw, haw!' Then he said, 'I know you went with your uncle Ulric. He coming in a minute, your uncle.'

'He said he was coming to meet me in school twelve o'clock.'

'Well I just sent to call him. When I saw him this morning he told me twelve o'clock, but a big man like me will sit down on my bottom and wait till twelve? I want to write out these charges and nail me man right away, I can't wait till twelve.' And he bent down and whispered to me, 'We put hand on the blighter right here in Mayaro.'

I nodded my head. He moved towards the door. He said, 'Come.'

I went out after him at the side door and we were in the yard. He pointed, and my heart suddenly gave 'voom!' and I had to turn and hold on to the wall. For as he pointed and I turned my head, there was the big round hole of the cell, and right in the

200

middle of it was Constable Cordner's head, peeping out.

Sergeant Peters laughed, 'Haw, haw, haw!' and he said to me, 'You squeamish? I want you to look at the man good. It will be a good lesson to you yourself as you growing up. "Thou shalt not steal", will be your own Commandment.'

I reeled away from the wall and I went back inside the Charge Room through the open door. Sergeant Peters came back in and said to me, 'That is the man who steal your gold chain and you sorry for him? Me – I'll nail him says the Lord. I'll crucify him. I'll hang his jack good and proper. I'll make him sorry he ever set eyes on my – on Mayaro.'

What he almost said made me jump, but it was a little slip. I sat down on the chair feeling terrified. The two wild-looking eyes and the agonised face of Constable Cordner seemed stamped on my mind. He had been right there, close, and when I looked he was staring like a terror-stricken beast. He had looked at me as if pleading for mercy.

Sergeant Peters said, 'Oh, Horace, just a little while, eh? I have to go over to me quarters with these charge sheets. I want to fix up everything this morning – in fact, since we have him here I waiting for Ulric to come. Now you sit down right here and wait for me. When Ulric come say I'm coming now. Now, now. Don't let Ulric go back, you know.' He moved off hurriedly, and then he stopped and looked back. 'And don't frighten – you all will get that blasted chain back. I, Sarge, working on that, don't 'fraid. If you don't get back the chain you'll get a heaping set of compensation. Sure as day.' Then he walked away, the three stripes on his grey shirt bending as he swung his arms. His back was broad, and his short black trousers showed thighs that were very thick. He walked jauntily.

I had already turned from looking at the sergeant and I was thinking of Uncle Ulric, wondering if the fellow with the message caught him or if he had already gone out to sea, when I heard a familiar voice. I swung around quickly almost saying 'Miss!' But I saw no one and realised the voice had come from the side of the Charge Room where there was the big round hole. I sat still, eager to hear who it was, and now between what sounded like sobs, the voice came again: 'Look at you, you damn two-timer,' it said. There was silence. I felt as stunned as if a rock had knocked me down.

Teacher Myra said, 'You are supposed to be a big Police Constable, and look at you now. In the cell. And they'll put you away for years, you'll see. You giving Mona gold ring and now stealing gold chain for her – well take what you get!'

I sat bewildered. A voice mumbled close to her and she said, 'Don't come with that – you could fool me once, not twice. You could talk love till you blind, that wouldn't save you. And don't bother with what you saying now because I know the facts. I know everything what happening down St Joseph, so you can't give me that. The little boy put everything in his composition and I know. I know all about Mona and I could tell you it really coming for you this time. I thought you was somebody good, but really, all that glitters could never be gold.'

The mumbling voice said something, and she said, 'I ain't telling Pa nothing. Not a single thing. And in any case he ain't want to know Mona passed you any chain. You thief it. Look, Pa has all the evidence and he'll hang your bleddy jack. You asking me to help you? Never! Look, Pa coming up the hill and I going. Stand you grind, Mister, and enjoy the calaboose. I never want to see you again. Never!'

And presently the frilly dress of Teacher Myra swept through the slice of space, and she was gone.